DEADLY DANGEROUS

The Life and Times of Detective Ian Stanton

DEADLY
DANGEROUS

Duncan Wherrett

ISBN: 978-0-9957792-2-8

Watchya Publishing
dncn@watchya.com

The Life and Times of Detective Ian Stanton

Book One

I

In Which Ian Wakes One Morning

One morning, Ian Jason Stanton wakes up early and knows he wants to be in the police and furthermore feels he needs to be in the police. He's 16 years old. He lies in bed looking at the ceiling simply turning this thought over in his mind. The idea still seems to hold firm. He lives at his mother's house in Guildford. She works in the local book shop four days a week and runs the book club in the library. Ian's father died when he was ten years old.

From then on, he starts to plan. What would he need to know, and be able to do, in order to make himself a good copper? You have to be good at self-defence. Some type of martial arts training he sees as a must – but which one? Research needed here.

First aid. There'll be first aid training in the police, but plenty in advance would be good.

Guns. No he doesn't want to be in any gun squad like some sort of disguised psycho, but knowing how to shoot might be useful. He could join an airgun club; that would be similar in many ways.

Education, yes, A Levels and a degree. He thinks you might not need to have a degree for the police anyway, but even without that he wants a degree. Ian never has a problem with studying, especially as he's a super-fast reader and is still able to take everything in.

About 18 months earlier, Ian had found an old harp in the school's music store room and he became fascinated with the instrument. Although old, it was undamaged and almost complete, with a few broken strings. The music teacher was able to tune it but could only give rudimentary instructions on how to hold the hands and play. Being so interested and resourceful, he began. In due course, it was decided the harp was of little use to the school so it was arranged he should supply the school with a reasonably good guitar in exchange for the harp.

While working on his A Levels, he starts to investigate various martial arts. He quickly eliminates judo as impractical and not useful enough; Kung-Fu, flashy and fast but too superficial; Taekwondo, too many kicks, a sport for yobs and no good for his purpose. Aikido he sees would be very fast, and effective for disabling an attacker and pinning them down quickly, without excessive force, but the learning process would be long. Karate is quick and direct but punching an assailant can have consequences, if used carelessly.

He decides to start with aikido and immediately joins the nearest club, taking to it easily and progressing well. He always likes running at school so starts to take that more seriously, along with some gym work for more overall strength and fitness.

Ian is 5' 10", if measured in the morning, and not impressive when people first meet him and could even be said to be easy to miss, merging in with the scenery. The uncharitable would say he is not too noticeable when no-one else is in the room. His clothes tend to be dull, showing no interest in any sort of fashion statement.

Off he goes to the University of Suffolk, Ipswich, aiming for a BA Honours in psychology. A keen student, he goes in for little in the way of social life. He's never been big on social activities, and has just one girl friend for a few months in his three years. That never bothers him because he has his hands full with college work and his sports activities. There is a karate club in town so he starts adding that to his portfolio.

Careful saving from holiday jobs enable him to buy a harp of better quality than the one he's been using and it makes a refreshing break from college work and sports.

He soon finds out that police training can involve competence with firearms, and it wouldn't hurt to practice with the airgun club and do a bit of clay pigeon shooting.

By the time he leaves university, he has a second dan black belt in aikido and it gives him an extra mental strength he was not expecting at first.

His real ambition is to be a detective and although no longer required to have first served in uniform in some areas, he feels it would be good to have that experience before becoming a detective. He's readily accepted as a trainee and begins.

They are a mixed bag in his training group, from a

range of backgrounds. Some of the men are big and brawny while Ian was fairly light and not of bulky frame. The women have a larger range of sizes but all seem very confident and assured.

Two of the men, who quickly pal up together, are somewhat rough-and-ready and start their private game of studying everyone else on the course, criticising and analysing them and giving them nick-names, which are rarely complimentary. The women are always giving some sort of sexual tag, followed by a number which represents marks out of ten for how good they think the woman would be in bed. The one black and one asian participants fair no better.

It isn't long before Ian overhears that his nickname is "Deadly Dangerous". It's not meant as a compliment but is developed out of sarcasm because they feel sure one thing he definitely would never be is deadly dangerous.

His new life begins . . . . .

2

In Which a New Life Begins

On completing training, Ian gets assigned to a station in north west London, and is disappointed to find that one of the rough-and-ready duo is there also. This man wastes no time in spreading around Ian's nickname of "Deadly Dangerous", which soon gets abbreviated to "DD".

Being one of the newest on the block, Ian has the most mundane tasks to do. He doesn't mind that, knowing it's normal and all part of the learning process. What he doesn't take to is night duty and trying to sleep in the day. With his time off it's off to aikido or karate training where he has now got his first dan black belt. There's also regular running with the occasional sprint thrown in, or having driving lessons.

Any time left for sitting around, he would rather read a novel or practise on the harp than sit in the pub with people from the station. This does leave him open to being labelled as a bit odd by the others and the tag of "DD" persists.

Ian Stanton proves to be effective in uniform, reliable and not intimidated in difficult situations.

Stanton soon starts to feel more comfortable and

quickly realises that most crime is petty and straight forward and most criminals are stupid. Then there's some frequent rough stuff mainly after too much drink over the weekends. With all his self-defence techniques and the added confidence of a protective vest, he has no trouble dealing with that. He's only paired up with a more experienced officer at first, a favourite being Sergeant Tom Innes.

Sergeant Innes is 35 and has been the police for 17 years. He's seen as one of the most dependable officers in the station, six foot two and very strong and fearless against knife attacks and violent assaults. The rumour is the only thing he's afraid of is birds flapping their wings near him, a circumstance nobody can quite understand. Frequently, Innes is given the role of chaperoning new young officers.

It's on one such day on the streets that Sergeant Innes and Ian have to try and find Jim Yule. At 17, he's already a regular minor thug and small-time thief. They knock on the front door of his parents' house. His mother answers the door with an aggressive 'What do you bleeders want?'

'Jimmy at home?' asks the Sergeant.

'It's Jim, not Jimmy, and it's Mr Yule to you.'

'Him then; is he in?'

'No he's not. Haven't seen him for a couple of days. He'll be with one of his mates somewhere.'

'Do you mind if we come in for a quick look round?'

'Of course I bloody well do. Got a warrant?'

The Sergeant says nothing at first and merely looks at her. 'You're all alone then?' he asks.

'Not that it's any of your business, but yes, just me and the Jack Russell. Nice and quiet like. Unless you want to arrest the dog.'

Instantly Ian forces the door open further, pushes pass Mrs Yule and starts running up the stairs. Mrs Yule shout at him, 'Eer you can't do that. Jim, watch out.'

As Ian gets to the top of the stairs, Jim appears suddenly and swings a metal bar at him. Ian is quick to dodge, grab his arm and twist him face down on to the floor. Mrs Yule is right behind Ian, with her fists raised, while he's clipping on the handcuffs. He quickly looks behind him and delivers a karate back kick into her stomach, causing her to fall back. Sergeant Innes is following and grabs her with his strong hands, preventing her from falling down the stairs. Ignoring her screams and shouts, he takes her downstairs and once in the hall, clamps the cuffs on her.

'This is assault! Police brutality! You saw him – the way he kicked me. I'll 'ave you for this.'

'Looked like self-defence to me. You were going to attack him.'

Ian comes down the stairs with an angry Jim and puts him in the living room. Mrs Yule is still creating.

'Right Martha, shut up. You're both on enough charges already,' says the Sergeant as he taps on his phone for a prisoner vehicle.

With a new vehicle taking mother and son to the station, Innes and Stanton get back into their own car.

'Did you know he was there or were you taking a chance?'

'Well either I can see through walls like Superman, or I saw a shadow move on the wall at the top of the stairs, just as she said she was all alone.'

'Good. Not too bright some of these folks.'

Sergeant Innes is always cautious when working with a newly-trained constable. Some are impressive from the start, some take longer to get settled and fit in, while occasionally it can be clear in a few weeks that the young officer has probably made the wrong career choice. He was not sure about Ian at the beginning but after this first incident, Innes feels much more confident about him.

Stanton has been on the job for five months when they are sitting in the patrol car, in a side street off the main road, just idly passing the time when a message comes in. "Suspicious character in the shopping centre, seen on the CCTV walking around looking nervous. A white male, with grey baseball cap and a blue rucksack."

The Sergeant starts the car, turns on the blue light without the siren and drives round to the Centre. The shopping mall has only two floors and the radio tells the Sergeant the man is on the first floor.

They go up the internal stairs and look through the small windows in the doors. A couple of reports from the security officer watching the monitors show increased anxiety at the man's behaviour.

Innes and Stanton see him walking towards them; he appears to be breathing heavily and sweating. It's approaching lunch time and the mall is busy in places.

The Sergeant says, 'Let him pass these doors, then we walk up behind him, you go to the left, me to the right. If he makes any suspicious move, just dive in and don't touch the rucksack. We hold his arms; keep him kneeling, pushing him face down on the ground might set off a trigger. You ready?'

'Yes.'

They go quietly through the double doors and walk towards the man who is walking erratically and looking from side to side.

When they are about three metres behind him, he suddenly turns round, sees them and his eyes widen in surprise. As his right hand moves towards the inside of his jacket, he shouts, 'Allahu Akbar' but at the same time Stanton leaps forward, grabs the man's right hand and twists his arm. Innes grabs the man's left wrist almost as quickly and they both twist his arms forcing him down on to his knees. They hold his hands and arms firmly out to the sides so he can't move.

The Sergeant shouts,

'EVACUATE GET OUT GET OUT EVACUATE.'

Five seconds later, the fire alarm goes off and over the tannoy everyone is told to leave the building immediately by the nearest exit. There's a rush of people running away and out. A few people actually pause to take photographs of the officers and their prisoner on their mobiles, causing the officers to keep their faces turned down. Stanton and Innes maintain their grips.

'Don't let up. We have to wait for the squad.'

The next seven minutes waiting seems like an hour. Suddenly a group of fully-armoured men dressed in black is running towards them. One of them carries an aerosol and says to the police, 'Look away'.

He sprays into the man's face and almost instantly he goes limp. 'Okay, we've got him. Move and get out.' Stanton and Innes don't hesitate.

Back in the car they start to get their breath back, but Stanton is almost hyper-ventilating and feeling particularly light-headed.

'Wait here; I'm going for drinks.'

In a nearby coffee shop, Innes has taken his hat off and asks for, 'Two white filtered coffees to go, and two of those cakes, and these two waters, please.'

Police sirens are going off up and down the street. The woman behind the counter says, 'What's going on, why all the police?'

The Sergeant looks at her. He's not supposed to say anything but thinks, Why shouldn't we get a bit of instant credit. 'Suspect bomber, me and my colleague had to hold him down until the bomb squad arrived.'

She stares at him open-mouthed, stopping what she's doing.

'Err, two coffees please miss.'

Back at the car, Stanton has started to shake a little.

'Here, get this down you.' They drink quickly and eat the cakes.

'You were good in there. You moved so fast. It was brilliant.'

'We don't know for sure yet if he was a bomber.'

'Yes we do. We had to take it that he was. That's why we did all that.'

'What was that stuff he sprayed.'

'A strong anaesthetic of some sort, to knock him out instantly.'

'That security man was good wasn't he?'

'Yes, really on the ball. We'll go and see him later. Now back to the station and we are going to see the doc. There's likely to be a nervous reaction soon so we'll need something to calm us down, although I'm more use to this sort of thing than you. How long have you been with us now, since your final training?'

'Nearly five months. It's a lot to happen in my first few months.'

'Well I won't say this has been a baptism of fire, fire's the wrong word to use here, but you know what I mean.'

'Metaphorically speaking then.'

'That's it.'

Two hours later, the news comes through that there was a bomb packed with nails. Not a huge bomb but anyone within six or seven metres would have been killed or cut to pieces. Now Stanton feels even more queasy.

The Inspector speaks to Stanton. 'You get off home now. Take those pills you got from the doctor. Come in normal time tomorrow. Best not to sit around at home brooding, and I'll put you on light duties for a few days.'

A week later, all the investigations into the bombing attempt are finished and Sergeant Innes and PC Stanton are called into the Chief Inspector's office. Standing there also is the Commander, who shakes their hands as they come in.

'The whole matter has now been fully examined and assessed. You'll know the charges that man faces. For your exceptional quick thinking and bravery, which doubtless saved many lives and showing no regard for your own safety, it is to be recommended you are both awarded the George Cross. Congratulations.'

Stanton and Innes both simply said, 'Thank you sir'.

Outside the office, almost in unison they let out a loud breath.

'How about that,' says the Sergeant. 'No less than we deserve of course. Come on then lad, the least we can do is celebrate with a cup of tea and a sticky bun. That's one grade up from what I got last time. I got a George Medal about eight years ago.'

'What's the difference?'

'Degree of risk. For the Cross there has to be at least a 90 per cent risk of death, so we were pretty close to the edge there. For the George Medal, the risk is considered less, although it didn't feel like that from my side. Fortunately for peace of mind, most days don't contain such volcanoes. Right, sticky bun time. You're paying – privileges of rank.'

Time moves on . . . . .

3

In Which there is no more Uniform

By the summer of the following year, Ian decides he wants to get on with being a detective. He applies and joins the detective training course in September.

After initial training, he moves on to supervised practical training in the same London borough. He's among a mixed group of officers under the supervision of Inspector Peterson and spends many weeks helping to investigate theft and burglary cases.

One February afternoon, Ian is in a small local park area. It's been raining a lot recently, making the grass areas very soft and muddy, but right now the sun's shining and it's unseasonably warm. Sitting on a park bench, he's reading a science magazine, one written by experts and aimed at non-experts, although he always gets lost trying to fully understand the articles on particle physics.

Walking along the footpath in his direction is a young man with a fat stomach and a rather cocky walk, wearing the familiar jeans and trainers, topped with a Liverpool football shirt and an anorak open at the front. Bounding along ahead of him is his dog, a large animal with long red fur and floppy paws.

The dog quickly approaches Ian, barking furiously and puts both its front paws up on to his lap depositing lots of muddy marks. Ian is not big on buying new clothes, but these trousers are new, having just been bought over the weekend. Not being best pleased he shoos the dog away with a wave of the hand and says 'Down'.

Mr Dog Owner approaches saying, 'Don't you hit my dog.'

'I didn't hit your stupid dog. You need to train it better.'

Instantly the man leans down to Ian as though to head-butt him but stopping a fraction of an inch from his face. With wide eyes he holds his right fist to Ian's chin. 'Well I say you did. Hit him again and I'll be hitting you pal.'

Ian was caught off-guard for only a moment, then he pulls the man's fist down and with his right hand scratches down his face. The man lets out a small cry as he stands up. Ian follows, stands, turns and delivers a side snap punch to the man's nose. The man falls back, partly on the muddy grass with blood coming from his nose.

Standing over him, Ian says, 'Stay there. If you move I will stamp on your trossachs. Now there are a few lessons you need to learn here, PAL. Firstly, train your dog better; secondly don't go round threatening people; thirdly never pick a fight with a copper'. He takes his warrant card out of his top pocket and shows it to him.

'What's your name?'

'Gerrard, Mike Gerrard,' he says, wiping some blood off his face.

'What are you doing with a name like that anyway? Head-butting like that can get you a red card. Give me your wallet.'

He hands it over and Ian looks for his full name. 'Now because I am so soft and kind hearted and the sun's shining, I'm going to walk away. But I've got an excellent memory for faces, names, Mike Gerrard, and dogs, so if I ever come across you again, make sure you are nice and polite. Understand?'

'Yes, right, sorry.'

As he walks away, Ian sees a middle-aged couple hesitating on the path a short distance away. They keep well to one side as he approaches and they look nervous. Ian takes out his warrant card again and says, 'Police. That man started to attack me, so I let him off with a firm warning.' He gives them a bright smile and walks back to the station.

Sometime over the second weekend in June, Alan Dimmock disappeared. The disappearance was both sudden and unexpected and after a slight delay, a police investigation was started. The officers soon established the order of events. Alan Dimmock is a partner in an engineering company and left work on the Friday around 6 o'clock. His wife left the house in the afternoon to visit her parents for the weekend. One of the other two partners in the company, John Fenshaw, visited Alan Dimmock at home on Saturday afternoon. He says they talked about a new project and he left at around 3.30. Dimmock's wife returned from her weekend to find the house empty. The two men are known to have frequent arguments. They used to get on well, but no longer. It is uncertain how the split occurred but suspicion is that one of them was playing around with the other's wife.

There are no unexpected DNA traces in any of the houses or cars. Dimmock's car is still at the house, no use has been made of his credit cards and there've been no sightings of him anywhere. There are no hints of Dimmock having a secret partner or life elsewhere. Whatever the suspicions, without evidence of foul play, the case has to be treated as a missing person for the moment.

There's a meeting of more than a dozen officers and support staff with Superintendent Swindale leading the case.

'Unofficially, John Fenshaw would be the main suspect, if there is a crime. We know he likes to take drives late at night. He's been doing this for years, once or twice a week. He enjoys driving, particularly late at night when there's little traffic. He always takes a cigar with him – his wife won't allow smoking in the house. Sergeant Chambers, summarise what we know of his drives after that weekend?'

'We've spent the last two weeks checking CCTV, fanning out from his house. On the next Wednesday night after the disappearance, he went south and into central London.' The Sergeant uses a laser pointer to illustrate the route on the map projected on a screen.

'The next Monday night he went north and took a large circular route home. The following Thursday, he took this route through Bushey, Radlett and then home. Since then he hasn't made any night drives.'

'No chance of dumping a body in central London,' says the Superintendent. 'Right now we have officers going over that third route. If anything is left lying around, it's likely to be found. There are so many people walking dogs and so on, a body would have to be buried. That can take a long time. The timings on the CCTV make that difficult. It's the same with this route to the north. We've had a good look along that route already. Unless something comes out of the search along this third route, we're getting to a bit of a dead end.'

'Sir,' says Ian.

'Yes.'

'That north route, where are the cameras in the area of the Beechgrove Wood?'

The Sergeant replies, 'There's one here, here and here,' pointing them out on the map.

'What are the times between the first two?'

'11.38 and 12.05.'

'How far between the two cameras?'

'Between five and seven miles, depends on the route. We don't know which route he went. He says he went down here and stopped for a cigar, but he could have gone via the Woods. But digging for a burial would take at least an hour.'

'We've been over those woods and found nothing,' says the Superintendent.

'Is the air raid shelter still there?' Stanton asks which raises some laughter.

'There's no such thing is there Sergeant?'

'No sir, and nothing on the OS map.'

'Any Anderson would have disappeared long ago,' adds the Superintendent.

'It wasn't an Anderson shelter. If anything it will be a Wilmot, four pound ten shillings for the basic model in 1939.'

And there is a little more light laughter.

'Who are you?'

'DC Stanton, sir.'

'You trying to be funny Stanton?'

'No sir.' Ian keeps his face turned down.

'Right, I want a few more officers helping out on the top route. Let's be very thorough there. Keep checking on his friends and we'll give this another couple of weeks. That's all.'

As the meeting breaks up, Inspector Peterson, gives nods to Stanton and Detective Sergeant Chambers to join him his office.

'What's all this about an air raid shelter that got you black looks from the Super out there?'

'I had an aunt who lived nearby and we used to visit. When I was about 11, I was friendly with the boy next door and some of his pals. In those woods was this old air raid shelter, built into the side of a small hill and covered with bushes and brambles. It was quite a dare to see if anyone would crawl up to it and go in. Only one boy would, although we couldn't be sure he did because all the growth around it was pretty dense.'

'But it won't still be there surely and why have an air raid shelter there anyway?'

'There used to be temporary buildings there, like prefabs. They went long ago, but the Wilmot shelters were solid; brick walls and lots of concrete. Secret places and often used to hide radio transmission gear during the war. My aunt's neighbours, there name happened to be Wilmot as well. Harry always pretended his granddad had the business that made them. Complete rubbish but we believed it at the time.'

'Can you remember the spot then?'

'Well, sort of, but it's only a small wood.'

'Right, Sergeant, you two go and check this place out. Stay there until you have got a definite answer, one way of the other.'

The wooded area is not flat but has several hills, hardly more than lumpy bits. One of them has plenty of vegetation growth around it and the area jolts something in Ian's memory.

'This could be it, but I can't be sure from here.'

'Well you had better get in there and have a closer look.'

'What? Me?'

'Of course you. This is all your idea and I'm the Sergeant. In you go.'

'Feel the power. Hang on, someone could only get through that lot by cutting their way in. Let's see if any branches have been cut recently. If not, then I'm wrong; I think that did happen once.' He raises his eyebrows and gives a slight grin to the Sergeant.

'Good thinking, and as senior officer I can take credit for that bit of insight,' says the Sergeant with a smile.

They start pulling at the branches and on one side they find lots of cuts in the vegetation, which create a small opening. The branches have been put back so the breaks don't get noticed. Ian starts negotiating his way into the middle then he calls from inside, 'I'm getting lots of scratches. You really need gloves and overalls here.' A minute later, 'Sarg, there's an old metal door over here. This is the place. There are steps and some of the door is below ground level. It's a small door, less than one and a half metres. It's covered with ivy.'

'Careful of any evidence. Don't go all the way in.'

'I've got forensic gloves.'

The steps are overgrown with grass and earth. Ian pushes some of the ivy aside and parts of it have clearly been cut recently. He pushes a metal handle down and uses force to push open the door, creating a creaking and squeaking sound as it slowly opens. He shines his torch into the shelter.

'Well?' asks the Sergeant. There's no reply, just the sound of Ian scrambling back through the vegetation. Once out in the open, Ian stands up. He's very muddy and has some tears in his clothes. 'There's a bundle in there, at the back, the size of a body wrapped in the green tarpaulin.'

'Holy shit.' DS Chambers gets out his phone.

'Inspector, it's Chambers. We've found the shelter, hidden in the undergrowth, and there's what could be a body inside.'

'That's good and bad news at the same time. I'll send along a couple of people to check. We won't say anything yet.'

'Tell them to bring some good hedge cutters; there's lots of brambles in the way.'

'Will do. If this comes to anything, tell Stanton to keep his head down around the Superintendent.'

The Sergeant turns to Ian. 'People on the way. The Inspector says keep a low profile with the Super if this is a body.'

'But he's in charge, he'll get the credit for any success here won't he?' Ian asks.

'Oh, he'll take that all right, but you'll have made him look stupid in front of everybody and he's a sore loser. He once broke a club just because he lost a silly game of golf against the Chief Inspector.'

'I hope he didn't break it over his head.'

'Not quite that bad, but the Chief had to pay for the lunch and all the whiskies just to placate him.'

'Will he turn up here?'

'The Super won't but the Inspector will,' replies the Sergeant.

'It would be quite a job dragging a body in here and he'd want to do it quickly,' says Ian.

'How much did he weigh, Dimmock that is, do you know?'

'The Path report said he was 5' 11" and weighed just over 11 stone.'

'Not so big then. Fenshaw is quite stocky and keen on rowing, so he's probably pretty strong, and he'd be desperate. I reckon he could do it all right.'

When two scene of crime officers arrive, they soon confirm it is a human body wrapped up. With the scene taped off, recovery of evidence is in progress when the Inspector turns up and takes Chambers and Stanton to one side. 'Whoever did this obviously has good local knowledge going back a long way.'

'You mean like Stanton?' says the Sergeant with a sideways glance at Ian.

'Yes, top of the list of suspects. And it would be hard to cut a path through all this undergrowth and then dump a body quickly. If it's a spontaneous crime, it's likely to need two or three trips, and after dark. At the moment, there's nothing definite to connect any absences or suspicious activity with Fenshaw, and we have only one record of him near this spot over the last three weeks – unless he hired a car.'

'But we checked all his movements sir,' points out the Sergeant.

'He was visiting sites and locations a lot over a period of several days. That's a routine part of his job. It's easy to lose a few hours that way. We've already checked all the company vehicles, so now I've got people at the office contacting all the car hire firms over a wide area and getting lists of everyone who hired a car or van over that period. We'll see if any names match up.'

And only one did – John Fenshaw, with a car hire firm more than ten miles away, leading to fibre traces from the tarpaulin in the boot of his hired car.

Time passes . . . . . with the usual everyday matters of domestics, break-ins, car thefts, card fraud, shop-lifting and stabbings.

4

In Which there is Cake with Coconut

In November, Ian decides to buy himself a Christmas present – an electric harp. He's impressed with the new sound possibilities of these instruments and researches for a good product. A modern instrument in electric blue is his eventual choice.

It's the following year and Ian is assigned to assist a large team searching for a young female student, gone missing in September, just at the beginning of the new term. There's no indication as to whether she's held captive somewhere or has been killed or has had some sort of breakdown and run off. Ian is one of the many officers checking house-to-house reports, collating them and looking for gaps or clues.

And there are too many gaps; some houses got no answer and were not revisited; some visits seemed too brief; some houses at the end of streets were not called on at all.

The 17 year old took the same route to and from college every day, except on Thursdays when she went home via the sports centre for a game of badminton. She went missing on a Monday afternoon or evening so the emphasis was on her regular route. CCTV cameras exist in abundance near the college, the sports centre and the high streets, but there are large gaps in between. Ian feels it's worth having a better look at the Thursday route – perhaps that's where she got noticed. Identifying the area and route he thinks is worth another look, he goes to clear it with the Inspector.

'Yes, that's fine; go ahead. Now the Superintendent and I have to do a media appeal.'

'Do they make any difference?'

'I don't think so, but it does keep the matter in the public eye and mind. The parents want to do all they can, of course. The media love them; there's nothing they like better than seeing distressed parents bursting into tears. The cameras will be clicking so much you won't be able to hear what they're saying.'

Ian and another officer, PC Prescott, work out a plan of streets and houses they want to cover, asking all the usual questions about recognising a face and remembering what they saw and did a week ago.

Prescott starts on one side of a street, with Stanton on the other. They spend their time knocking on doors, talking, going back where there was no answer and slowly ticking houses off the list. Early in the day, when Roger Prescott knocks at one house, an old lady answers the door, just a small amount. He introduces himself the normal way and explains about the search. The old lady simply looks and says nothing. Prescott isn't sure whether she has understood. Then she says, 'Would you like a cup of tea?' She has an anxious expression, as though she's afraid he'll say no. Prescott takes a moment to decide between getting on with the job or being kind and saying yes to the tea.

'Well thank you, that sounds very nice.' She opens the door to let him in. In the kitchen the woman enthusiastically fills the kettle and gets out china cups, chatting all the time and asking everyday questions. She's obviously very lonely and rarely has a chance to entertain someone. From the cupboard she produces a new packet of Rich Tea biscuits and spreads them out on a large plate. While drinking the tea and accepting a third biscuit, Prescott makes a note to get in touch with AgeUK to arrange a volunteer visitor for the old lady.

'This has been a good break, thank you. I must get on now, we really need to find that missing woman. What's your name?' he asks.

'Emma Davey, thank you thank you will you come again?'

'I'll try and do that.'

For his part, Ian even asks to look around some of the houses, partly to see how people react to the request. People don't seem to mind and it only takes a couple of minutes.

At one house, he senses the man is a little too keen. His smile doesn't look genuine; the smile is all with his mouth and there's no movement around the eyes, which would happen with a genuine smile. Ian feels he's not to be trusted.

'Do you mind if I have a quick look round?' he asks.

'Don't you need a warrant?'

'Oh, yes, you're quite right; it's fine if you refuse. But people usually let us in for a quick look around

The more places we can definitely cross off the list, the sooner we can spread out farther afield.'

'Okay then,' he replies, not wishing to arouse any suspicion. 'I'll have to get the dog first and tell him you're a friend.'

He opens the kitchen door and grabs the dog by the collar. It's a Staffordshire Bull Terrier and is already growling. Speaking to the dog he says, 'Jackson, friend, friend. If I shake hands with you, then he knows you are a friend.'

The man shakes hands with Ian and the dog starts wagging his tail.

'Well this is a good trick. It makes a change to see a well-trained dog. I guess he must be perfect against burglaries.

'Yes I trained him myself.'

Ian has a quick look in the rooms upstairs, keeping it very casual and not appearing to take much interest. Then downstairs into the two living rooms either side of the hall, and into the kitchen. The man says, 'That's it then.' He looks away for a second and Ian quickly opens the back door and goes into the garden which looks a mess.

'There's nothing out here. I'm not too brilliant at gardening.' The man is sounding concerned.

'Nor me. I like gardens but I don't like doing all the work,' responds Ian with the same casual manner. Around the garden is a high fence on one side and two high hedges. There's a shed close to the kitchen door and he notices the shed window is completely covered inside by a dirty sheet.

The man is now appearing more agitated. 'Look, that's enough. I want you to get out now.'

Ian thinks he hears a slight noise from inside the shed. 'What's in there?' he asks.

The man ignores the question but says, 'Jackson, guard.' The dog starts growling and baring its teeth.

'Okay, yes, that's fine. Let me pass and I'll leave,' says Ian showing caution.

The man stands aside and Ian walks back into the kitchen. Ian has his own customised belt when he's out and always wears a jacket to cover it. He likes to have two pairs of handcuffs, an all-purpose penknife, an LED torch and a small aerosol of pepper spray. He slips his hand under his jacket and takes out the aerosol, and in the hall turns suddenly and sprays a blast into the dog's face. The dog whines and collapses on the floor and splutters. Ian goes to spray the man as well but he's quick enough to turn away and run into the kitchen. Ian grabs the dog by the collar, picking it up and dragging it into the dining room. By the time he closes the door, the man is running towards him with a kitchen knife. Ian steps aside, grabs the man's wrist, twists his arm and forces him on to the ground, causing him to drop the knife. Ian cuffs him, marches him into the garden leaving him face down on the long grass.

'You move from there and I'll break your neck.'

Ian picks up an old garden fork and breaks off the lock to open the shed door. Lying on a camp bed is a young woman tied up and gagged, wide-eyed and looking terrified. He instantly pulls out his warrant card and says, 'Police police. It's all right.'

Taking out his penknife he cuts the ropes, then takes a length of the rope and ties the man's legs together. Immediately back in the shed, he picks up the young woman and carries her to the living room and lays her on the settee. 'What's your name?' he asks.

'Annie, Annie Carter. The dog, where's the dog?' she says, sounding very scared.

'Locked away; we're safe.' The first errand is to get her a glass of water. As she gulps it down, he's on the phone to the station.

'Sergeant Chambers, please – emergency.'

'DS Chambers.'

'DC Stanton, Sergeant. I've found the girl and she's alive.'

The Sergeant jumps up. 'What? Where?'

'27 Harvey Road. One man in custody.'

'Right,' says the Sergeant, putting down the phone. He's in the operations room, which contains about 20 officers and civilian staff. He calls out, 'She's alive.'

There's a spontaneous cheering and applause from all in the office.

'You two. Get four cars, no five cars; two officers in each; two WPCs to 27 Harvey Road. Seal off the house back and front. You – two ambulances to the same address.'

Someone shouts out, 'Who found her Sarge?'

'Stanton,' as he runs down a short corridor, gives a cursory knock on an office door and barges straight in. Swindale is now a Chief Superintendent and is in discussion with Inspector Peterson.

'We've found her – alive.'

Back at the house, Ian drags the prisoner into the shed and leaves him sitting on the floor. He thinks to call PC Prescott. 'Prescott, it's Stanton, I need you here – 27 Harvey Road.' A police car arrives in a few minutes to find Ian standing at the front door holding up his warrant card. 'In here,' as he leads them into the living room.

'It's DD isn't it? Where's the arrest?' asks one officer. 'You stay here Frank.'

Ian leads the way through the kitchen and to the shed. 'I'm only a DC so I can't give you orders, but it would be good if you could stay here and keep an eye on him. He has not been cautioned.'

'Right, well done.'

PC Prescott comes running up the path. 'Prescott, there's a dangerous dog in there. Don't let anybody in. I hit him with pepper spray. When he recovers, he's going to be angry,' Ian says.

'Right, I'll call for the dog handlers,' says Prescott as he takes out his phone. At the same time, a second car arrives with a WPC. She sits beside the woman, who's starting to calm down a little now, but is crying quietly.

PC Knight asks Ian, 'How did you manage to find her?'

'Doing door-to-door. Talking to him, it didn't feel right, so I asked to have a look around.'

'He let you in?' Knight asks with surprise.

'Yes. I guess he didn't want to arouse any suspicion and people don't see me as a threat. When I showed too much interest in the shed, he threatened to set the dog on me and came at me with a kitchen knife.'

'Brilliant. Great job.'

Suddenly several cars arrive. While the Inspector is outside with DS Chambers organising sealing off the street and house, Chief Superintendent Swindale charges into the room. Quickly he looks around.

Someone says, 'Prisoner out the back sir'. He goes to see and returns immediately.

'Right, there too many people here. Who are you?' pointing to Ian.

'DC Stanton sir.'

'DC? Oh yes, I know you. Get out. I only want uniforms and seniors here.'

'What?' says Stanton, looking curious.

'Don't "What" me. Just get out. Get yourself back to the station.'

'Yes sir.' Ian looks at officer Knight and the WPC, then at the woman on the couch who has her eyes closed with tears on her cheeks. The junior officers look at each other but say nothing. Ian leaves the room, then the house.

Sirens are sounding and ambulances arrive, as the Inspector enters the room. He looks around and takes it all in.

'Are you Annie Carter?'

She replies with a nod and a weak, 'Yes'.

He taps into his phone. A woman answers, 'WPC Grey.'

'Grey. We've found her; she's alive.'

The officer shouts out with delight and repeats the news into the room.

'Is Mrs Carter there, put her on.'

The Inspector hands the phone to Annie. 'Here, it's your mum.'

'Where's Stanton?' Inspector Peterson asks the others.

There's a long pause. PC Knight says 'The Superintendent sent him back to the station, sir.'

'So who knows what's happened here?'

'Only Stanton, sir,' says Knight, with a certain amount of bravery.

'So DC Stanton did all this and he's not here?'

'One prisoner out the back sir,' continues Knight tactfully.

After a quick look at the prisoner and at security around the back, the Inspector returns to the living room.

Everything takes its natural course after that. An ambulance takes the girl off to hospital with a large police escort, the crime scene is sealed off and a car is sent to take the parents to the hospital.

'Sir. The press will be swarming in no time. Shall we direct them to the station, rather than here and you could speak to them on the front steps?'

'Yes, right. I've got enough to keep them going for now. Keep in touch if anything new happens,' as he leaves the room.

The Inspector watches the Chief Superintendent get into his car and drive off.

'Sergeant, get Stanton on the phone and tell him to get back here Now.'

'Yes sir.'

★

Ian walks back towards the station about a mile away. He's annoyed and upset at first, but then a wonderful feeling of peace and success washes over him. He walks along, feeling elated. When on the main road, he comes to a corner café. In the café he asks for a coffee and picks a cake with icing and threads of coconut on the top.

Police sirens wail up and down in the background. At the counter, the man says, 'Something big going on here.'

'They've found that missing girl, alive, so someone said,' says Ian, not wishing to let on he's in the police and involved.

'Fantastic. Hang on, I must tell Maureen.' He shouts out the back, 'Hey Maureen, they've found the Carter girl alive.'

Maureen comes into the café, looking excited. 'Really, they've found her? Where?'

'Oh I don't know. Somewhere a few streets away. I suppose it'll be on the news soon.'

Ian is about to pick up his coffee and cake when his phone rings.

'Right-o, on my way,' which wasn't quite true as he sits down to quietly finish his coffee and cake before doing a bit of speed walking back to the house.

Finally returning to the police station, Ian walks into the operations room. When he's spotted, people stand and applaud. One of the woman rushes to him and gives him a big hug, much to his embarrassment.

'Come on, tell us what happened.' Ian gives an

outline and how the Chief Superintendent told him to get out. 'I had better write everything down now while I remember it all.'

Someone says, 'My typing's super fast. You just tell it and I'll type.'

After the excitement and tension of the rescue, Ian is soon back to earth with more routine police matters. Now up to Third Dan in aikido, he maintains the sport on a regular basis, along with karate and his airgun practice. One thing he has always been nervous about is swimming, for some reason never having learnt at school. The politest thing that could be said about his swimming is that it's like a doggy paddle gone wrong. A visit to the local pool tells him that swimming improvement lessons are available for a modest charge. He decides that if he could do the breast stroke and front crawl to a competent level that would be a good idea.

Routine time passes . . . . .

5

IN WHICH TRAPS ARE SPRUNG

It's now July of the following year and Ian Stanton is in his third year in the CID. He's on the phone as Sergeant Innes approaches.

'Ready to visit this Hemmings character?' he asks. WPC Walker is coming too.'

Beatrice Walker is what can only be described as an absolute stunner. Tall and curvy, long wavy ash-blonde hair, which is always tied up into a tight bundle at work, vivid blue eyes and a beautiful and exactly symmetrical face with perfect teeth. If her beauty doesn't scare most men, her intelligence certainly will. First class honours degree in philosophy and economics, fluent in three languages and an expert in medieval art around Europe. She's in her last week in uniform before she transfers to detective duties. In uniform or any form of plain clothes, she finds it difficult to tone down her looks.

'I've just got to finish this call Sergeant. You go on. I'll follow right behind in my car then I can go straight home after.'

'Right. Don't be long.'

The street they are going to has semi-detached Victorian houses with front gardens, which mainly contain small areas for off-road parking. The street is only wide enough for cars to be parked on one side, so Ian has to park 50 metres away from the house. As he approaches, he notices the unmarked police car Innes will have used and just then his phone rings.

'Ian, this is Goodall. I've just heard that Nick Peters was released yesterday. He's known as Nick the Flick and he's a complete psycho. That address you're going to, he's put it down as the place he's staying. If he's there, his brother will be too; he's nearly as bad. There's going to be more in that house than you expect. I've called Innes but no answer and Walker, no answer.'

'Okay, I can't see them so they must be inside. I'll go round the back first. If I don't call you in two minutes send backup.'

'I'll send a car anyway.'

Evening is drawing in and the curtains are closed. Stanton switches off his phone and goes round to the back of the house and finds the kitchen door unlocked. Of course he doesn't know what's happened already.

While Innes and Walker were talking to Hemmings at the front door, there was shouting from inside, sounding like someone was being violently attacked. Innes pushes his way into the hall and goes into the room with the noise, closely followed by Walker. Hemmings pushes Walker hard in the back so that she falls on to Innes and they both lose their balance.

They were immediately jump on by four men, knocked to the ground, punched and kicked. In no time, they were handcuffed behind their backs and gagged with tea towels.

Nick psycho said, 'Right you can 'ave him 'arry and we'll 'ave her'.

'Great,' said Harry. 'He's a good one, I like big boys.'

A phone rings in Sergeant Innes's pocket. 'Get their phones and turn 'em off.'

'We 'aven't got long before they get missed then we take the bodies to the Hatfield site. We'll fix alibis with Mike. Fucking coppers, I hate the bastards. This one's a beauty. Let's get 'er next door. I'm 'aving 'er first. After six years in the Scrubs I'm bursting. Turn the radios on. Not too loud but loud enough.'

As they start to pick up Walker, she kicks out which gets her more punches in the stomach and face. After being dragged into the other room, she's dropped on the floor.

This is when Stanton comes quietly into the kitchen. He hears the radios and excited voices. Going into one room, he sees Sergeant Innes on the floor with blood and injuries on his face.

'Who the fuck are you?' Harry asks.

'Friend of the family – he said I could join in here.' This gives Ian just enough time to get close enough to Harry to deliver blows. A kick on the knee is followed by a hard punch in the face and as Harry falls down he hits his head on the wall and lies unconscious. Ian quickly searches the man but finds no gun. Stanton always carries two keys for handcuffs, one on a key ring and a second in an otherwise empty pocket. He rolls the Sergeant on to his side and undoes one half of the handcuffs.

Quickly, he goes next door. In a split second he sees

the layout. There's surprise on the faces of the men inside. Man-1 is the nearest to Stanton and moves towards him.

Man-2 is by Walker's feet and is taking her shoes off; her trousers are already around her ankles. Man-2 puts his hand into his jacket to pull out a gun. Stanton grabs Man-1 and pulls him in front so the two bullets fired by Man-2 hit him in the back. Stanton pushes Man-1 on to Man-2 who falls back and drops his gun. Stanton is quick to pick up the gun.

By now Man-3 has pulled Walker up by the hair and is crouched down behind her, with a gun at her head. He shouts, 'Stop. Drop it or she's dead.' Stanton knows instantly to stop now would be the death of all of them. As he drops to the ground, Ian snaps out a shot hitting the man in the face. Such quick shots from awkward angles is something he's practised a lot with his airgun.

Walker falls back on to the dead man's body. Her clothes have been ripped and cut down the front exposing her breasts but she seems fully conscious. Stanton points his gun at Man-2 and shouts, 'Face down. NOW. Face down!' He fires one bullet near the man's head. 'Hands behind your back Now!'

In panic, the man says, 'Yes, yes, don't shoot.'

Stanton jumps forward, picks up the loose gun and slides it across the floor under the sideboard. After rolling Walker on to her side, he undoes one of her handcuffs, while saying, 'Get out to the street.' He quickly puts cuffs on the man lying down while Walker struggles to pull up her trousers, then he goes back to the other room to help Innes. Harry is groaning and starting to move. Innes was too heavy for him to lift, so Stanton put his hands under his arms and drags him out into the hall, through the front door, down the path and through the gate to the pavement. Walker staggers to the door and out of the house and with lots of blood over her face she looks about to faint any moment. She holds her torn clothes over her front and has only one shoe. Stanton gets her to sit down on a low wall. With gun in one hand and keeping a close eye on the house, he presses buttons on his phone to call the station.

'Hello Ian.'

'People hurt. We need three ambulances and gun squad.'

'On the way,' replies Goodall and cuts off.

Stanton keeps a close eye on the house with his gun ready.

After around five minutes a patrol car arrives, closely followed by an ambulance from the other direction. By now there are plenty of people standing around in the street but keeping well back. Stanton shows his warrant card to the ambulance medics and shouts, 'Police. Two coppers hurt. Take them and get out.' He barely takes his eyes off the house. Sergeant Innes is carried to the ambulance and Walker manages to stagger there. The ambulance pulls away and after a few more minutes, a black van arrives. Ian is quick to show his badge, knowing that these men will jump out of the vehicle with guns level and wouldn't like the sight of him holding a gun. Half a dozen firearms officers take over.

Stanton makes his way back to the station while Inspector Peterson starts to find out the sequence of events. There is no early night for Stanton.

A few days later, Stanton is at his desk looking at files; he's relieved to be doing mundane tasks while investigations take place. The new Detective Constable Walker approaches, with plaster on her face and some nasty bruises. 'May I have private word, please?' she asks. Stanton follows her round to the back of the station where they sit down on a bench.

'There's really only one thing I can say, and that's Thank You.'

'You're welcome. I'm sure it won't become a habit,' he says in a light-hearted way. 'How's the Sergeant?'

'I saw him yesterday. A broken cheek bone and concussion, but they'll be letting him home today. His pride is hurt more. He can't understand how he fell for that trick and how we ended up in such a mess. I don't blame him. He reacted like that because he thought someone was in trouble.'

They sit quietly for a moment.

'Your aren't a full AFO are you?' she asks.

'No.'

'I remember exactly what happened. Strangely it was all in slow motion to me. That man Peters was right behind me and very close. You were dropping to the floor and you fired. How were you able to hit him and miss me?'

'I guess I must be a rotten shot.'

Beatrice Walker hesitates then bursts out laughing. It looks as though the laughter might become hysterical but she manages to control it.

'How did hubby take all this? Is he in the police?'

'No, he's a computer security expert. Anyway, a WPC went round to the house. She was good and played it down a lot so as not to worry him. Said it wasn't much, they were just checking me over to be sure. It wasn't until later he started to hear more and he still doesn't know the full story. He will in time of course, as I hear there's talk of you getting a George Medal.'

'Oh. What only the Medal, you mean you and Sergeant Innes aren't even worth a George Cross?'

She starts laughing again. 'Look, laughing hurts my face so stop it. There will be an inquiry of course, what with the guns and two people killed. The Inspector says it'll be a formality. Have you seen the police doctor yet?'

'No. Why should I? I wasn't hurt.'

'Not physically, but it's not every day you shoot someone.'

Ian simply shrugs his shoulder.

'In the meantime...' Beatrice pauses for a couple of seconds. 'Will you let my buy you a coffee and a doughnut?'

'With jam inside?'

'With jam inside.'

'Perfect reward, thank you.'

Soon after, when Ian gets awarded the George Medal, it's nearly five years since he first started his police training.

Time elapses . . . . .

6

IN WHICH THERE IS PLUCKING OF STRINGS

Ian is driving to a house where a break-in has been reported. There's a light dusting of snow on the ground and it's a crisp February morning as he turns into the drive towards a large Edwardian detached house.

A smartly dressed woman lets him in and explains how she and her daughter were out for only about an hour and didn't bother to put the alarm on. They got home to a broken window and several valuable items missing.

While Ian is writing down the details, a police forensic van pulls up to the house. Jack Nowak is very experienced and he's accompanied by a trainee, Alison. They immediately start to examine the break-in area, a small conservatory at the back of the house which doesn't have double glazing. Ian is shown into the living room where the house owners have a list prepared and photographs of some of the stolen items for Ian to examine and take away. In the living room, the daughter is lounging on an easy chair. She looks to be in her late teens and is sulky.

But Ian's attention is immediately drawn to a full-sized harp near the French windows. He moves over to the harp and looks closely at it for about a minute.

'May I give it a pluck.'

The daughter shrugs and says, 'Sure'. Obviously everyone always wants to give it a pluck and she's not much interested.

With his right hand, Ian gently draws his fingers over the strings towards himself, then away from himself with his thumb. He makes a continuous circular motion with a perfect glissando. Then he does the same with his left hand and continues with each hand in turn in an expert rhythm. At this point the two forensic officers walk into the room.

The young woman perks up, looks at her mother, then to the new arrivals, then back to Ian. She stands and moves closer to the harp as Ian's plucking merges into a tune. One tune blends into another with perfect technique and using an unusual range of chords. He moves on to Bach but playing it much faster than normal.

The young woman is standing there with her mouth open, while her mother leaves her chair to come and stand behind her daughter. They notice how Ian has his eyes closed all the time.

After several minutes, he stops playing and stands quite still for some seconds. He turns to the young woman and says, 'Thank you. It's certainly a beautiful instrument. I've never played on 47 strings before.'

She seems speechless and gives a small bow.

'Have you finished?' he asks the technicians, and Jack nods in reply. 'We had better be going. We'll let you know as soon as we have any news.' He turns to go.

The mother speaks. 'Where did you learn to play like that?'

'Mainly the internet, books and I taught myself.'

The daughter says, 'You had your eyes closed. How can you play like that with your eyes closed!' almost shouting at him.

Ian shrugs. 'That's the only way I can play.' The three of them leave the room and when outside the house, next to the vehicles, Ian asks, 'Think you might get something out of that?'

'Possibly. I reckon there was a spot of blood on the broken glass.'

'Wow, that would definitely be something, if we could actually get a burglar on a charge for a change.'

When the two technicians are driving off, Jack says, 'That harp business was a bit special wasn't it?'

'Yes,' replies Alison. 'You know, that's the chap who saved my cousin's life, and Sergeant Innes's. She's DC Walker. He took on four men with guns. Got a George Medal for it.'

'Blimey. Never go by appearances then, eh?'

Ian is having a few minutes in the canteen when a woman in civilian clothes approaches. He thinks she must be a Support worker.

'It's Ian Stanton isn't it?'

He nods and she sits down opposite him.

'A quick word please. My name is Joe. Rumour has it you are quite useful at playing the harp.'

'Are you in forensics?'

'No, but I heard this from Alison.'

'I play the violin – quite well actually. I'm seeing if I can get a few musicians together to make up a small group, just for the fun of it.'

'Oh. What have you got so far?'

'Someone who plays the drums, very cleverly in fact. And a brilliant, brilliant singer. That's all so far.'

'How does one hit something with a stick cleverly?'

'Not all drummers are gorillas.'

'Some of my best friends are gorillas.'

'Indeed? Do you have a harp?'

'Yes I do. It's electric and it doesn't sound quite like a normal harp.'

'That's good. I'm not after a normal sound, like some chamber ensemble which couldn't really make it. My friend, Don the drummer, is an electronic whizz-kid. He works here in technical. He's made an amp with all the normal effects plus something of his own. What it does is to repeat the notes played, almost instantaneously and maybe a fraction higher or lower so that one violin suddenly sounds like 20 violins playing together in an orchestra.'

'Interesting. So one mistake can be heard 20 times or perfect playing can be heard 20 times with no mistakes.'

'Exactly, but let's leave out the mistakes.'

'And will it do the same for an electric harp?'

'I should think so. Want to give it a try?'

'Sure. And who says you are a good violinist, if I may ask such a rude question?'

'Fair enough. I managed two years at music college. I suppose I wasn't good enough to get a top orchestra job, and I also got bored playing many of the same pieces all the time. Now I play socially with a few other string players, but here I'm really after a different sound.'

'What about this singer?'

'That's Sarah, she works here.'

'But but but, hang on,' says Ian. 'We'll do this later. I have to go. What's your number.'

'272.'

'I'll call you later. Could we meet some time over the weekend?'

'Fine.'

Joe lives in a semi in a smart suburb and on Saturday afternoon Ian arrives with his electric harp. She takes him into the living room. Joe is slim and has a face of sharp features and short dark hair. Her clothes are an around-the-house casual track suit in mauve and she favours bare feet.

'Tea, coffee?'

'Not yet thanks, let's see the gadgets first shall we.'

'Okay, this is my normal violin, a pretty good instrument and this is my electric violin. It looks wild doesn't it?'

'Certainly different and it's got five strings.'

'Well spotted. Gives a wider range, and I wanted one that looks a bit unusual.'

'This is a normal violin.' She plays for about 30 seconds. It sounds good to Ian's non-expert ear.

'Now this is the electric violin.' She plays the same piece again. 'Sounds very similar on this instrument but there is a subtle difference. Now I switch on Don's magic box.' Joe plays the same piece again and suddenly it's like a small orchestra of violins all playing in unison.

'Flaming heck, that's amazing; suddenly it's like the Sorcerer's apprentice.'

'Yes, now listen to this.' She presses another button on the amp controls and plays again. This time it starts with one instrument and slowly more instruments are added to it until all 20 seem to be playing. 'This dial makes it anywhere from one instrument to 20.'

'It's bluetooth. Will it work with any instrument?'

'With the right connections.'

'So who's the singer then?'

That's Sarah, she works in Support. She lives here and we're partners. Gone to visit her parents for today and tomorrow, in Reading. They don't like me; they think I'm an evil influence having led their precious innocent daughter astray.'

'Are they right?'

'Mmm yes. I didn't know what an amazing singer she is until I heard her singing in the shower.'

'People actually sing in the shower?'

'She does. She's very nervous about singing in front of people, even me, so that needs to be worked on. She takes private singing lessons because she enjoys it so much. She does cross-over and even some fairly raw rock.'

The door bell rings. 'That'll be Don. He'll want tea straight away.'

'I've was able to make a recording of Sarah and a few songs. You can listen to it while we have our tea and scones. Don's heard it already.'

She plays the recording.

'Wow. Wow and double wow,' says Ian clearly impressed. 'What was that last piece she was singing?'

'A bit of modified Steffani.'

'And I've never heard The Sound of Silence sung like that either.

'She can't keep up such a raw voice for long but it sounds really good added in like that. She can fill a large hall without a microphone. Now it's your turn. Come on, start plucking those strings.'

'We'll be the examiners and executioners, with our arms folded and looking intimidating,' says Don.

When Ian takes the cover off the harp, Don says, 'Well that is one striking-looking instrument.'

'I can put it on a stand and I usually do for practice, but I'm going to use these straps to hold it. Then I can move around and pretend I'm heavy metal and in front of 80,000 hysterical fans in the Olympic stadium. I'll need to do a few minutes warm up.'

He plays a couple of tunes, the first at a modest speed, the second much faster.

Don is the first to speak 'It definitely doesn't sound like a normal harp; much more gutsy and there's some reverb on it, and there's plenty of bass.'

'The bass has been modified with double strings an octave lower.'

'Right. At times you seemed to be playing bass and treble at the same time. I'm glad to see you don't do all those silly harpist arm movements.'

'Alison was right then. Well I reckon we can do something with this. How about you Don?'

'Definitely.'

'Can you read music Ian?'

'Just about, but not instantly for sight reading and playing.'

'That's all right. The big question is will Sarah play ball and get over her fear of singing in front of people?'

'Can I meet her then and see what persuasion she needs?

'She's already scared you – she's seen your police record.

'But I'm a pussy cat really'

'Of course you are dear – a tiger in disguise,' says Joe.

The following Saturday, Ian arrives at their house to meet Sarah. She has a pleasant but plain face, blinks rather a lot but perhaps that goes with the stammer. The stammer is only slight and not bad enough to get really irritating to the listener. The three of them are sitting and talking when Joe says, 'How about some coffee Sarah?'

Sarah says nothing but obediently gets up to go in the kitchen.

Ian says, 'Look, why don't Sarah and I go to the coffee shop down the road and have a little chat.'

'What, just the two of you?' Joe frowns and Sarah looks from one to the other and back again.

'It'll be fine, I'm sure I'll be quite safe,' he says.

'What?' again from Joe, obviously not pleased at being out of this loop.

'Come along Sarah, we won't be long.'

Joe watches them walk down the path. At the gate, Ian turns and as a tease says to Joe, 'I'll bring her back in a week or so.' Sarah smiles and Joe looks serious.

Walking down the road, Ian asks 'Is she the jealous type.'

Sarah replies with a weak, 'Yes'.

The coffee shop is fairly busy and there's some soft background music.

'Have you and Joe been together long?'

'About, nearly two years I think. It's Joe's house. Her parents have lots of money. I don't pay rent, just buy all the food, share the bills, do the cooking and most of the chores.'

It sounds a little one-sided to Ian but he says nothing.

'Playing and singing in front of people can be daunting,' says Ian. 'I mainly play on my own and I've never played to a crowd. I think the trick is to treat it like an adventure and not a terrifying ordeal.'

'I think it will need more than that for me.'

'Some actors claim to be very shy but then they get on stage and do the business because they're playing a part and hiding behind the character, with a different mind, different clothes and someone living a different way of life. How about if we created a completely new persona for you, some sort of fantasy character?'

'You mean like pretend I'm a movie star or made-up comic book character?

'Exactly. What secret fantasy do you have about yourself? One that you've never dared tell anyone.'

Sarah is quiet at first, looks around, hesitates then says, 'Walking down a street in skin tight leather with long white hair down to my waist and Goth make-up and everyone moving out of my way because I look so scary.' Then she giggles.

'R-i-g-h-t. That would work. What colour leather?'

'Black.'

'No, not black, too ordinary.'

'How about a bright green, long black boots and long very red hair. And exaggerated make-up that makes you look wild and unrecognizable.'

'Okay, if you can get me dressed up like that, I'll see if I can give it a go.'

So the plan is in motion.

Over the next few weeks, Joe works out music and arrangements and they start practising and developing their sound, with their target being the police Christmas concert.

Ian finds a supplier of custom motorcycle leathers who measure Sarah and make her the outfit. Wig and boots are bought and her new make-up designed.

Joe is not told exactly what they are working on. When Sarah is ready for a public viewing, they all gather in the living room. Sarah goes off to get changed, but she goes via the kitchen. From the fridge she takes out an opened bottle of white wine and has three big swigs. Fifteen minutes later she comes down stairs, grits her teeth and walks in the living room.

Sarah has a trim figure with a flat tummy. The leather jacket and trousers are a strong green and are a tight fit while she's put a little extra padding over her boobs. Then there are the black boots with half-high heels and matching black leather gloves. The wig is long and full of waves and looks a natural red colour rather than a dye. The bright red lipstick and exaggerated eye and eyebrow make-up have transformed her face, particularly without her glasses. She feels embarrassed but puts a brave face on it.

Ian smiles, Don cheers and claps, Joe just stares, not sure how to react.

'You look amazing. Give your hips a wiggle,' says Don.

Sarah obliges.

'Brilliant. Will you marry me?' he asks and Joe slaps his arm.

'Well look at her. Everybody's going to want to give that leather a stroke, and drag her off home,' says Don.

'Super hot or what,' says Ian.

Sarah blushes and looks away.

'Now the rest of us have got to have something that fits in with that. Let's all dress in green and black and white. I fancy a green bowler hat,' finishes Don.

'And . . . ?'

'Nothing else, just the green bowler hat.'

'What do you think Joe?'

'Well it's certainly eye-catching. This is what you two have been up to is it?'

'Can you still move all right in that suit?'

'Yes, it's easy and I love the feel of the leather.'

'Do you mind if I'm the first to stroke it?' asks Don.

'I've stroked it already,' says Ian.

'Why don't you make some tea Joe and we'll stay here?'

'That's enough from you two – get control will you?'

The men laugh and nudge each other.

'Sarah and I will both make tea. Come on madam features,' says Joe.

After Sarah has been bundled off to the kitchen, Ian says, 'When you get a chance, stroke down her thigh; it really gets you going, and Sarah loves her new skin.'

'If Joe ever finds out such details, you'll be investigating your own murder,' warns Don.

'I hope Joe doesn't feel too threatened and take it out on Sarah.'

'I'll go into the kitchen and be the diplomat; I've known Joe for ever,' offers Don.

Time progresses . . . . .

7

In Which a Misper Case Resurfaces

In Ian's mind, crime can be put into three categories. There is the easy and obvious crime; somebody virtually caught in the act holding the smoking gun, including the stupid person who left a simple clue or bits of DNA behind, or that shoplifter caught on CCTV. Such events can be wrapped up in a day or so.

Next are the more long-term investigations, involving lots of door-to-door, the persistent tracking down of witnesses, and elaborate forensic work, leading, eventually to a result.

The third category is the unsolved. Weeks and months of plodding police work and no result at the end of it, except an open file.

A fourth category of computer and cyber crime is well outside Ian's range. Although he's good with computers and can do coding, it's not an area of crime he's involved in. The worlds of international drug smuggling and international terrorist organisations are not in his compass at all.

The category of the unsolved is the situation with young Anthony Bradshaw.

Autumn is quite well advanced when Chief Superintendent Swindale is called in to see the Assistant Chief Constable.

'Do you remember the Anthony Bradshaw case George. Boy went missing over five years ago. Never traced. You were in charge as DCI then weren't you?'

'Oh yes, I remember it well. We had a couple of serious suspects for that. Bits of circumstantial but nothing strong enough for a charge. No body found and the file is still open.'

'That's it. Well Charles Bradshaw, his father, is a friend of mine at the sailing club in Lymington. We tend not to talk much about work; it's boats, sailing or golf. But when he found out I'm ACC here, he mentioned his son. He thinks about him all the time of course. He knows the case hit a wall but suggests maybe new forensic techniques might help now. Possibly. Anyway, for diplomatic reasons, I said we'd give the case a review. Now there is no suggestion that the case was not handled properly, but I am going to put some fresh eyes on it for a while, and they can run new tests.'

'I can't image we missed anything but it'll be worth doing new tests. Who's going to run it?'

'Not sure yet, but keep well clear please and don't put ideas in his head, all right. It won't be a large team.'

'Yes, sir.'

Chief Inspector Gibbons is given the task. He has a reputation for being precise and finicky over details to the point of OCD. He chooses Detective Sergeant Blake and DC Stanton as his foot soldiers, because of their similar approach. There are several piles of files they have to work through in detail.

'Ian, do you reckon you are a bit OCD?' Sergeant Blake asks him one day, over his desk piled up with documents.

'A bit? Watch the insults please. It goes with the job but I can be so OCD that I'm CDO.'

'That makes all three of us then. Maybe we should all go to the same therapist and try for a discount.' And do they laugh.

They are having a break from the files with drinks from the machine. Malcolm Blake goes for the very strong tea, while Ian feels safer with the hot chocolate.

'That psychology you did at university, it's all about the way people think and behave isn't it?'

'Yes that's right.'

'At lunch, Adam Border was having a rant about sentences, the way he does. Thinks they all should be so much longer as a good warning to other criminals. Nothing new in that idea.'

'But it doesn't work. People don't think of consequences. Look, if someone invited us to take part in a robbery and says we could make an easy £20,000, we'd turn it down for all sorts of reasons. Some people would jump at the chance even though underneath it they know they would get 10 years if caught. The length of the sentence would make no difference to their behaviour, they just won't think of such consequences. At the end of the 18th century there were some 200 offences which could get you hanged; for stealing something worth more than 5 shillings, that's 25 pence, or even writing someone an offensive letter.'

'We could use that against internet trolls.'

'We'd run out of rope. Anyway all the hangings really made no difference, nor would longer sentences, except in keeping the public safe from persistent offenders, but it doesn't actually stop crime.'

'And video games and movies are all packed full of mass killings. It's just fun, cartoon violence with no consequences.'

'Exactly.'

'Then what will work? Are we all wasting our time?'

'To some extent. You have to change people's mindset at a much deeper level. And that's for another day, if I am ever to get through this box.'

Ian is a fast reader with a near photographic memory and doesn't miss much. It's early one evening, Ian is on his own and working his way through documents, when DCS Swindale approaches his desk.

'Stanton.'

'Yes sir.'

'How's it going? Anything new?'

Ian pauses for a good five seconds before replying. 'It's not for me to say sir.'

'It is for you to say constable. I am your senior officer and I expect you to give me a proper answer. So, anything new?'

'With respect sir, DCI Gibbons is my senior officer here. I have to keep him up to date.'

'Really. And you need to remember what's good for your future.' After giving Ian a serious look, he walks off.

The next day, when the three of them are talking in the DCI Gibbons' office, Ian asks, 'Why was this man David Forester even considered a suspect?' Ian asks.

'Andrew was very much a home boy; didn't go wandering off a lot on his own; had only a few pals locally, which reduced the likelihood of a stranger attack. So very soon, focus went on close relatives and friends. David Forester fitted into this point of view. That seems to be the main reason for it. He knew Mrs Bradshaw from work and was a family friend who used to visit quite often. He lived on his own a few miles away; had the occasional male friend staying and once in a while went to male clubs. I think it was just prejudice and they were clutching at a straw. He had no alibi for when the boy went missing, and that was all. We don't have to visit him again at this stage,' replies the Inspector.

'And Jenkins the builder is a slightly stronger case. He lived several doors away and they all new each other. Andrew was often there because he had a young boy's crush on the daughter, Samantha, and Andrew would help her in the garden. The situation with Jenkins is a little less vague but not much.'

A receipt showed how Jenkins bought oak floor-boards and renewed the floor of his living room two weeks before the 12 year old went missing. A neighbour spent some time in the house chatting and drinking tea with the builder while the job was being done, so there's no question over the timing. Jenkins' wife and daughter went to stay with her parents in Pinner while work was being done and stayed much longer as a trial separation. It seems his wife was fed up with his moods and bad temper, which meant Jenkins was on his own in the house at the time the boy disappeared. Ian and the Sergeant keep reading and checking movements with a few new forensic tests along the way.

'Ian, we might have something here. We need to see the Inspector,' said the Sergeant one morning.

'Inspector, there's a copy of a receipt here, look at this. It was in among some door-to-door reports, completely unrelated. It's for new wood flooring, oak, the same specification as Jenkins bought for his floor and the same quantity. The supplier is nearly ten miles away. The buyer collected and paid cash, over £1250, and one day after the boy went missing.'

'So what are you suggesting, that the floor was renewed a second time because it had to be?' said the DCI.

'One constable certainly spread his net and felt this could mean something.'

'Tricky to deliver all that wood, pull up a floor and dispose of the old stuff with nobody noticing.'

'The houses in the street are quite well sheltered. Detached, short private drives and plenty of hedges and high fences,' chips in Ian. 'And as a builder if he was always doing things in the house or garden, a bit more noise wouldn't be noticed.'

'But if there was blood on the floor, why wouldn't he just patch in a new bit?'

'Well he wouldn't want to go back to the same supplier; anyone checking would find out. And getting a little wood from somewhere else, chances are it wouldn't match for grain and colour.'

'Good point. And why would anyone pay cash for that amount, unless they didn't want to be traced?'

'To avoid VAT?'

'Not with a trade merchant. They wouldn't get involved in that. They don't pay VAT, they just pass it on down the line.'

The Inspector says, 'If the floor has been changed, it implies there was blood. Some killings don't create any. Sergeant, go back to this supplier, get them to check their records and see if anything else turns up. The accountant at least will still have everything. And paying over £1200 in cash sounds odd so ask about that. And get a sample of that wood. Stanton, you keep on with the files.'

Sergeant Blake returns with a similar sample but little new information.

'I spoke to the accountant and the manager. It is unusual to have that size of cash payment but does happen. Sometimes builders offer to do jobs for cash to avoid VAT on the work, but there's still VAT on the materials. They don't like such cash payments – too much cash around and it has to be put in the safe.

The manager thought it strange someone would go so far to buy the wood; there are more local firms which stock the same range, but suggests they might have been out of stock.'

'It's tongue and groove. That could stop any blood flowing through, unless there was a lot of it. Jenkins doesn't live in that house any more, does he? Now he's in Marshfield Grove. We'll have to go to the house and persuade the new owners to let us cut into their floor. We'll need to be prepared to renew the whole floor for them.'

The present owners are not pleased about the implications of the task, but reluctantly agree in the hope the matter would be cleared up quickly.

DCI Gibbons is as discrete as he can be, turning up with a couple of builders and a forensic vehicle with no markings. They start cutting and pulling up the boards near the centre of the room at first and it's not long before they find a few small blood marks. The room is sealed off as a crime scene while tests are done. These test soon show a DNA match with the missing boy.

'Sergeant, come with me. We have to bring Jenkins in for questioning. Stanton, get hold of the station solicitor and tell him what's happening.'

Nearly two hours later, Jenkins is in an interview room with a solicitor next to him. DCI Gibbons and Sergeant Blake are sitting opposite, and Ian Stanton is sitting to one side, just observing. Recordings are switched on.

Under questioning, Jenkins keeps denying all knowledge, cannot explain the blood, insists he didn't buy the second supply of wood and suggests errors in the testing. After an hour they are going round in circles. Jenkins gets sent back to the cells and the officers return to their office.

'There was something there sir. When you asked him about a body, he kept thinking about a patio,' says Ian.

'What do you mean thinking about a patio? He said nothing about a patio,' queries the Inspector.

'Not out loud sit, I said thinking about it. And pink, pink kept coming into my head.'

'Are you saying, while he was in there you were reading his mind?'

The Sergeant smiles and looks down.

'Erm, something like that. His thoughts were very loud.'

'Fine, very good. Get back to those files will you.'

'Yes sir,' and Ian walks out of the office and back to his desk.

'He's done it before sir, at least once to my knowledge. Stanton can be pretty sensitive like that. That's how he found the kidnapped woman 18 months ago,' says the Sergeant.

'Look, I know a body under the patio is good for crime stories and comedy sketches, but in all my years I have never found it a reality. It's just too obvious. Any resourceful murderer is going to find something better, especially a builder with machinery, there are going to be lots of way to get rid of a small body. And what's that about pink?' the Inspector asked.

'Pink decorative concrete or pink house?'

'Pink houses are more common in East Anglia. Sort of a traditional colour. They used to mix some pigs blood into the whitewash.'

'It's worth a look, sir, and right now that's the best we've got and we can't hold Jenkins for long unless we come up with something.'

'Okay. We'll look for pink houses first, before pink

patios. Jenkins gets most of his work from locals, through recommendations. You and Stanton drive around those streets working your way outwards and make a note of all the pink houses you find. There probably aren't many. And I hope I don't have to apply for a search warrant on the basis of a bit of mind reading.'

Stanton and Blake spend the rest of the day on the task. Of the four houses they find, one was built recently, one had no patio and with the other two there was no-one in. As a cover story, so as not to start off on too sour a note, they suggest they are investigating bad financial practices in the building trade.

The two officers have to return in the evening where they are told that one of the houses was built with the patio nearly ten years earlier. In the forth house, they are quietly excited to hear that the patio was built five years ago. It covers a large area with a low wall all round.

'I can't remember the firm's name but he was a fairly local builder. But we weren't around at the time. You see, we didn't want to be here with all that mess, so we hired a villa in Italy with a couple of friends and had a month's holiday. They didn't have to get into the house so we left them to it. By the time we got back it was beautifully finished.'

Blake and Stanton say nothing at this news and try not to give anything away.

'That's all for now. Thank you very much. We'll be in touch,' says the Sergeant.

Back in the car, they are just about punching the dashboard in their excitement. Blake then gets on the phone to call the Inspector at home.

'Right, first thing in the morning check Jenkins's records. If he's involved, we'll probably find nothing. And we have a look at the house owner's bank statements. And we see about doing a radar search first,' says the Chief Inspector with definite enthusiasm in his voice.

All three of them are in early next morning and there's an extra buzz to their activities.

'One of the men working for Jenkins at the time is still with him; the other's now a joiner at WTK Builders.'

'If either of these financial accounts shows Jenkins built the patio, bring them both in.'

Jenkins's accounts show no record of the job. It's over a day before they can check the house owner's bank statements which show a large cheque paid to Jenkins six months after the boy's disappearance. The two workers are questioned but claim they can't remember anything of use about the job.

By now the house owners have been informed as to what's really going on and are horrified at the possible outcome – the thought that there might have been a body in their back garden for the last five years.

Structural imaging radar is brought in but the most the experts can say is that there is something of different properties and densities in the soil and under the two feet of concrete. That's enough for the police. The area is screened off and drills have to be brought in to break through the concrete. The police have mixed feelings, for they are now fairly certain what will be found. They are correct – the body of a young boy.

It seemed as though the body must have been hidden in a cold storage for a long while before being buried.

The Chief Inspector spends an hour with the Assistant Chief Constable, explaining all about the case, including the insights Ian had after the interrogation of Jenkins.

'That's going to sound odd in the report,' comments the ACC. 'Some clever lawyer might find it all a bit suspicious somehow. Perhaps you should play down that part of it and build up the part about going round the neighbourhood looking for sites where Jenkins did jobs at the time.'

'Yes sir. We'll do that. Stanton will be all right about it. I'm sure he won't want to be branded as some sort of psychic, not outside the department anyway.

Ian decides to pay an unofficial courtesy call on David Forester and explains the latest developments to him. After hearing the course of events, David is very quiet and his eyes are moist. Finally he says, 'At least this is some sort of conclusion for Mary and Charles. It was a terrible time for me too. I was questioned so much and it was all very aggressive. They had no evidence against me and kept trying to make me confess; that was the only way they might have had a case. It almost drove me to suicide. And I lost all three of them as friends.'

'Your name won't be mentioned in any of the recent proceedings so you should be safe from the press but you never know with them. According to strict police procedure I shouldn't really be here, so please be discrete.'

'Thank you. This is kind, but I do have a couple of places I can stay while this balloon is up, just to be safer.'

Chief Superintendent Swindale felt very embarrassed by the whole business and although not everyone felt he was at fault for the previous failure, he took it badly.

Time continues . . . . . with more everyday matters.

8

In Which there's Leather and Leg Irons

Ian, Joe, Don and Sarah have been practising hard on several numbers, with Joe the chief music arranger and composer. Don favours having two side drums of different sizes hanging from his shoulders and that's enough for him to drum good rhythms. He's made Ian one of his special amps and Sarah is much more confident about singer with people around. She loves her outfit and often walks around the house wearing it. It makes her feel empowered. A few times, she's taken a couple of glasses of her favourite wine and gone for a walk in the streets with it on, only leaving out the outrageous make-up.

Joe is pleased with the way things are going and decides she wants them to make a recording. She feels it will concentrate their minds and efforts and improve the performance. 'And we should do it in our show gear. That way it'll feel more genuine.' Everyone is fine with this so off they go to a recording studio. It takes them a couple of hours to lay down all the tracks and they have the added bonus of a photographer on the premises photographing them both playing and as a band.

The police concert and party is taking place in early

December.　They have to present themselves for an audition, no less.　Although there are only three people watching, this is the first time they have done any performance in front of others, apart from the recording.　Sarah is the most nervous and keeps her eyes closed at first, but after a minute or so she really gets going.

The Christmas event itself takes place in the local Town Hall, a fairly small but smart and traditional building.　Doors are opened at six o'clock on Saturday evening and families start off with drinks and nibbles. The organisers know that a lubricated audience will be a happy and a more easily-pleased audience.　The main room in the building has a stage and two hundred seats, plus standing room.

With everyone seated and ready soon after seven o'clock, the compère walks on the stage.　Everyone knows him and claps.　He's a popular police constable of long standing who's a very good story telling.　He talks about police experiences, some real, some invented, but all with a good comedy touch.　With everyone warmed up, he introduces the first act.　The curtains open to a man at a honky-tonk piano and a woman in a flamboyant music-hall dress.　She sings rather bawdy Victorian songs while he pounds away at the piano with great enthusiasm.　The younger members of the audience can't understand the sexual innuendos in the words and the whole crowd applauds wildly.

The compère delivers five more minutes of his anecdotes, then introduces the Barber Shop Choir. They are six men standing in line and dressed in white satin shirts, black bow ties, black trousers, shoes in black and white and with their hair heavily greased and brushed back. Hanging in the background is a giant pair of scissors, nearly three metres long made of thick plywood. They sing in harmony and do small dance steps along the way.

Another five minutes from the comedian compère, and then comes the magician. He's dressed in a gold lamé suit including a gold lamé top hat. He does the traditional tricks of producing rabbits, doves and streams of silk scarves, then making things disappear again. The younger audience in particular is thrilled.

While the comedian compère does another few minutes, Don quickly sets up all the gear and electrics behind the curtain, because now it's the turn of "Eversley Green". That's the name they've given themselves; Eversley from the street the station is in and Green because that's their theme colour.

While the curtains are still opening, Ian and Don start playing with a strong fast beat. The group makes a striking sight. Don has his green bowler hat, a white jacket, a black shirt, black shoes and green trousers, which he had to buy from a women's fashion shop. Not too many green trousers in menswear. His side drums have highly polished copper sides.

Ian wears a green shirt, black trousers and green trainers. Joe has a loose green dress and matching ballet-style shoes. She wears the same colour wig as Sarah but tied at the back out of the way of the violin. She starts playing soon after the other two, and the sound of 20 violins swells out of the speakers.

But most eyes seem to go towards Sarah. For days, Ian has been saying how this is a new adventure and how the mind loves new experiences; anything to take her away from the fear of performing in front of a crowd for the first time. She daren't look at the audience but keeps her eyes looking over them into the distance, which gives her a superior, haughty look. The tight green leather outfit, black boots and black leather gloves make her look like a famous sexy rock queen. Although she doesn't realise it at the time, she's getting all the whistles. She's gone to town on the theatrical make-up and wears the wig of long wavy red hair. Although many people know who the other three are, no-one recognises Sarah.

The first song is one of Joe's, and Sarah's voice carries well across the hall even with no microphone. As she sings, Sarah jerks and wriggles her body to the music, and a lot of the men in the audience, and even some of the women, suck in their breath. The song is strong and tuneful and many a rock vocalist would be proud of it.

Joe can't keep still while playing but bounces around continuously on the balls of her feet. As the song comes to an end, they keep playing more softly, not giving any time for applause but merge into the next song. It's "The Sound of Silence" but played slightly faster than normal. Sarah's voice starts off almost sweet and gets louder and stronger as the song progresses; until she gets to the last lines, "And the sign said The words of the prophets are written on the subway walls And tenement halls and whispered in the sound . . . . " As she sings them, she leans forward and virtually screams out the words with a hard rough edge to her voice. Almost at the end, there's a pause as she stands still and tall, then she says the final words "of silence" with soft delicate high notes.

The playing carries on further and this time it's a pumped-up piece of Steffani, with its fast dynamic vocals. Sarah doesn't sing words, just notes in mezzo-soprano style, very pure and very fast. She finishes on a long note, then they all freeze. In unison they take one step back and make a small bow.

There is silence for a few seconds, then the mass of applause and cheering really shocks the four of them. Some people are even standing and applauding with shouts for more. They take a couple of bows, look at each other and walk off the stage. Emotionally it's all too much and they don't feel they could play another song, even if they had one prepared. Off stage, Sarah sits on a chair and bursts into tears. Joe puts her arms around her, but Sarah jumps up and is jumping on the spot with excitement.

'That was amazing. Wasn't that so amazing?' She goes to each of them in turn and gives them big hugs, then she goes back to Ian and says 'Thank you, thank you', and when hugging him again, whispers in his ear, 'I need sex'.

'I can't help you here little miss hot tits', replies Ian very quietly. At the same time, the compère is winding up the show and inviting everyone back to the food and drinks. With the performers still in their costumes they are expected to mingle with the audience. Sarah has to straighten her make-up first and wants to ensure no-one can still recognise her, just to keep the mystery going.

Ian speaks to Joe, 'Before we get back in there, are you going to put handcuffs on Sarah?'

'Yes, and leg irons. I think we've all been upstaged.'

Time advances . . . . .

IN WHICH A BURGLARY TURNS NASTY

Burglaries and robberies are all too common and some burglars have their own routine. They can even regard it as a craft with its own code of conduct. That has always been the approach of Ben Cameron. As a young teenager, he was a light thief, then became a regular burglar. In and out of prison for more than 30 years, he was one of the main adversaries of Chief Superintendent Swindale. Swindale wants to see him bundled out of the way for ever. When there's a burglary in a large old house, bearing all the hallmarks of a job by Cameron, Swindale becomes convinced Cameron's responsible and is determined to make sure he's convicted for it. This is made perfectly clear in the strongest terms to Inspector Peterson, who's handling the case. Swindale even attends a couple of the interrogations of Cameron, much to the irritation of Inspector Peterson, and wants charges applied immediately.

Cameron continually protests his innocence, insisting he was at home on his own all evening and all night. The big difference between this case and Cameron's normal burglaries is that the elderly women in the house was severely injured and not found until the following day. Cameron has never ever used violence and any sign of trouble or resistance he would be out of the window and gone. With his record, a crime like this could get him 12 years or more. They know the robbery occurred before 10 o'clock at night because the old lady always went to bed before 10, and she was fully clothed at the time.

Cameron has no alibi. 'I didn't go out or phone anyone, did no emails. I had a pie for supper and watched television. I can tell you what I saw.'

'That doesn't count,' says Swindale, 'you could catch those up on the repeat.'

Inspector Peterson is instructed to keep on at him before their time runs out, until he confesses.

Ian also feels this is a very weak case and is not convinced Cameron could do such an attack. He goes into the man's cell for a quiet chat and he asks the duty officer to remain in the doorway.

'Look Ben, let's go through that evening again minute by minute. You had an early drink at the pub and got home what time?'

'Soon after six.' He lists what he watched on television until he heated up his pie and beans. 'Then I watched the motorbike racing, until nine. After that I changed channels and watched that reality show, you know the one with all them glamorous women. In the first break, I checked the weather then watched the rest of the show.'

'You checked the weather? You never mentioned this before. How did you check the weather?'

'Well on my small computer of course. It's on my

Favourites list. I love watching the weather. I check for here and Newcastle and I place little bets with myself on how right they get it.'

Ian's head drops down on to his chest. 'So you went on to the net. At what time would this be then?'

'During the first break – about quarter past nine.'

'You didn't use your smartphone; we checked your phone'

'It was on charge.'

'We didn't see a computer in your place.'

'It's a small laptop. I keep it hidden; you know away from all them break-in chaps.'

'Very funny; so where is it?'

'Behind an extra panel at the back of the small chest of drawers in the front room. Does this make any difference?'

'Slightly. Does it need a password.'

'Yes, I'll write it down.' Ian stands and leaves the cell, smiling at the officer by the door, who smiles back and shrugs his shoulders.

Hearing the news, the Inspector reacts in the same way. 'All right, get hold of his computer and check the times with the server. In theory he could have taken his computer with him, checked the weather in the street somewhere, using that as an alibi. This is all a bit clever for Ben and the case is getting weaker and weaker. Nothing links him to the scene, so if the server checks out, we'll have to let him go. If the Super wants to charge him, he can build the case and sign the papers, we can't.'

And that is how Ben Cameron was release, with

the Chief Superintendent quietly fuming and bearing another grudge against DC Stanton.

In April, Inspector Peterson is taken ill with cancer and it's clear he'll be away for months, at best. That leaves a temporary gap in his section, but Chief Superintendent Swindale immediately divides the workload between two other Inspectors, one of whom is particularly close to the Chief Super himself.

When it becomes known that a station in east London is very short of officers, Swindale is quick to suggest that DC Stanton must fill one of the gaps. The transfer is arranged much to Ian's dissatisfaction but he can do nothing about it.

Sergeant Tom Innes stops him in the corridor.

'Ian, I want a word, let's go in here. Sorry to see you go like this.'

'Me too. I hope there won't be any sort of Do on Friday. It won't be a happy day for me.'

'No, Okay. The thing is, unfortunately, among the officers, the junior ones at least, the place you are going to is known as a dirty station.'

'Bad cops you mean?'

'Some of them, yes. Bribe money, too close with the gangs, drug samples missing from the evidence room, you know the type of thing. It's a rough tough area and some of the coppers fit in there well. Not all but some. It depends what group you end up with. You might be all right. If they are a bad lot, they'll wait a while just to size you up, then likely pass you a fat envelope full of notes. If you take it, they'll know they've got you. If you don't take, they won't trust you and then they'll try to stitch you up. That means planting something on you, or making it look like you fiddled the evidence, that sort of thing. So watch your back.'

'Right, thank you Sergeant. I'll see how it goes. If it's no good, I'll put in for a transfer.'

'You won't get one too close after this one.'

'Then I'll leave the force and apply again elsewhere three months later.'

'Anyway, keep in touch. Maybe you can come back here soon, then.'

On his last Friday afternoon, Ian goes into his Inspector's office to say goodbye; it is brief and courteous. There are only two other detectives in his general office and he keeps the farewells brief. Along the corridor he looks for Sergeant Innes. He's out, so that's it. Ian leaves the building feeling very low, and somehow he's certain he will never be back at this station. The sun is shining which gives him the right excuse to put on his sunglasses.

It's early May, and the following Monday Ian comes out of the Underground and takes the ten minute walk to his new station. Some of the streets he goes through make the area look like part of a second world country; boarded up shops, "For Sale" signs every third building, wheelie bins and bundles of rubbish scattered, but the station is reasonably new, which is more encouraging in a certain direction.

He asks his way round and goes to introduce himself to his new Inspector, DI Latham. The other officers watch him as he enters the Inspector's office and he's not what they expected. He looks so unassuming, and neither tall nor broad. They know his record and were expecting someone to stride in and be more of the "I'm the big man now, and I'm in charge" sort. They are doubtful, except one officer who remembers the old maxim: "In a scrap, knock down the biggest man first but watch out for the small man – he will be the best fighter". It's not that Ian can be labelled as a small man, it's more that he looks ordinary and not particularly threatening or intimidating. The officers in the open general office look at each other. Some have frowns of scepticism, some have cocky smirks on their faces.

Time drags . . . . .

10

In Which Bad goes to Bad

Ian doesn't go to the pub for all that boozing and bonding business and just wants to get on with the necessary work and see how everything fits together. He decides to keep his existing flat for now and put up with the long Tube journey to work. After a long day, he always returns home tired and has even less contact with former colleagues than before. With any spare time, he wants to keep up with his own activities. The aikido he always finds relaxing; the tumbling around on the mats being like a full body massage. The karate and running are more tiring but he makes a point of doing them once or twice a week. And the harp practice, that's always a good way for his mind to drift off.

He's been at the new station for about a month, when he goes in one morning, opens a drawer to take out a file and finds a fat envelope. There are only two others in the office at the time so he pretends not to notice the envelope. Soon after, he takes a sneak look and sees it's stuffed with £20 notes. An hour later, there are different officers in the room, when someone says, 'That's your's in the drawer mate'. Ian stands up, takes the envelope out of the draw, walks across the room and drops the full envelope into the general waste bin, then walks back to his desk. He knows he's raised his colours.

Ian remembers the advice from Sergeant Innes about them planting something incriminating on him. He thinks ahead.

The office is usually busy with people coming and going, files moving around and being examined, phones ringing, calls made, officers making visits. Three weeks later, one of the team returns to the office, and there's the smallest of looks between him and a colleague at a desk. Ian's senses are too astute not to interpret this a certain way. Discretely he leaves the room with a few documents and goes downstairs to the changing room. He opens his locker and hidden behind a pullover is a small package. He puts on forensic gloves to look in the outer bag and sees a plastic bag of white powder, then replaces everything the way it was.

From his pocket he takes out a tube of super-glue and the front part of a key. It's one of his locker keys he has previously broken in half. He puts a few drops of glue on the key which he pushes into the lock and closes the door, leaving it unlocked. He quickly goes to the toilets and makes sure the tube of super-glue flushes away properly. After making a couple of copies on the photocopier, he returns to his desk and carries reading files as normal, looking the picture of carefree innocence.

In early afternoon, the Superintendent enters their main office with a detective Sergeant and two uniform constables. 'Everyone here, stop what you are doing and come with me now.' He leads them downstairs into the changing room, with the three junior officers keeping an eye on everyone.

The Superintendent calls out each officer in turn, gets them to open up their locker and thoroughly inspects everything inside. Then it's Ian's turn.

'DC Stanton, let me have the key,' he demands.

'It's open sir.'

'What do you mean it's open?'

'It's always open. The key broke and got jammed in the lock weeks ago. I never leave anything valuable in there and the door is always unlocked.'

'Sergeant, have a look.'

The Sergeant opens the locker door and examines the contents, and very quickly finds the package.

'How do you explain this?'

'Well I don't. Best to ask the person who put it there. Anybody could do that when the door is never locked.'

The Superintendent hesitates. 'Let's look in the last two.' Nothing else is found.

'All right, get back to work. Stanton you come with me.'

Back in his office, the Superintendent sits behind his desk.

'What do you have to say about this Stanton?'

'I could never be stupid enough to do anything like this sir.'

'No.'

'Anonymous tip-off was it sir?'

The Superintendent looks at a picture on the wall

and says nothing for a good ten seconds.

'Okay, just get back to work now.'

'Yes sir.'

At this stage, Ian sees the Superintendent as a decent man and an experienced copper. He's nearing retirement and looking tired after years working in this rough and tumble area with reduced budgets.

Time creeps along . . . . .

11

In Which Knives are Everywhere

Ian is dealing with a burglary case. A man is in the cells with evidence against him. A search warrant is issued to search his house and property in the hope there might be links to other crimes. The man's wife is in hospital after an accident. Walking along and intensely looking at her mobile, she stepped into the road and was hit by a fast cyclist, suffering a broken leg, lots of bruises and concussion.

Ian, DS Harper from the office and a uniform officer make a search of the house. They are use to searching and are wise to all the likely hide-aways thieves adopt, if they are careless and stupid enough to retain stolen goods for any time.

Although still married and in the same house, the Moffat's very much have separate lives and seem to keep their distance from each other. Ian is in the wife's bedroom and checking a chest of drawers. At the back of a drawer under some underwear he finds an A5 notebook. The book is more than half full and it's all written in shorthand. Ian starts to read a page at random. After a few minutes, Sergeant Harper comes into the room. 'Having fun among the knickers Stanton?'

'Yeh.'

'What's this then, is that shorthand?'

'Yes, Pitmans.   And it's very neat and carefully written, not scrappy and rushed like it might be from dictation.'

'You can read that stuff can you?'

'Yes and listen to this. "I was glad of the rain. That's always good in my business. He was wearing a thick coat so no blood came out" and this "that was an exciting one, having to stab her twice. I was still buzzing two hours later and could not sleep well that night with the excitement". It's like some sort of gruesome murder story.'

'Well some people get their kicks out of writing and reading that stuff. It'd be different if they had to work with it every day.'

'And there are these numbers on some pages, like chapter titles. 3/24 and 10/11 and 12/15. Could be dates.'

'They must be in reverse then, American style, with the month first. What was one of those, 10/11? Then it'll be the eleventh of October. Hang on, that's my birthday. I remember, I took the day off and me and the wife went down to Brighton for a day out. And the following day, when I turned the radio on over breakfast, there'd been another of those serial stabbings. Let me check.' He starts tapping into his phone. 'Yes, woman, 43 stabbed in Billericay. That's some way from here. What are those other numbers again?'

'Twentyforth of March.'

'19 year old man stabbed in Brentwood. The killer is

labelled "The Phantom Slasher" by the tabloids.'

'Try December 15.'

'Woman 26 also in Brentwood. Bloody hell,' says the Sergeant.

'Well either this is some weirdo who enjoys writing about murders or there is something more to it.'

'Right, bag it up and we'll get back. We've got a couple of items from the shed we need to check on.'

Back in the Inspector's office, they report the details to DI Lathom.

'Stanton, how long will it take you to type up all that stuff?'

'Quite a while on my own. If someone can type while I read it, that'll help.'

'Right, has anyone handled this book?'

'Only me with gloves.'

'Get it checked by forensic first. Get them to do it now, not in two days. Wait there for it. I'll give them a call. Then make some photocopies. And Reg, ask around for anyone else who can read shorthand, although not many people bother any more. I'll find out who's dealing with these serial killings. There might be stuff in that book which wasn't released to the public. Even if we think there's nothing to it, we hand over that book. Let them make the decision.'

Twenty minutes later, Ian has made photocopies of the book. Two copies get passed on to Sergeant Harper who gives them to shorthand experts for transcribing. One copy is to use himself. In fact he makes a forth copy which he tucks away at the bottom of a drawer.

He's not sure why but it seemed a good idea as a little insurance.

'Sergeant, I called in at the hospital on the way in this morning and Mrs Moffat will be discharged later today. I was looking at more of the book last night and came across this passage "that's number five – things are going well. I was going to make it 20 to set a new record but if I go up to 15, then stop, that will certainly keep them guessing". I didn't do a full search of her room. Once we started talking about the book, we left. Have they ever found a murder weapon?'

'Don't know; they probably haven't said. But there have been eight killings.'

'As soon as she gets home, she'll soon find the book missing. If there's more evidence, she'll destroy it.'

'I'll tell the Inspector, then let's get over there. Go and get one of those metal detectors from the stores.'

The Inspector wants to cover his back and get credit for what might be a major breakthrough. He immediately bundles up the book, the photocopies and the transcripts as far as they have gone and sends them with two officers to be delivered to the investigators of the serial killings. 'Both be there when you hand them over and get a receipt from the senior officer.'

Sergeant Harper and Ian Stanton are soon back at the house and searching the bedroom. Going round the room with the metal detector, it starts getting hyper-active around the wardrobe.

'There's a small step ladder in the spare room,' says the Sergeant as he rushes out to get it.

Ian takes down a couple of small suitcases, and the Sergeant climbs the steps.

'There's a loose panel up here. Fucking 'ell,' he says as he looks under it. 'Take a look at that.'

Ian goes up the steps.

'How many there, seven isn't it?'

'Yes. And the book said she'd stop at 15.'

'Right, let's get out of here and get this place sealed.'

'I'll just take a photo and you'd better do the same Sergeant.'

The investigating team looking into the serial killings keep hitting dead ends, so with the new information they grasp it eagerly and take over the situation. After two weeks, Mrs Moffat gets charged. She's an avid reader of crime stories and television police dramas and has been able to keep her tracks well covered for over a year.

DI Lathom writes his report on the whole episode and it transpires that the Sergeant found the book written in shorthand and wondered about its significance. Following that, he claims the Inspector and the Sergeant were the ones who returned to the house and found the knives.

In due course, Ian comes across the report and protests to the Sergeant. Harper simply shrugs his shoulders. 'He's the Inspector and you ain't.' Ian complains to the Inspector, who tells him to shut up and that the Sergeant will back up everything in the report.

Ian leaves it at that but decides to get prepared.

There can be just too many incidents in the madness of the streets.

Ian is on his way to work. He's already in a bad mood over the report, then the Underground train sits in a dark tunnel for nearly half an hour. Finally it arrives at his station and he's getting off the train through one of the single doors. The train stops, the doors open and immediately a young man starts to push his way on before Ian and another passenger have a chance to step down. Ian pushes him to one side 'Do you mind if people get off first?' The young man just scowls and waits to let them off.

Ian starts to walk down the platform and another young black man, about 18, is overtaking him. He has a cocky swagger with rap music coming through his player, then he pushes Ian on the shoulder. 'Hey, he's my cousin man, leave him alone, he's my cousin.'

'Don't do that again,' replies Ian.

He does. Another push, 'He's my cousin, he's my cousin.'

Ian pushes him back and even without full aikido power, the young man tumbles back and falls over against the wall. Other people around start to keep their distance.

Ian is in the process of saying, 'Now you are not going to do something stupid are you?' but without any hesitation the young man pulls a knife and lunges at Ian. A quick side step, grabbing of wrist, twisting without being too gentle, pulling him round in a circle so Ian can see if there's another attacker near by, pressing him face down and cuffs behind the back. Holding and twisting his other arm, Ian takes no notice of the shout of pain as he pulls the arm towards the cuffs.

He puts his foot on the knife and takes out his warrant card. 'See this – police. You are under arrest.' Ian recites his rights. The train is still in the station with the doors now closed and everyone watching.

Ian pulls the young man to his feet and picks up the knife. 'Do anything else and you will get seriously hurt.' He moves the man along the platform and up the escalator. At the top near the ticket office is a PC he recognises from the station. Ian explains what just happened.

'Now we have all that paperwork to do and you are going to get five years,' says the PC as he gets on his radio calling for a vehicle.

Time gets tense . . . . .

12

In Which Dark Plans Lie

Inspector Latham and DS Harper are off on a call and take Ian Stanton with them. They have to visit a small garage business and expect to be making an arrest. They are in a short quiet side street, with rubbish and a few old cars littered about. The Sergeant turns the car round and parks about 100 metres from their target garage, which has a large shutter fully closed down.

'All three of us will go in there. There's an entrance round the back; that's where we all go in nice and casual like. All three of us will be needed in there. You hear that Stanton?' says the Inspector.

'Yes sir, quite clear.'

'Stanton, have you got a private phone on you?'

'No sir, only the police issue.'

'Hand it over to me,' Lathom orders.

'What? What for?'

'Don't argue, just hand it over!'

Stanton passes the phone to the Inspector in the front seat.

'I want it make sure it's turned off before we go in there.' He turns off the phone and puts it in his pocket. 'Right, let's get out.'

Walking towards the garage, when they are nearly there, Lathom says, 'On second thoughts, Stanton, you go and wait by the car, in case someone does a runner. The Sergeant and I can handle this.'

The two of them walk towards the garage, leaving Stanton a little bemused. After a couple of minutes, a man comes quickly out of the metal door in the front shutter, runs to a nearby car, jumps in and drives at speed towards Stanton's position. Ian takes the number and a description of the man and lets him pass. Soon after, the two police come from around the back leading two men in handcuffs. As they approach, Stanton can see blood on their faces and damage around their eyes. At the car, the two prisoners get pushed roughly into the back of the car and the door is slammed after them.

'Where were you Stanton? I said all three of us had to go in there?'

'You told me to wait here.'

'Shut up. I said the three of us had to go inside. Did you not hear that Sergeant?'

'Yes sir, every word. I've even got it recorded on my phone,' says the Sergeant as he pulls his phone out of his pocket.

'Did I ever say that I didn't need him and he should return to the car?'

'No sir, you never said that,' confirms the Sergeant.

'And why are their faces covered with blood?' Ian asks.

'They resisted arrest and look at this,' continues Lathom pulling a gun out of his pocket. 'We had to face this and you were too scared to come inside and do

96

your duty. Where's the third man?'

'He drove off at speed.'

'And didn't you stop him?'

'What, jump in front of a speeding car?'

'He would have stopped. More cowardice. You're going to be on charges here, disobeying my orders and cowardice and anything else I can add to that. Right now you're suspended. Stand over there and keep out of the way.'

By now, Sergeant Harper is on the phone calling for a prisoner vehicle.

Ian has to return to the station in the front of the prisoner van with the uniforms, while Lathom and Harper return in the police car. The Inspector puts his charges into motion while Ian goes home for the infamous gardening leave.

As soon as Ian gets notification of the charges and the misconduct hearing, he approaches Unison to get help from a solicitor experienced in such matters.

Meeting the solicitor, Ian outlines the events of that day.

'So the Inspector and the Sergeant confirm that you were told to enter the garage with them and the Sergeant has a recording to that effect, and they both deny that you were subsequently told not to go with them but to stay by the car.'

'That's it so far,' agrees Ian.

'So far? So what's your defence here?'

'Hang on. Let's not spoil the punchline. Let me give you a little bit of background. Here is a brief summary of my record while I was stationed at Eversley Road.' He passes the solicitor a single page document which he quickly reads.

The solicitor looks at Ian over his reading glasses. 'Mmmm, well that's certainly not the history of a coward, but they might simply say it's old history and you suddenly lost your nerve with some sort of minor breakdown.'

Ian continues, 'It was not my choice to go to the Ryburn Road station, and before I went, someone at Eversley Road warned me there were some dodgy officers there and I should be careful. It would depend what group I ended up in. After a month, an envelope full of £20 notes was left in my desk. I threw it in the bin in front of everyone, which didn't go down well. A month later drugs were planted in my locker, but I got wind of it and fixed the lock so that it appeared the locker could never be locked so anyone could have access there.

Trying to plant stuff on me got them nowhere, but after that I took extra precautions. You remember that woman serial killer caught recently? I found the evidence and realised its significance as crucial in finding the killer, but the Inspector filed a false police report saying he found the evidence and did all the detection work. He was not even there, but the Sergeant backed up his version. Said I had nothing to do with it, except I was wearing a secret recorder and I can prove my version. These gadgets can be incredibly small now. Everything is on tape, or chip in fact. And now we have this.'

Ian puts a small player on the desk and presses the start button. 'I haven't touched this at all which means there are a couple of gaps while we wait for something else to happen.'

A recording of the whole event comes out of the player. There's all the conversation in the car, as they walk towards the garage and as Ian is given further instructions to stay outside. There is also Ian's commentary as a man runs out of the front door and drives off at speed, and all the events after the two police return with the two prisoners.

At the end, the solicitor is quiet for a few moments.

'When did you start doing these recordings?'

'After the business of the drugs planted in my locker, so the middle of June. Not all the time, but often, especially during meetings or on assignments.'

'I suppose he took your mobile so there was no risk of you recording something. They didn't think ahead when they took you on, did they? It looks as though this is going to be fairly clear cut.'

'Should I have a barrister at the hearing or do you think that's unnecessary?'

'We have to make statements and give all evidence to the investigators before the hearing. You won't be able to suddenly produce this rabbit out of the hat at the hearing like some television court drama.

'There has to be a good reason for presenting late evidence or it won't be accepted at the hearing. What I'll do is plan all this out in the most effective way and we present all this evidence at the interview with the investigators. They will ask why you felt it necessary to make secret recordings, then we can bring in those previous incidents which led you to believe you needed such insurance. I am sure it won't take the panel long to decide, then those two characters will be in serious trouble. They won't be able to stay in the force.'

'One thing about those garage men arrested. They have no history of violence, certainly not of carrying guns. They were all about welding bits of cars together and fiddling the numbers. Nothing links them with the gun; I think it was planted.'

'After your hearing, after your successful hearing, most of the case against them will collapse. At the hearing, there will be a legally qualified chair person, who might be a barrister, a lay person and a police officer, who will be a Superintendent or higher. The chances are all three of you will be questioned. I'll need to copy of this recording and the other recording over the serial killing evidence, because that can show the Inspector has some history of lying.'

Ian goes into his small briefcase. 'Here are the recordings on a memory stick and I've written out transcripts of everything on them. And this is a copy of the police report where the Inspector claims all the credit for the murder evidence.'

'I'm starting to feel redundant here,' said the solicitor with a smile. 'As for getting a barrister, we have a strong case and solid evidence, but I'm sure you know these hearings are not like a criminal case where guilt has to be proved. It's like a civil matter, going for the balance of probability. We don't want them winning on a technicality and us having to go to appeal. We want to win this on the first round and have you coming out cleanly. I suggest a barrister will be a good precaution and it's hardly a massive case so the fee won't be outrageous, but I don't suppose legal fees will be your main concern at the moment.'

'Hardly.'

And that's the way it went.

The Inspector and Sergeant make some attempt to say the recordings are fake, which doesn't get them very far, while the Sergeant tries to say he wasn't close enough to hear everything the Inspector said. Ian is immediately cleared whereas the two accusers are suspended pending their own hearings.

With the hearing over in early November, Ian has no intention of staying even one more day at the station, but goes in for the last time, to see the Superintendent.

'Whatever normal procedure is sir, I shan't be coming back here. It'll just be too awkward and perhaps not safe.'

'That's fine, I'll sign all the papers.'

'One final thing, this is my report on that Mrs Moffat serial murder case and how we got on to it. It would be good if this could go on record.'

'I'll give it a look. Better luck in your new posting Stanton.'

As Ian walks away from the station, he's relieved the last six months in that place are over. He walks for a while, missing his usual Tube station and going towards the next on the line. By way of a minor celebration, he enters a coffee shop for a drink and two cakes.

Time thaws . . . . .

13

IN WHICH FORCES GO WEST

By December, Ian gets a new posting in central Bristol. The building is only six years old and the general atmosphere in the work environment feels good to him. He's been there just two days when he's talking to his Sergeant who looks at someone behind Ian. He looks back at Ian and smiles then looks behind him again. Ian turns round slowly and sees Beatrice Walker smiling at him.

'Hey, what's this then?'

'Hi-yer Ian.'

'You stationed here now?' He holds his hand out to her and she takes it in both her hands. She wants to give him a hug but that's not possible here.

'Yes, for nearly two months. I couldn't believe it when I saw your name in the newsletter. I'm DS now too.'

'Wow, those eyelashes work wonders don't they?'

'Watch it,' as she holds up a fist. 'Are you here all day?'

'I think so.'

'I'll see you at lunch?'

'Sure thing boss,' he agrees.

'That's better.' She smiles and walks away.

As soon as she's out of the room and out of earshot, there's some mild whooping and cheering from the others in the room.

'What's this with you and Super-Barbie then?' asks the Sergeant.

'Super-Barbie, is that what you call her?'

'Not to her face; we wouldn't dare make a sexist comment about her eyelashes like that. You must be well in there to get away with it.'

'Well, friend of the stars, you know,' says Ian with his nose in the air.

Ian and Beatrice sit opposite each other in the station canteen and there's a lot of smiling at first.

'Okay, Madam Sergeant, explain yourself first, how come you're here?'

'Leo was offered a partnership in a computer security firm in Bristol. I was made Sergeant in June. We came here for the weekend and I thought why not have a change? He came here, staying in B & B and did some house searching.'

'You mean you left him alone with all these hot west country women?' chips in Ian.

'I terrorised him first so there was no real risk. Anyway, I applied for a transfer and we put the house on the market. Eventually everything fitted together. You didn't think of going back to Eversley?'

'No, I thought maybe somewhere new. Fresh start and all that.'

'Swindale's still there so he probably wouldn't let you return anyway.'

'No. It's good here, is it?'

'Yes it is. I followed your hearing, but how did it come about? What were they after?'

'Tom Innes warned me there were some bad officers in that station and I was unlucky enough to end up in one such unit. How is Sergeant Innes by the way?'

'Oh, he's good. Still as solid and reliable as ever.'

Ian tells Beatrice about the anonymous bribe and the drugs in the locker incident, which amuses her greatly.

'Then there was the evidence over that woman serial killer, the one in the Essex area.'

'Those killings weren't on your patch.'

'No, she was very crafty. She bought the knives months and months before, one at a time, quite innocently from different kitchen shops, then wrapped them up in plastic bags, completely untouched. All the knives had long, very thin blades. She would drive 20 miles or more, park, then walk two miles or so along side streets to find her victim. No killings in the summer, only when evenings and nights were darker. Also in colder weather when people were wearing coats. She'd pass someone in the street and one stab low in the chest into the heart or from the back into vital organs. Completely random killings. She'd leave the knife in the body and calmly walk off. No blood immediately because they were wearing a coat, and she would make her way back to the car avoiding main roads and cameras. It was just coincidence we searched her house because her husband was arrested for burglaries. They didn't really get on; separate rooms and separate lives.

'I found a book, like a diary, hidden in her bedroom.

It was written in shorthand so I started reading it.'

'I didn't know you knew shorthand?'

'One of the many secrets I still manage to keep from you. Anyway, at first the book might have been either a record or a fantasy story. Just as a precaution we went back next day and then we found knives hidden in a panel in the wardrobe. Everything was handed over to the squad in Essex working on the killings and that was that as far as we were concerned. Except, my Inspector wrote the report and claimed how he and his Sergeant discovered the book and the knives and worked everything out, claiming all the credit for himself. I complained but the Inspector and his Sergeant stuck to the report. By then they were thinking I was too much of a risk to all their rackets. That's why they pulled that cowardice stunt to get me dismissed, but thankfully I had already started making those secret recordings.'

Beatrice puffs out her cheeks with a loud breath. 'What a carry on. Perhaps you were lucky to get out of there alive.'

'I was certainly glad to leave.'

After a pause Beatrice says, 'Inspector Peterson is back.'

'What, healthy?'

'Seems like it. Much thinner and not much hair, but he's got the all-clear. Back to his old job. Sarah, Joe and Don missed you when you stopped joining the practice. You know Don was killed?'

'No! How?'

'On his bike, cycling to work. A large van suddenly turned into a one-way street the wrong way and ran into him. Case pending. Probably get a suspended, when it should be five years for manslaughter.'

Ian looks down, obviously shocked by the news.

'I stopped going to the practice. There was all the travelling and strange things happening there, then I was worried about the hearing so I wasn't really in the mood for it. I just got out of the habit. I'm still playing the old harp though.'

'Well I suppose I must do my bit to change the world for the better. It's great to see you. We'll talk again soon. Bye for now.'

Whereas Beatrice and her super well paid husband have bought a beautiful house straight away, Ian lives in digs to start with. He has a large room in a comfortable old house and the only other people there are the retired owners, Mr and Mrs Trewarne. He gets an evening meal as well if he's around in time. He arrived with just two suitcases and his harp, which is enough until he sells in London and buys a flat.

One evening, Thomas Trewarne is out and Sandra Trewarne has a friend around. Sandra and Martha have known each other since working together in their twenties. Ian is also sitting in the living having joined them for a pot of tea. Ian certainly can't compete with them in a chatting competition but that doesn't bother him. Martha tells him how she was born in Bristol in Elmers Park Road in fact, "whereas Sandra is a new girl having been here only 50 years".

'Do you know Elmers Park Road Ian?'

'Isn't that the street next to the common, with the big Edwardian houses?'

'Yes that's it. I was born in one of those larger houses just off the common. They were the first houses to be built when it was a new street. Detached, five bedrooms, high ceilings, kitchen, scullery and a basement – very grand. Apparently the builder went out of business after that first five, and when another builder came along he built smaller houses at first, then when he sold them and made more money he built larger ones but not as big as the first five and with no basements. That's why the houses in that street are so different.'

Sandra likes to hear Ian practice on the harp. Rather than being set to full blast electric mode, the harp is on soft and gentle, and the music comes downstairs as subdued sound.

Ian is well settled into the new station when one morning in June he's walking along a corridor and sees someone coming towards him he seems to recognise. The woman is smiling as she approaches him.

'Sarah? It's Sarah isn't it?'

'Yes of course it is.'

Ian grabs her round the waist and gives her a big hug lifting her off the ground. 'This is amazing what are you doing here?

'Working here now.'

'And Joe?'

'She's in Bristol, but not here. She couldn't get a job here at the time. You heard about Don?'

'Yes, Beatrice told me.'

'Joe was really cut up about it. They had known each other since nursery school, went to all the same schools, even lived in the same street at one time. They were more like brother and sister. That's one reason why she wanted to move – for a complete change of scene. And she wants to get our little group going again.'

'Good. Look, right now I'm heading off out. I'll catch you later, where are you?'

'Top floor, main office.'

That evening , Ian visits Joe and Sarah at home.

'Okay, so the two of you in the wilds of the west,' says Ian.

Joe speaks first, 'Well, we were very sorry when you stopped coming to our practice sessions, but you obviously had lot on your mind. Then we lost Don. We both took that badly.'

'Yes, I only heard about it recently from the new Sergeant Walker.'

'I carried on playing with my violin and viola friends and Sarah continued with her singing lessons, but we missed our strange band. Then Beatrice told us how you were joining this station and we thought "why don't we have a change as well?" so we decided to do a bit of stalking.' Joe gives Ian a big grin. 'And here we are.'

'Do you fancy playing again Ian?' Sarah asks. 'We could probably find a drummer or something contrary that fits in.'

'Sure, let's do that. Can you still get in the leather suit?'

'Yes, cheeky. I wear it sometimes, secretly, and the wig.'

'Good.'

Joe and Sarah seem much the same but Ian notices Joe doesn't appear to look at Sarah quite as much as before. Perhaps they are just so use to each other.

Two weeks later, Sarah meets someone at the station who plays trumpet in a jazz band and his wife plays drums for fun in a women's relaxation group.

When they all meet up at Joe's house of the first time, Jake comes along with a standard trumpet and a Baroque trumpet. With its novel sound, the Baroque trumpet looks promising to the others and maybe his wife can work with two side drums. With this in mind, they start meeting regularly.

Time flies along

14

In Which Hints turn to Facts

Ian is one of the many officers in the district involved in looking into trafficking of young girls and exploited overseas labour.

People go missing all the time; some only because they want to, some vanish for no known reason, others disappear when its obvious something bad has happened. That was the case with Veronica Bruce. Twenty three years old, a satisfying job, happily living at home with parents and just become engaged. Suddenly she wasn't there. An hour after when it is thought she vanished, her very basic phone was found on a grass verge 11 miles away.

Resources have to be divided between where the phone was found and nearer home, although the general view is that the location of the phone was a deliberate false lead.

For ten days in July, there are the usual door-to-door enquiries, all movements traced, tracked, and retraced, with many apparent sightings being called in. Then interviews and door-to-door enquiries have to be re-examined.

Ian is just one of the officers checking the interview

results, partly because that's one of the jobs that falls on the shoulders of constables and partly because he is too good at picking up on details to get out of it. He's reading through the results when he comes across Elmers Park Road. There are the usual gaps, where residents were out and there was no follow-up, but overall nobody saw anything unusual or recognised the woman in the photographs. It's then Ian remembers the former chat with Martha, the friend visiting Sandra Trewarne, and obscure basements are always worth a little consideration.

'Sergeant, there are some gaps in Elmers Park Road; I'd like to go back there and ask around.'

'All right. Take WPC Khatri with you.'

Driving over there, Ian asks, 'How long have you been with us Khatri?'

'Three weeks sir; just finished final training.'

'Good, but don't call me sir, I'm only a DC. Stanton will do.'

'Oh. It doesn't seem right somehow – I mean, yes all right, Stanton it is then.'

Ian can see she's nervous so says no more about it.

'Now all the streets around here have been pretty well covered but there's something I want to check. The grand old houses at the end of the street would be a cliché in a creepy film, at night, full moon and a gale blowing, so we're just going to make sure they are only occupied by little old ladies.' He looks at her with a smile.

'And we check they haven't got hatchets hidden under their cardigans?'

'That's the spirit.'

Ian parks the car just round the corner from Elmers Park Road. 'Got your folder? Good. This is what we do. We look very casual, not at all threatening, because I want them to let me into the house just for a friendly look around. If they say no, that's all right, and doesn't mean anything sinister. I'll knock on the door and do the chatting. You stay back a bit, just hanging around. When I give my name, I'll show my badge. Then I'll introduce you and you hold up your badge and look friendly. I'll go in alone and the front door will be left open, with you waiting on the front path. Get the idea?'

'Yes sir, err Stanton.'

At the first house, the door is opened by a man in his early seventies. Ian introduces the pair of them and explains they are working on the missing woman case.

'Someone's called already and we couldn't offer any help.'

'Well we have to keep asking and checking. People can remember things later and might not consider them important. Now I understand these houses have a basement; do you mind if I have quick look, just to get the lie of the land?'

'Yes all right. It's only used for storage really.'

'The notes say you live here with your wife? Just the two of you is it, sir?'

'Yes. My wife's in the kitchen there. But we often have visits from our son and daughters with their families. This large house is a big adventure for the smaller grandchildren. This is the door leading down to the basement.'

Under the stairs is a smart panelled door with a brass door knob. The basement is brightly lit with fluorescent lights and half full of boxes and some furniture.

'The families tend to keep too much stuff because they know we can store it for them.'

Ian has no concern that these people are secret kidnappers of young women, so he thanks them and leaves.

Walking down the path, Khatri says, 'No bodies under the patio then?'

'If you knew my history in detail you wouldn't make jokes like that.'

'No, right, sorry,' and she makes a mental note to check later.

The house next door has not received a successful visit and the front door is opened by a smartly dressed middle-aged woman. Ian goes through the same patter and takes names. One couple, and a son away at university, but right now in Thailand.

'I've seen all the pictures of the missing woman and been following the story but there doesn't seem to be much good news yet.'

'We are still taking the matter very seriously. Do you have an attic here?'

'Yes, but I've never done more than poke my head into it. Would you like to see it, well the hatch at least.'

'Yes that would be good, thank you.'

'It needs a long step ladder actually to get into it.'

Mrs Harrington-Swift leads the way to the stairs and they go on to the first floor. Ian can hear a vacuum cleaner at work. 'That's Katrina, she's a regular.' A woman looks up at them from inside one of the bedrooms. The areas Ian can see are beautifully and tastefully furnished and not cluttered with too many ornaments or fussy bits.

The attic hatch is quite small in the high landing ceiling. 'Not too suspicious, I think.'

'Not really,' agrees Ian.

Back in the hall, Ian says, 'And the basement, I think you have a basement here.'

'Ah, the basement. Well I want to make it clear that anything in the basement is nothing to do with me,' she says with a smile.

This woman is such a tease, thinks Ian. 'Intriguing,' he says and they move to the basement door. The layout is the same as the previous house. As she opens the door, a light automatically comes on. 'There we are.'

'You first please.'

At the bottom of the steps, Ian pauses before speaking. 'Ah.'

'I know. My husband's little sanctuary away from business.'

'Well I suppose it's better than always being down the pub or bookmakers.'

'Yes, and I play a lot of golf so I do get my own back.'

Spread out over most of the large basement floor is a model railway scene, tracks, train stations, grass, trees, hills, even little ponds.

'Originally he said it was for our small son, but I never did believe a word of that.'

'Thank you. We'd better go before we get accused of sacrilege,' says Ian.

'Very understanding of you.'

At the front door, Mrs Harrington-Swift says, 'The Whittakers next door are away at the moment. All five of them went to Corfu at the weekend.'

'Good, thank you.'

'That was amusing,' Ian says to Khatri. 'I'll tell you more later,' he continues when back on the pavement, as they look at their lists. 'She says these people are on holiday and they've all been seen properly anyway. Drew a blank on the photos, and said nothing useful. Number 7; the notes say it's empty and up for sale, which it is. We'll have to get the key from the agent and check it. But the next house got no answer.'

As they get past the high hedge towards the gate, Ian sees how a figure in an upstairs window quickly disappears. The figure knows it must have been seen. Ian rings the bell. With no answer he rings it again. After a minute, the door is opened cautiously by a man in his thirties. Ian introduces the pair of them as normal.

'Mr and Mrs Wilson, isn't it?' Again he explains what they are doing and shows photographs of the missing woman. Ian's super antennae are so well tuned to a person's body language he can feel something's not right here.

'It's Brendan Wilson and your wife, isn't it?'

'Yes, and Susan.'

'Good. May I have a quick look round, please, see the attic and that'll be it?'

'Are you looking in every house?'

'Oh yes, within a certain radius of the missing woman's house, then we cross them off the list and never bother them again. It only takes a minute.'

Mr Wilson just nods and opens the door further.

'We'll leave the door open, my colleague will stay outside.'

As soon as Brendan Wilson turns to move away, Ian quickly turns to Khatri who is a little way down the path. Ian looks at her and points to the door step, which tells her to come closer.

Ian has a quick glance into the two large living rooms downstairs, trying to show no real interest then they go up the stairs.

'These houses are amazing. It must be wonderful having so much space. Have you been here long?'

'Most of my life. My dad had a successful electrical business. I worked there for a while. He died and left me the business, but I wasn't much good at all that management business so I sold it.'

'Very wise. Let someone else have the stress.'

The main bedroom is enormous, being two rooms joined and created into en suite.

'Is your wife in?'

'Err, no, at work, she's manager at the local Aldi.'

He sounds nervous.

The door of the final room is half open and Ian sees it's being used as a workroom. Going into it, there are woodworking benches, tables and models of ships and galleons.

'Did you make these, what from scratch?'

'That was my first. That was a kit. . . but the others are from scratch.'

Ian looks closely at them. 'They're beautifully made

– and you carved all the wood and made these tiny metal parts?'

'Yes.'

'You're a genius. They should be in a museum so you can get the credit for them.'

Mr Wilson just shrugs his shoulders.

On the landing, Ian looks up at the small attic trap door, which would obviously be difficult to get into.

'It's just got . . . water tanks and cobwebs.'

Ian has seen a step ladder in the work room.

'I'll just get that ladder and stick my head through the hatch.'

The ladder is high enough for Ian to look in the loft and a quick scan with his torch confirms what Brendan Wilson has told him.

Downstairs, Ian takes a brief look into the kitchen and then goes to the door under the stairs, which can't be seen from the front door.

'Do you have a basement here?'

'No. The first four houses have basements. The rest of us in the street don't,' Mr Wilson says.

As Ian opens the door under the stairs, Wilson says, 'It's only a small broom cupboard.'

Ian holds the door open wide and it looks like it's only a broom cupboard, with an upright Hoover, a couple of brooms and old coats hanging on hooks on the rear of the door and on the back wall. With barely a hesitation, Ian takes the Hoover and brooms out of the cupboard as Mr Wilson starts to panic. 'What are you doing; it's only a cupboard. Stop it, get out.'

As Ian is taking hold of the coat on the back wall,

Wilson shouts and rushes towards Ian with his fists flaying about in the air. Ian grabs one arm and starts to twist it but gets a severe blow in the face from the other fist. Wilson is soon face down on the carpet, with cuffs being attached to his wrists behind his back.

'Khatri, Khatri, Now!' Khatri rushes in, drawing her taser as she runs. 'Shut the door,' he says.

Ian takes a second pair of cuffs from his belt and attaches Wilson to a central heating pipe. Ian stands and feels his face where he took the punch. 'Call in. We want another patrol here.'

While Khatri is making the call, Ian takes everything else out of the cupboard and finds a small handle in the back wall. He turns the handle, picks up a broom and standing to one side, he pushes on the door to open it fully. There's a low level of light from down the steps and a switch near the door which produces more light.

'Give me that taser.' With the broom, Ian starts prodding the steps for any possible booby trap. 'I'll go down first. Wait till I call you.'

At the bottom of the steps, he calls up. 'All right, come on.'

The basement looks rather chaotic, with old chairs, boxes, an old workbench, the largest item being a wrought iron bed against a wall with a duvet cover spread over it and woman lying under the duvet. She looks unconscious and her wrists are tied to the metalwork at the head of the bed. While Ian takes a penknife from his belt, Khatri pulls back the duvet.

'She's naked.'

The woman's wrists and ankles are tied with rough

sisal string causing her skin to be red raw and bleeding in places. He cuts all the strings.

'Put her in recovery. I'll call in. Keep the taser and watch the steps. I'll call out before I come down.'

Ian runs up the stairs, and presses the quick dial for Sergeant Walker, who's one of the sergeants on the case.

'DS Walker.'

'It's Stanton. We've found the woman.'

'Hey, success! Where?'

'Nine Elmers Park Road. We need the ambulance first.'

'Right,' and she hangs up.

'Khatri, it's Stanton, I'm coming down.'

Back in the basement, Khatri is standing on guard with taser in hand.

'How is she?'

'A weak pulse. I think she's been drugged.'

After a few minutes, sirens can be heard. 'That's probably the car you called. Stay alert.'

There are two uniform officers in the first car and Ian puts them in the picture. 'That's the arrest. Will you stay with him? The crime scene is down here. It's Stanton, we're coming down.'

'I hear you,' replies Khatri.

It takes a moment for the new constable to take in the whole scene. 'Is this Veronica Bruce?' he asks.

'We think so. I'll go back upstairs and wait for medical.'

In five minutes, the ambulance pulls up and the medics take over downstairs. The new officer says, 'Can you treat her here until senior officers arrive?'

'Yes, as long as they're quick.'

Soon after, the Chief Inspector arrives with lots of officers.

'The arrest has not been cautioned and the house could do with a better search,' says Ian. The Inspector takes control, meaning Ian and Khatri can now step back. They are standing quietly in one of the living rooms, letting everyone else do all the organising and running around. Ian goes up to WPC Khatri, who's smiling and has tears in her eyes. He gives her a big smile and with a very light touch on the shoulder with his fist, he says, 'Feels good doesn't it?' She gives a big cheerful nod, wiping tears off her cheeks.

Sergeant Walker comes into the room looking more emotional than Ian has ever seen her. 'You all right Khatri?'

'Yes Sergeant.'

'She did well,' says Ian.

Beatrice points a finger at Ian and says sternly, 'As for you DC Stanton, how did you manage to find her when nobody else could? Tell me later.' Then she throws her arms around him and gives him a strong hug. 'Any more discoveries like this and we might have to bring you in for questioning.'

'And you get a hug as well. Well done,' as Beatrice hugs Khatri.

'Sergeant,' says Ian. He's got a wife. She must know about all this. She's manager at the local Aldi. The name is Susan Wilson.'

'I'll get it,' says Beatrice and disappears out the front door with two uniform police.

Khatri smirks. 'Hugs from Super-Barbie indeed.'

'Keep it to yourself.'

'And I don't care what you say, I'm going to call you "Sir" just for today.'

Back at the station, there's all-round satisfaction at the outcome, nothing riotous like footballers celebrating a goal, but smiles and nods towards Ian and WPC Khatri. Ian had to put up with comments about his bruised face and black eye, and about getting too old and slow for this kind of job.

When someone congratulates Khatri, she says modestly, 'I didn't do anything, DC Stanton did all the clever work.'

'Yes but you were there and you did your bit, so you get some of the credit.'

A couple of days later, Ian buys a huge bunch of flowers for Sandra at his digs and another for her friend Martha. He visits Martha with Sandra and explains how her little story about the basements in those houses sowed the seed for his suspicions and led to the happy outcome.

'The press aren't allowed to say anything until after the trial, then they can run your story. It should be worth a few thousand to you but don't take their first offer.'

Time is pleasing . . . . .

15

IN WHICH SARAH TRIES NEW WATERS

By the middle of September, Ian is finally able to conclude the sale of his London flat and the purchase of a new place in Bristol.

When he has a complete day off, Ian likes to do a lot of lounging around. Work can be hectic and stressful. He's been in his new home for a couple weeks and sitting on the sofa simply gazing at the ceiling, quietly sucking on a large piece of dark chocolate, when the phone rings.

'Hello.'

'Hello Ian, it's Sarah . . . green leather Sarah.'

'Hi, how are you doing?'

'I'm on my own and I was wondering if we could m.meet for coffee and n.chat this m.morning.

'Yes sure, shall I come round to you?'

'No I have to go somewhere first, so I'll come to you and see your new place. In about half an hour?'

'Fine, see you soon.'

When the buzzer goes, he tells her to come to the first floor. Ian opens the door to see her dressed in her full stage gear of green leathers, red wig, reasonably strong make-up, black boots and gloves. She looks a little nervous, but completely sexy with it.

'Come in. Good to see you. I love you in this gear – you look fantastic.'

Sarah is delighted with the comments, steps closer to him, unzips the jacket all the way down and kisses him in the lips. She puts her arms around his head and carries on kissing. He puts his hands under her jacket and round her body. She's only wearing a bra underneath. The message is perfectly clear, so he leads her into the bedroom.

In the bedroom, she sits down on the side of the bed.

'I'll draw the curtains.' There are net curtains but now the room is more subdued.

'Stand up will you.' With her standing beside the bed, he kneels down in front of her, unzips the leather trousers and slowly pulls them down to below her knees. He holds her legs and kisses her thigh. She sits down to let him take off her boots, followed by the trousers and socks.

'You had mm.better just get on with it before I lose my n.nerve. I'm quite safe, my period's due tomorrow and I'm very regular.' This is the first time she's spoken since arriving and still has her stammer.

'All right – up.' As soon as she stands, he pulls her knickers down with one quick move 'Lie face down will you.'

She drops her jacket on the floor, throws aside her bra and lies on the bed. Ian takes off his clothes, kneels beside her and starts rubbing her back with long smooth strokes and squeezes her bottom gently.

'Okay, turn over.' He gives her tummy a little rub, and they have sex immediately.

When they've both finished he lifts himself off her and she rolls over on to her front, breathing quickly.

'Do you want to get into bed. Do you want cuddles?'

'Mmm.'

He pulls her half on top of him and rubs her back some more.

'Well this is a wonderful surprise.'

'Was I all right?'

'You were and are fantastic. Hot, soft and sexy.'

She giggles. 'I don't often get called hot and sexy, never in fact.'

'Hot, soft, juicy and sexy. And you have a delicious bit of pussy down there.'

'Oooo I do love dirty talk. Can you get that carved into stone and give it to me as a wall plaque?'

'What would a certain person say about that?'

'She'd kill me, kill both of us.'

'Does she knock you about?'

'No, but she is bossy and can get a bit rough during certain activities.'

'So where is she now? Anyway how come you are here?'

'Gone to visit parents for the weekend.' She pauses. 'For some reason I put the gear on this morning; it always gives me more confidence and quite suddenly I wondered what it would be like having sex with a man. Never had it you see; only ever done it with Joe. And then I thought of you, you were the natural choice. At the very least you deserve a reward for finding that woman, so I thought I'd volunteer myself for the task.

'Mind you, I was so scared I nearly didn't ring the

bell, but the taxi had already gone so I had to really.'

'This sex with a man was something on your bucket list was it?'

'Only since this morning. Actually things seem to be a little cool with Joe and me at the moment and I definitely needed the attention and company.'

They are quiet for a while.

'Ian, I'm hungry.'

'Sure, what do you fancy?'

'Don't know. A sandwich will do.'

'All right, and I've got some special English sparkly – it's like champagne.'

'I love champagne. Yes please.'

'What do you want in the sandwich?'

'I don't eat meat.'

'You've just had a piece of meat inside you.'

She laughs. 'And you certainly know how to ram it in, but maybe men are always like that.'

'Not the fat ones, certainly; too much stomach in the way. Have you got any allergies?'

'No, but I am supposed to be allergic to men. Surprise me with the sandwich.'

'You had better use these tissues; I pumped quite a lot of juice into you there.'

'Oh hell, it's all going to come out isn't it? Men are so disgusting.'

'Nonsense, you loved it.'

'Yes you're right there. All that throbbing was great.'

Ian returns with a tray, a plate of sandwiches, a bottle and glasses.

'Do you like chocolate?'

'Depends; what type is it? Organic dark. Oh yes, I surrender.'

The bottle goes pop and he fills the glasses.

She takes a sip, 'Mmm it's good,' then she polishes off the whole glass. 'Another please,' and she drinks half of it.

'What's in these then, they are enormous? I've only a little mouth.'

'I'm not going to tell you, Make it a blind tasting.'

She closes her eyes and takes a large bite.

'Mmm. Slices of date, with a mild blue cheese and nuts of some sort.'

'Pine kernels.'

'This is amazing. You ought to open a sandwich bar. This is good; I think I like being waited on like this. I'm normally doing all the serving. If I come again, will I get the same treatment?'

'Good heavens, no. This is a one-off. Next time you'll be ravaged and abused and locked in the cellar until I want more sex with you.'

'Just like home then.'

When she's finished the sandwich, he offers her more wine.

'Are you trying to get me drunk and take advantage of an innocent girl?'

'Yes, with luck I'll be able to have you again in a few minutes.'

'Can you do it again? I thought men could only do it once a day.'

'Certainly not. If you were to stay the night you'd probably get fucked half a dozen times.'

'Cripes, I wouldn't be able to walk. I could never stay the night anyway. Joe usually rings up to check on me.'

'With a mobile you could be anywhere.'

'No, she'll ask me what I'm doing, what's on tele, could I get her a phone number from her book – that sort of sneaky stuff.'

'And she's at her parents is she and not humping someone else now.'

'That's a point. I never thought of that. How would I ever know. Spoken like a true detective. Suddenly I don't feel guilty.'

She stretches her arms up and arches her back sticking her breasts out. 'Now I feel like a groupie who's just had sex with the star, and it's heavenly.'

'Ready for more sex then?'

'Now already?'

'Sure, if you can get me hard. We'll have you on top this time.'

'Let me have another swig of sparkly first.' After she empties her glass, she says, 'I'm not usually allowed on top. I've see it done like that in the porn videos.'

'Give me your hand.' He puts her hand on his penis and she holds it gently. She throws the bed clothes to one side, sits up and hold his penis and balls on both hands, stroking and squeezing until he gets properly hard.

'Oh it's amazing how big it gets.'

She leans forward, gives it a lick then puts it in her mouth, rolling her tongue over it. Then she kneels over him and put his tool into her and starts moving up and down slowly a couple of times. She starts bouncing up and down getting faster and faster while Ian jerks his hips up at times to meet her movements. Finally she climaxes and flops down on to him. Ian wraps his arms around her, and rolls them both over so he's on top. He starts shagging her and pushing harder and harder. It's a good minute before he comes, and Sarah is getting somewhat exhausted. When he finishes, he lies down on top of her and a minute later she pushes him off.

'Christ, that was certainly more than I bargained for.'

'You all right?'

'Yes. I'll live. Actually it was good.'

'That'll be another first for you then. Does Joe know about these fantasies of yours?'

'Definitely not. I told you. She'd kill us both.'

'So, I've got some blackmail material haven't I?'

'You wouldn't would you?'

'No. As long as you come round here twice a week for the next 10 years.'

She laughs and gives him a light punch on the chest. 'Any more champs.' She snatches the bottle and drinks the remainder straight out of the bottle.

In due course they get up, Ian putting on a shirt and tracksuit trousers while Sarah puts on the wig, her black knickers and the green leather jacket completely open at the front. At one point she's standing with her hands on her hips looking at him.

He bursts out laughing. 'What's funny?' she asks.

'The contrast of you standing there looking so hot and sexy and you at work in sensible clothes, sensible shoes and glasses.'

'Joe doesn't like me too dressed up.'

'I want to photograph you like that.'

'Don't you dare. That'll be evidence.'

'Yes, now stand there or I'll call Joe right now and tell her what we've been doing. Stand up, feet apart more and put your hands on your hips, head up.'

Sarah pouts as she takes up the pose while Ian takes the snap on his mobile.

She sits beside him, looking concerned as he shows her the picture. 'Look at that. Don't you think you look sexy?'

'Spose so, but you won't ever do anything with that will you? I mean I'll have more sex with you if that's what you want.'

'No of course not. I promise. This is our special secret.' He puts his arm around her and kisses her on the forehead.

'You know once you've had sex and most of a bottle of bubbly, you don't seem to stammer at all.'

'That will have to be my new medication from now on. You certainly gave me a good pounding there.'

'You're worth every penny. Was I too rough with you?'

'No. Firm but fair. A great experience.'

They have a simple lunch of soup and coffee.

'Do you think you and Joe will want a kid or two?' he asks.

'Joe does. It'll be me who has to have it. It'll be IVF of course. How about you, would you be the donor?'

'Sure, but only if we could do it the proper way.'

'Joe wouldn't allow that. She'd go mad!'

'We wouldn't tell her. We'd be very sneaky about it.'

'Ooo yes, that's a thought. I'll put you on the waiting list.' They laugh.

'Now I'm very curious, have you ever had sex with Sergeant Beatrice Walker?'

'No of course not. She's way out of most people's league.'

'Really? What league am I in then, third division slut?'

'Erm, erm.'

'Careful now.'

'Erm, you'll be in anyone's first division dear.'

'Perfect. Perfect cobblers, but it'll do. Anyway, you did save her life. I thought maybe she would throw her arms wide open, then her legs and say, "My hero. Take me", just like in the movies.'

'No chance of that sort of thing with Beatrice, and she's devoted to her husband. You have your bossy-boots, so do I. Beatrice is more like a bossy sister.'

'If you were a super-hero with five million pounds in the bank I bet it would be different story.'

'Well, she did buy me a coffee and a doughnut.'

'What more could a super-hero ever want?'

They sit down on the settee for a few quiet moments.

'I think I'll go now. That's enough excitement for one day. I'd better go home and calm down in case she comes back early. It can happen if there are rows at home.'

'I'll drive you back.'

In the bedroom, she gets fully dressed. She opens the wardrobe door to look at herself in the full length mirror and touch up her make-up.

Ian admires the finished article 'You certainly look red hot like that and very fuckable'.

'Thank you kind sir and can you add that to the plaque as well?'

'The singing in that green leather has definitely made a big difference to you hasn't it?'

'Yes, every shy timid woman with a slight stammer should get one.'

Getting into the car, Sarah says, 'There could be one snag. Our neighbour; she's very nosy and gossips a lot. If she sees me coming and going like this she's likely to mention it to Joe. I should have a story ready.'

'Okay. Tell her before the neighbour can say anything. Say you rang me up this morning and asked to meet for coffee, chat and lunch. Then you decided to meet me wearing all this show gear just for a laugh and to shock me. The taxi brought you here and we went to the Crescent coffee shop, then the Park for lunch, much to my embarrassment of course. We had soup and sandwiches in the café then I took you home.'

'That sounds good.'

'We had better go back via the Park and check out the café, just to make sure it is open today and not closed for refurbishment or something.'

'Good thinking detective You would make a great criminal.'

'Then you could be my Moll.'

'Perfect.'

'Do you think you might take up men on a full or part-time basis?'

'Don't know. It's certainly been an adventure. I'll see how I react later.'

Time plays on . . . . .

16

IN WHICH THE BAND HITS A HIGH

The group practices for the little musical gang carry on once a week. Joe is very insistent about how much practise they must do individually in the meantime. That's Ian with the harp, Joe on the violin, Jake with the Baroque trumpet, his wife Petra with two side drums similar to those used by Don, and Sarah with the vocals.

Joe has composed what seems like a mini-symphony. All the instruments merge in and out at various stages, like new layers. At times, the violin and trumpet are playing at a slow pace while the harp and drums play at a faster pace, then they all merge together. The pace changes from quiet and gentle to loud and exciting, and the lyrics tell a romantic story, with Sarah having the opportunity to display her full range.

It takes some learning and practice for the musicians, because the idea is to play it without any sheet music. Their target is the up-coming police concert for the West Country region. Performers have to be members of the force and their families, which means Joe and Petra qualify.

They now call themselves "Westcote Green", after the street name for the station.

By the middle of November, they are all pleased with their progress, especially Joe and she's the hardest to satisfy. She suggests they get the piece recorded professionally in a studio, the way they did last year; it certainly helped tighten up their performance on that occasion. With studio time booked, they want to play the piece in one go and Joe suggests they should do it twice and choose which version turns out better. The only person to object to this is Sarah, saying that some passages can be quite a strain and her voice might not hold up for two performances, one after the other.

They present themselves for the concert audition in their full show gear. The decision making panel is impressed and surprised by what they see and hear. One of the assessors asks, 'Are you all in a station?' Another assessor says, 'I recognise you Ian Stanton, and I think I recognise you with the trumpet.'

'Yes, Jake Harris, I'm in soco and this is my wife Petra.'

Ian says, 'Joe here used to be in the Eversley station in London and now is a partner. The little green devil here is also at our station. She wants to keep a bit of mystery going, but you probably see her several times a week.'

Sarah stands with her feet apart and the hands on her hips, looking rather cocky. She does one of her sexy wiggles and gives a big smile.

'Perhaps not dressed like that I think,' responds the assessor.

'Only for church,' chips in Joe.

Joe points out that if they are chosen they would

like to go on first, to give them time to get everything plugged in and set up properly. This seems to suit the organisers because they have another band comprising 15 musicians, 13 of whom play different brass instruments accompanied by two drummers. They all dress in black, white and scarlet and the intention is to have them as the final act.

In early December when the concert starts, it's only Beatrice and Leo who have any idea what to expect, apart from the small number of organisers. "Westcote Green" open the show and their music starts with a blast, a full relay of 20 violins, the harp music repeated five times through Don's gadget, the Baroque trumpet with its unique pitch and a strong driving beat from the drums. Petra never takes her eyes off her drums, looking at them with concentration and rattles out the beat with great intensity. Many people notice how Ian has his eyes closed while playing but only the musicians among the audience realise the significance of this.

But it's Sarah who seems to get all the whistles. Her moves and wiggles are much stronger and sexier than previously and she makes the most of them. They only play the one piece lasting over 20 minutes and it's a rousing success.

Time gathers momentum . . . . . until

17

In Which Woollies turn into Hot Metal

In January, the Sales are on. Ian is not much of one for buying lots of clothes but thinks he could do with a thick winter pullover. He's off duty and in a local shopping centre on the first floor, just inside one of the stores selling women's and men's woollen clothes.

Suddenly there's gunfire from upstairs, quickly followed by screams and more gunfire nearby. A gunman runs into the clothes store firing an automatic rifle almost at random but hitting a number of people. Ian is behind a rack of garments, but immediately steps out, runs towards the gunman a few feet away and punches him on the back of the head. The gunman falls to the ground, dropping his rifle. Ian picks up the gun and steps back a couple of paces. There's the possibility that the man is wearing explosives so Ian shoots him in a safer place. He turns the body over, takes the man's pistol from a holster and a bullet magazine, then runs to a side wall.

He finds himself next to a young woman, who is uninjured but terrified. While Ian is getting organised by putting the pistol in his belt and the spare magazine in a pocket, he speaks to her. 'I'm police. I'm not firearms but I'll have to have a go.' He looks her in the eye, hesitates and says, 'My name is Ian. Have a good life,' then he runs out of the store into the open mall, where all the shooting and screaming are loud and clear.

As he rushes towards the doors leading to the stairs, he gets a strange sensation. Everything seems to be moving in slow motion. He knows in reality all is chaotic and terror but it doesn't feel like that to him. He even recalls having heard racing drivers talking about it, how although they are driving at 200mph, they have plenty of time.

In the stairs area, there are several people crouching in corners as much as they can, because there's no emergency exit near them. They see him with the rifle and freeze, even more fearful.

'Police,' he says and runs up to the next floor. Looking through the small window in the door, he sees a gunman about 40 metres away, looking in the other direction and firing. Ian is reminded of the situation several years ago with Sergeant Innes and the bomber. Keeping a constant eye on the gunman, he goes through the door and, passing several bodies, runs towards the gunman. Several bursts from Ian's gun and the man is down, and there's no explosion. He snatches up one of the gunman's weapons and slides it towards a man keeping low by the wall. Ian shouts to him, 'I'm going downstairs. Fire this in the air a few times to make a distraction.' Gunfire persists, most likely from the ground floor as Ian quickly goes round to the escalator.

On his way down, he struggles to disconnect the old magazine and engage a new one, then he fires one shot to ensure it's still works properly. Going down the next escalator to the ground floor, he's stooping low, trying not to be seen. Stepping on to the floor, while at the same time looking in all directions for the gunman, there's a brief lull in any shooting. He turns just as the gunman turns towards him some 12 metres away. For the briefest of moments the gunman hesitates, obviously not expecting another gunman here. Then they both fire simultaneously. The gunman explodes and Ian takes several bullets. He drops the rifle but has the sensation of rising up and looking down on the scene while still controlling his body; it's like being in two places at once. He knows he's hit in the right shoulder and the right part of his chest – he must get to a wall and lie on his right side. Staggering but strangely not feeling any pain, he moves to the nearest wall, taking the pistol out of his belt with his left hand.

At the wall, he sinks down on to his right side. He's aware enough to know that with a chest and lung injury lying any other way would cause him to drown in his own blood. Still just about conscious, with gun in hand and not wanting to be mistaken for one of the killers when the Armed Response Unit comes storming in, he pulls his warrant card out of his shirt top pocket, lays it on the ground, and then he fades.

From the first gunshot, to the moment when Ian lies on the ground is less than two minutes. It's after a further two minutes when the black-clad armed police rush into the building, determined to show their mettle. With the building secure, dozens of paramedics take over the carnage.

★

Ian's mother is taken by police car from Guildford to the Bristol hospital. The WPC with her tries to play down the seriousness of his injuries, but mothers being mothers she has a jumble of fears running through her mind. At this stage it's thought that Ian is simply another innocent shopper caught in the attack.

Ian is one of many in intensive care, but the only one with an extra police guard. He's out of surgery by the time his mother arrives and after getting a report from the doctor, she starts her vigil.

Over a day later, the Assistant Chief Constable and the Chief Superintendent enter the general office where Ian has his desk. Some of the officers are there, others are still interviewing witnesses from the shooting. The Inspector comes out of his office when he sees the senior officers enter.

'Good morning everyone. I am able to give you an update about the shopping mall incident. We have been with the investigating officers and looking at the CCTV which have now been compiled in sequence. We know the terrorists entered the building through the main entrance, at 12.03, then they went into a stairs area. They removed their overcoats which they were wearing to cover their weapons. One went to the second floor, one went to the first floor, one stayed on the ground floor. All at the same time, they entered the shopping area and started shooting.

'On the first floor, there was an unarmed police officer in one of the shops and when a gunman entered the store this officer attacked the gunman, took his gun and killed him. It is an officer from this unit. His name is not to be made public for his own protection both from possible reprisals and from excessive attention from the press. He did speak briefly to a member of the public and it was clear to her he was frightened but he knew he had to do his duty. He took a couple of weapons and went up to the second floor and killed that terrorist. Then he went down to the ground floor and was involved in a gun fight, killing the third terrorist but sustaining severe injuries himself.

'Looking at the videos we were all amazed and impressed with the completely unselfish bravery of that officer, who is not a fully trained AFO. It would be good to think we all could have acted that way, but to be honest I certainly wonder if we all could. After surgery, the officer will remain in intensive care for some time, but the doctors appear optimistic. Thank you, carry on.'

There is light applause from those in the room.

DC Betty Nicholls had switched on her phone as the ACC started talking. Now she switches it off and immediately leaves the office to go and find Sergeant Walker.

'Beatrice, the ACC has just been in and given us an update. It was DC Stanton. It's amazing, listen to this.'

Beatrice listens with her eyes closed. 'The silly bugger's done it again hasn't he? Who'd ever marry him – how could they put up with the stress? Thanks Betty. I'm going to the hospital.'

There are lots of uniform police around the hospital and it's not difficult for Beatrice to find where Ian is. There's a large officer outside the door.

Beatrice walks up to the door and nods to the officer. 'Hello David.' She points at the closed door. 'DC Stanton?'

'No comment. A complete embargo.'

'You mean I can't go in there?'

'Not a chance. You know the phrase "More than my job's worth, guv". Orders from the biggest chief. Only certain doctors, nurses and his mother.'

'Is she here?'

'No comment. But if you take a seat over there, you might see her pass some time. That woman down there is police, but don't tackle with her.'

Beatrice gives him a small nod and smile and walks down the corridor. She easily works out that the woman she's approaching must be a minder assigned to protect Mrs Stanton from the press and they will be staying in a police safe house somewhere. Beatrice sits next to the woman and takes out her badge. 'DS Walker. I've known Ian for years. We were at Eversley Road, London, together. He saved my life once, four years ago. I'd like to have a chat with his mother if I could.'

'Not today. I'll have to get clearance. Perhaps try tomorrow.'

'Thanks.' Beatrice leaves.

The following afternoon, Beatrice is allowed to see Mrs Stanton and has permission to fill in some details for her. They are sitting in the hospital canteen with tea and scones. Mrs Stanton's face looks lined and drawn with worry, taking small sips of tea and merely nibbling at a few crumbs from her scone.

'Actually, it seems Ian stopped the slaughter even

before the armed police arrived. They'll be running out of medals for him soon.'

'What do you mean?'

'Well he's already got that George Cross and George Medal, hasn't he? I don't know how they can top that now.'

'What medals? Ian hasn't got any medals.'

'Ah, hasn't he told you about them? Have I just put my foot in it?'

'Now that you have, you might as well leave it there.'

'That's the sort of comment Ian would make.'

'He never talks about his police work,' says Mrs Stanton. 'He knows I'm nervous about it. He probably doesn't want to worry me further. So just what do you mean?'

'All right, he can fill in the details if he wants to. There was an incident six years ago when he and Sergeant Innes stopped an atrocity. They both got the George Cross. Nearly four years ago Sergeant Innes again and I, I was in uniform as a constable then, well we got caught in a trap; Ian appeared from nowhere and literally saved our lives, against four men. Ian saved my life. He got the George Medal that time. We think it should have been higher, but still.'

'He's not in the gun police is he?'

'No, but we can still get trained how to use them.'

Mrs Stanton sits quietly for a while and looks rather tearful. 'I don't see him very often these days. He suggested I should move to Bristol, then he could visit me more.'

'That sounds a good idea. There are some attractive areas out and about.'

'I was relieved when he became a detective. I thought it would be safer than being on the streets all hours. Shouldn't he be a sergeant or something by now?'

'Yes, he should be. He's always wanted to stay at ground level. I feel he doesn't want the responsibility of rank. He's never taken the Sergeant exams but this incident might change all that. He might get promoted whether he likes it or not.'

Time drags slowly . . . . .

18

In Which Sarah helps with Recovery

It's early March and Ian is still on medical leave recovering from his injuries and regaining his strength. It's nearly 8 o'clock on a Friday evening when his phone rings. 'Hello Ian – it's Sarah.'

'Hello sex pot.'

'Oh I wish everybody said that to me. How's the recovery?'

'Slow but progressing and boring, with so much sitting around.'

'Are you busy this evening then? Joe's away again and I need someone to talk to.'

'Yes of course, good idea. Come on round.'

'Thanks. See you in 20.'

When Sarah arrives they have a modest hug.

'Cup of tea?' Ian asks.

'Mmmm please.'

'And I have fig rolls and dark chocolate gingers.'

'Oooo, complete seduction.'

Sitting down with tea and biscuits, Sarah is soon on her second biscuit.

'So how's the recovery then? All patched up are you?'

'Yes all patched and working and starting to do some

light exercise.'

'Joe and I tried to visit you in hospital but it wasn't allowed, then you seemed to disappear.

'Yes, security, and they wanted to keep me anonymous. After hospital I stayed with someone from the station then at my mother's house. To the world I was just another victim in the mall.'

'How many m.medals did you get this time?'

'I'm not allowed to say.'

'Fiddlesticks. What about pillow talk with Marta Hari?'

'She hasn't turned up yet. What about Joe, where's she off to then?'

'Not sure. She was away two weeks ago and came back with a touch of perfume on her. She never wears perfume. And she was very cool with me. I know she's at it with someone else now. She says she's gone to her parents again and her mother is ill, but I doubt it.'

Sarah picks a chocolate biscuit from the bowl and moves to sit on Ian's lap. 'Bite,' as she puts a biscuit to his mouth. Then she takes a bite herself and carries on alternately until the biscuit is finished. She goes a little bit coy. 'Ian, could I stay here tonight?'

'All night? What about Mrs Adolf, won't she check up?'

'No, not tonight, probably tomorrow. Besides I accidentally knocked the phone off the hook, so it won't ring. Please let me stay. I need the comfort.'

'Okay, but I have to warn you, as for comfort I'll probably do more than hold your hand.'

'Thank goodness for that. Now for the first one, if

you could do it the same way as last time, when you had yours arms under my legs and really pressed down on me – that was great. And then I'd like to be on all fours with you going in from behind – I love having it that way.'

By now, Ian is laughing. 'Lucking for me you're so scandalous. Who have you done it with on all fours?'

'Only Joe. I've still had only Joe and you.'

'And I'm your secret sin, remember?'

'Sure, is it bedtime yet then?'

'Yes and I'm going to start off by massaging your back and your tits.'

'Heavenly heaven.'

When they wake in the morning, Ian puts his arm around Sarah and holds her close. 'You all right dear?'

'Mmmm. That one in the middle of the night was a bonus.'

'Yes I woke up to find a hot and sexy woman next to me and the equipment seemed ready, so I had no choice did I?'

'None at all. Last time you said I was hot, juicy and sexy.'

'Indeed you are.'

'Now can I put on my Marta Hari persona? Are you going to tell me what medals you got after that shopping centre business?'

'No. It's a very sensitive subject. Six naked virgins managed to drag it out of me once and now they're pushing up daisies. It had to be done I'm afraid but I wouldn't want the same fate to happen to you.'

'Recycling; very good; I approve. So it's classified is it?'

'Yes and top secret.'

'How exciting. I feel like that groupie again who's now being fucked by a superstar in a Madison Square dressing room. It's wonderful. Now for the finale, it's me on all fours. I would like some strong coffee first, to get me nicely pepped up, then you do the business, then breakfast. How's that?'

'All right, strong coffee coming up.'

Sitting at breakfast, Sarah looks a little vacant.

'You all right, Sarah?'

'Yes fine. Just a bit drained. That last one, heck. You certainly know what to do with your hands, while you're shagging a girl. I didn't half explode. Joe's ever so rough at times, almost violent. You're not, you give me a good pummelling but it stays kind. That one was the best of the lot.'

'Write me up a testimonial will you and I'll start a website with it.'

'Well there's nothing wrong with your recovery; the important muscles are in good working order. You might as well get back to work immediately,' she says with a laugh. 'Are going to be my full-time secret lover then?'

'No, you're far too dangerous for me, and perhaps we don't actually have enough in common for regular business.'

After more tea and toast, Sarah says, 'I suppose you're going to throw me out now, after you've sexploited me to the full?'

'Heh! You've sexploited me, little Miss Hot Stuff. I've simply been giving you some therapy.'

'Will that be your defence with St. Peter?'

'Definitely.'

'Actually it has been good therapy. And I love being called hot and sexy as you ram into me again; it's a real ego boost. Joe's always finding fault with me.'

'Now, we could take a walk in the park, have early elevenses then I can throw you out.'

'That'll do. And I'll try not to be a nuisance.'

It's the end of March before Ian is back in the office and doing light duties. Gradually he works towards getting back to fitness with more exercise, running, cycling and then aikido and karate. He leaves out swimming, being rather self-conscious about his scars from the bullet wounds and subsequent surgery.

Time moves along . . . . .

19

In Which Paris gets a Visit

Detective Sergeant Walker is in the office of Chief Inspector Chandler.

'I've just had a call from Inspector Wallis. He's meant to be going to France with you on Monday isn't he?'

'Yes sir, over this Bolton murderer.'

'Well he seems to have come down with flu. He's been feeling worse over the last couple of days; now it's got really bad. So we need to find you someone else.'

Beatrice thinks quickly.

'How about DC Stanton?'

'Stanton? He's only a DC. We can't really send two junior officers on a job like this. The French will find it insulting and won't take it seriously.'

'I think they will sir. They have a double murderer walking around their streets and the chances are he's involved in something criminal there. By sending two juniors we're making it clear that it's their show. If we send someone very senior, it might look like we're checking up on them or trying to take over. The French will see it as our mistake letting him get away and will love the chance to show us how it should be done.'

'Yer, that's a good point. So you think it might be a diplomatic move?'

'Yes sir, I do. We'll only have passive role anyway. Besides, Stanton's not your regular DC.'

'True enough. You think he's properly recovered?'

'Yes he's pretty fit again.'

'And has he got a valid passport? Give him a ring and check will you.'

She makes the call and confirms he has.

'All right, Inspector Wallis doesn't speak French so you were always going to be the main link there anyway. I see your husband's going too isn't he – in a private capacity?'

'Yes. Why do you suppose he doesn't trust me in Paris among four million romantic and passionate French men?'

'I really can't imagine. What's he going to do with himself while you're dealing with this case?'

'He'll work. He can do his computer work anywhere. That'll keep him happy for hours and he speaks reasonable tourist French.'

'Okay, call the Inspector at home to make sure you've got all the files and bring Stanton up to speed, and let's hope you can come back with a head on a plate.'

Beatrice sits down with Ian in the Inspector's office.

'All right, Constable,' she says smiling, 'you are coming with me to Paris next Monday.'

Ian rubs his hands together in a comic manner. 'Oooo gossip galore.'

She gives him one of her frosty looks. 'And Leo. There's this character George Bolton, already guilty of murder; killed a dealer in Bristol and later killed a policeman escaping from a prison van. After that he disappeared. His brother Alan was visited recently by some criminal from France. The Boltons had a French father and both speak decent French. All the signs are that George Bolton is in Paris, doubtless working with French criminals. The Paris police have been keeping an eye on the man who came here to visit Alan Bolton, so we have to go and help, if we can, and hopefully start extradition.'

'Is there a timescale on this?'

'No. Until we get a result one way or the other. A lot might depend on how much the French have been able to find out in the meantime.'

'Still got all your French have you then?' Ian asks cheekily.

'Just about. Now what we have to do is march in there and give a strong impression. The very first impression we give will make all the difference as to how we're treated. That means, firstly, super smart stylish clothes. What have you got in the way of suits?'

'I bought a new suit for the last medal award. Not special, but looks all right because it's new.'

'What colour is it?'

'Mid-grey. Nothing very striking, otherwise there's only this thing.'

'Then we have to go and buy you something which has more impact.'

'We? Who's paying?'

'You are and I'm choosing.'

'This sounds like a highjack.'

'That's right, I'm a Sergeant remember?'

'All right, but not black. I don't do black.'

'You just about wearing black now.'

'That's for work; I need to fit in and not get noticed. Otherwise I prefer lighter shades and colours, but they are really hard to get in men's clothes.'

'So, who knows, we might end up in the women's department. Now here's the file. Unless they change it, the contact will be Commissaire Maurice Albert at this address. The nearest rank here would be a Superintendent. Get your teeth into that and first thing in the morning, we'll hit the shops. Bring a healthy credit card.'

'Can't I get this on expense?'

'Nope. I do love spending other people's money. My husband says it is one of my most endearing qualities.'

Meeting in the morning, Ian says, 'If I'm about to be fleeced of piles of money, I'll want a decent coffee first.' So off they go to a coffee shop.

As soon as they sit down, Beatrice starts taking pins out of her hair. For work she always has it pinned back tightly in a very prim manner. Pulling out the last pin, she shakes her head, just like they do in the movies and her hair tumbles down in its waves.

'What's that for?' asks Ian.

'Shopping mode. Sometimes it works better.'

Ian doesn't mind. Walking around with a woman like Beatrice when people might think you're married is good for any man's ego.

'What you are going to be wearing?' he asks.

'That'll be a surprise, but I do intend to make an entrance.'

'You could manage that wearing an old sack.'

'How come you're still single with lines like that?'

'It's these modern women you know. They just can't cope. One weekend with me and they're completely burnt out.'

Beatrice almost spills her coffee through laughing.

They try a couple of department stores in the High Street and although they feature all the famous designer labels, everything seems to be black or gunmetal grey with the occasional bit of beige. Ian doesn't want these drab colours and Beatrice agrees that there's nothing which will make the right sort of impact.

'Right, we'll go to Jeromes.'

'Jeromes?' They don't even have any prices in the window.'

'Of course not, they're far too expensive for that. Look, it's like torture, eventually you start to enjoy the pain. Come along,' as she takes his arm and leads him into the shop.

The men's suits follow the normal colour code of black and dark. There are a couple in maroon and a couple in blue. The more expensive examples have attractive and subtle checks. One in duck egg blue catches their eyes and it's the only real choice for their needs.

Ian looks at himself in the long mirror. He sees Beatrice nodding with approval, and to his surprise he likes it also. 'Dare I look at the price tag?'

'I'll do that.' She turns over the price tag. 'Mmm, you'll live.'

Beatrice goes over to the shirts. 'Collar size?'

'Steady on now.'

'Collar size!'

'15.'

After making a choice, she moves over to the ties. By now, Ian has given up. She chooses a bright colourful silk tie and says, 'Right, that'll do here,' he says.

'I'm not sure I like that word "here".'

Speaking to the assistant, she says, 'We'll take this suit and this shirt and you can throw in the tie free, can't you?' and the smile on that beautiful face works wonders.

'Yes, madam.'

She snaps her fingers at Ian for the credit card.

Outside the shop, Beatrice looks very pleased with herself. 'I think that's the best we'll get short of something bespoke in Savile Row. What about shoes?'

'I've got good shoes, honestly I do. I've got some excellent shoes for best. What colour, black or brown?'

'With this suit in France, brown and light socks.'

Although they have met briefly, Ian hasn't met Leo properly until this trip to France. He's tall, fair, hand-some, intelligent, easygoing and genuine – any reasonable man's hate figure. He's just the sort of husband you would expect a woman like Beatrice to have. They've been together since their second year at university.

They catch an early flight and settle into the hotel in time for lunch. With their appointment to meet the Commissaire at 3 o'clock, Ian is in the reception waiting for Beatrice. He's in his new designer suit, complete with coordinated shirt and colourful tie. Although not use to being this smart, he feels good about it.

When Beatrice steps out of the lift, to say she looks dressed to kill wouldn't do her justice – thigh-high black boots, buccaneer style, with large stiletto heels; a suit of beautifully-styled jacket and skirt in dark blue vicuña, yellow silk blouse, and the waves of her long ash-blonde hair flowing freely. A neat exclusive shoulder bag matches the colour of the jacket and skirt. There's a good amount of leg showing between the top of the boots and the hem of the skirt. Heads turn as she walks towards Ian. She stands in front of him with her hands on her hips. 'Well?'

Ian takes a step back and looks her up and down several times and says, 'Walking in like that, you're going to cause heart attacks.'

'Do you know, that's the nicest thing you've ever said to me.'

'They might not let you in. Those heels look like a lethal weapon and now you're two inches taller than I am.'

'You're looking pretty sharp yourself. Let's be off then. Got all the papers?'

'For goodness sake. Any more insults?'

'Very sorry officer, I'm sure,' says Beatrice.

'And if we sit down in his office, whatever you do, don't cross your legs. That'll be going too far.'

'No it won't. No such thing.'

This is just normal banter for these two.

Time moves quickly . . . . .

20

IN WHICH THIGH-HIGH BOOTS WORK MAGIC

The Commissaire's phone buzzes. Marie-Edith, the support assistant sitting just outside his office, takes the call. *'Sir, the British officers are downstairs. Do you want me to go and fetch them?'*

'No, I'll do it. It'll be more polite,' says Commissaire Maurice Albert.

At reception, he speaks to the desk officer who points out the visitors and he's immediately struck by their appearance. Beatrice stands out of course, but Ian looks distinctive too.

After greetings and handshakes, he takes them up one flight of stairs. When they enter the large open office area, it quickly quietens down as everyone in the room turns to look. All eyes follow Beatrice in particular, while she smiles at people and greets them as she passes, shaking hands with a few on the way.

Ian thinks, How to work a crowd; with technique like this she could win an election. The Commissaire leads them into his office, just about keeping a straight face because of the reaction they are causing. Marie-Edith has stopped what she's doing and watches like everyone else. Ian gives her a bright smile and she blushes.

Once the Commissaire closes his office door, there's a collective letting out of breath in the main office. Some people cast glances at each other and everyone quietly goes back to work.

'Please sit down,' says the Commissaire.

And they do, with Beatrice crossing her legs and giving the Commissaire a good smile. He looks at them both in turn a couple of times. 'Well, Sergeant, I am very impressed with your French. That doesn't usually happen with visitors from Britain.'

'I can believe it. But my mother is French and I was born in Paris.'

'Really, that's amazing. Welcome home.' The Commissaire looks extremely pleased with this information. Ian is impressed with the way he manages to avoid looking at her legs.

'My father is English. We moved back to England when I was four but I've been to Paris and France dozens of times.'

'What about your colleague?' asks the Commissaire.

'No, DC Stanton doesn't speak French, but believe me he is an officer with awesome skills.'

'No offence Sergeant but the British didn't want to send a senior officer?'

'They saw this very much as a French operation sir, and I think it was felt with a very senior British officer it might look like we were trying to interfere. You know what seniors are like for getting in the way.' She gives him a huge grin.

'Quite right, we are nothing but trouble aren't we?' and they both laugh.

'Well down to business. We've been watching this man Semenoff, the one who visited Alan Bolton in England. He shares a flat with another long-term criminal. Two friends, one with a record, visit every few days and they drink and play poker for several hours. We are listening to the house, the phones and emails. None of their messaging is encrypted. Of course encryption would just make people like us more suspicious. They get emails from different sources ordering clothes and they appear to be innocent enough. We've checked up some of the products and they have a small website and a warehouse in Toulouse. It seems a legitimate business, but small and dealing with low-end fashion. We don't know what they do with the orders, though. They don't send them out by any means we're covering. Maybe they deliver them by hand but we can't keep tabs on that. We don't have enough resources. You will know how difficult it is to watch people for days and nights without being noticed and there's no definite crime yet. There certainly has never been any mention of your man Bolton, if he is still using the same name. It's not very French, so he might be using another.

'I can give you the transcripts of their calls and emails going back several days ago. And the latest batch will be ready later this afternoon. I have to see my chief at 4, so I'll give you these papers and maybe you can make something of them. We could meet again in the morning, say 9 o'clock and discuss the next move. If that's all right, I'll escort you downstairs.'

After handshakes all round, Ian and Beatrice are walking down the steps of the police offices when

Beatrice says, 'Let's find a café bar for a while, then I'll call Leo.'

They sit down to drinks and Ian asks, 'Were you happy with how that went in there?'

'Yes, it went quiet didn't it?'

'The men looked scared and the women wanted to kill you.'

'That's just the way I like it.'

'I dare say I should be safe though; they probably hardly noticed me, as usual.'

'That's partly why you are such a good detective, but I think some people noticed you. Now we'll all have dinner together tonight and tomorrow night Leo and I will be meeting a couple of my cousins. Will you be all right on your own?'

'Fine. I'll walk around a bit looking at the lights, have supper in the hotel so there won't be a language problem and have an early night.'

'Your first time in Paris, ever, and you want an early night?'

'I'm not suddenly going to turn into a party animal or even become sociable.'

She smiles. 'Most unlikely.'

Some time later, back inside the police office.

'Sir, I've had a good look at their records and made a summary here.'

'Good, thank you. Detective Sergeant Walker. Good record all round. Several Commendations. Intelligent and soon promoted. And DC Stanton.'

There's silence while he reads. *'Good heavens.*

George Cross, George Medal for bravery. Saved the lives of Sergeant Innes and WPC Walker.' He raises his eyebrows and looks at Marie-Edith.

She nods *'The same.'*

'Loads of Commendations. Discovered and rescued a kidnapped woman, and a second. What's this about a terrorist attack?'

'That's all a bit under wraps, sir. I had to do a lot of poking around. Three gunmen attacked a shopping mall some months ago and it seems DC Stanton dealt with it even before the armed police arrived. He got another George Cross and a Sovereign Medal, but none of that is officially admitted,' the assistant explains.

'I've never even heard of a Sovereign Medal. So how did you find out all this anyway. No no, don't. Best not to tell me. Some amazing detection successes, even uncovered corrupt police. What is he, Superman? And she looks like Superwoman. These two should be police partners in a Hollywood movie. No wonder they didn't bother sending a senior officer. I wonder why he's still a constable; that doesn't make sense. If he spoke French we could give him a job and make him a Capitaine straight away. Well, Marie-Edith, we're really going have to be on our game here.'

'Yes sir, you are aren't you?' She laughs.

'And you as well, don't forget that.'

Beatrice and Ian decide to keep dressed the way they are for the rest of the day and when they meet up with Leo later, he says, 'Look, let me take a photo of you two mannequins while you're still dressed up. This street's good, with the sun coming through the trees. Stand over there will you. Try not to look too intimate or I might be able to use it in any divorce proceedings.'

'Very funny,' says Beatrice. 'We'll discuss that later.'

The two of them stand close together, with Beatrice square on taking up a strong assertive pose, and Ian at a slight angle, while Leo takes the pictures on his mobile. Just as he's taking a third picture, Ian suddenly puts his hand on Beatrice's shoulder, much to her amusement, especially as Leo didn't notice.

At dinner, Beatrice, Ian and Leo talk about the meeting with the French police.

'You know Leo, your wife is such a flirt, and that's with me not understanding the language.'

'I know. She's out of control.'

'And what about those three women loading their guns and waiting for you to turn your back?' jokes Ian.

'Rubbish. It's simply a question of style. Language and manner are just different in France from Britain. And I saw you smiling at that assistant and making her blush.'

'Hey!' says Leo. 'So it's my turn next then?'

'What?'

'Nothing precious, only joking.'

After dinner, Beatrice reads and translates the documents from the Commissaire but no clues jump out immediately. Ian wants Beatrice to go over the transcripts a second time while he writes everything down in English.

★

On the next day, Beatrice and Ian go into the offices at the agreed time to see if there's been any progress.

'If you check with the Commissaire, I'll wait here, until there is something interesting to report,' says Ian.

'Why not come in?'

'Because I'm just standing around, saying and doing nothing, following you like a lap dog.'

'I can't see anything wrong with you following me like a lap dog,' says Beatrice trying got make a joke out of it.

'Don't lap dogs normally get stroked a lot and fed with treats.'

'And sometimes they get a smack. All right, wait here.'

But there's been little activity with only one man at the house. On her return Beatrice says, 'Nothing to report so we have to do some hanging around until the Commissaire calls later. What do you fancy doing then?' she asks.

'After elevenses you mean?'

'We've only just had breakfast.'

'Irrelevant; elevenses are a craft skill and can be had any time, and several times in the morning if you're well organised.'

'Okay, café time, then we come up with something useful.'

Nibbling at his croissant Ian says, 'You know I've never been to Paris before?'

'Right.'

'Well I'm really sorry about this, but it means I have to go up the Eiffel Tower and at least stick my nose into the Louvre.'

'Oh Gawd; how embarrassing,' groans Beatrice. 'All right, we'll do that. In fact I haven't been up the Tower since I was about 12, so that's all right. Leo wanted to go once and I made him go on his own.'

'You know the Tower becomes 15cm taller in a hot summer?'

'No I didn't know that, and you are not allowed to come up with interesting facts about Paris, that I should already know myself. Say, "No boss".'

'Yes boss, I mean no boss.'

'Good, and as for the Louvre, we'll do one room which I will choose. It's like the British Museum in that it would take weeks to look at everything. And we are not going to make any attempt to see the Mona Lisa.'

'Suits me; as long as I come away with a new fridge magnet, that's all that matters.'

Beatrice laughs. 'What a peasant. We're seeing Leo for lunch and if there's no call from the station, I want to visit the National Library. It's beautiful and I want to look at some of the old calligraphy.'

'You're interested in that are you?'

'I do some calligraphy. I went to classes on it.'

'What illuminated manuscripts and so on?'

'Well not exactly to that level, but the writing at least.'

'I didn't know that was one of your talents.'

'I'm not just wavy hair and long legs, you know.'

Ian laughs, 'Yes I know. I'm not overlooking your brain.'

The Eiffel Tower gets the full tourist treatment and there's a token visit to the Louvre for an hour and a half.

They are in the National Library in the late afternoon, with Beatrice examining a rare illuminated manuscript intensely when the phone vibrates in her pocket. It's a call from the Commissaire.

'There've been several messages at the house. If you come in first thing in the morning, we'll have the transcripts ready.'

'Good news, Ian, something's happening, so we're back there tomorrow morning,' reports Beatrice.

Next day at the police office, Ian and Beatrice are wearing more normal everyday but extremely smart casual clothes. As they enter the office, Ian decides to tease Marie-Edith a little. He gives her another big smile, causing her to smile back, blush and quickly turn her face down to her keyboard. If Beatrice notices, she's discrete enough not to let it show.

'There've been many more orders for clothes in this last batch,' says the Commissaire.

'What sort of conversation are they having?' asks Ian.

'Still lots of general chat, mainly about the clothes trade,' replies Beatrice, reading through the transcript.

'Come on now, Bea, details. Let's have the exact words translated shall we.'

Beatrice has mixed feelings when she gets ticked off by Ian, but starts reading and translating.

'They just look like orders for the garments, with strange names for the fun of it, I presume. Although some of the quantity numbers seem a bit odd.'

'Let's have some of those names again. One was "Screaming A" wasn't it?

'That's how it translates; it's a long jacket. Then

there's Maria M, another jacket, Joan of Arc raincoat, Holly H trousers, Herring B scarf, Gianluca V, a man's bomber jacket.'

'They mentioned capes several times in the last batch. Are capes in fashion at the moment?'

'Not particularly I think.'

Ian sits quietly for a minute. 'Once translated into English, these names sound a bit like rhyming slang.' He starts walking around the room. 'Screaming A could be Screaming Alice, meaning Crystal Palace. Herring B stands for herring bone meaning telephone..and..and.' He pauses.

'And Maria, that's Maria Monk. One of these might be accident but several of them is more than coincidence.

Screaming Alice, Crystal Palace, crystal, crystal meth. Maria Monk for spunk or skunk. Gianluca Vialli for charlie, a common name for cocaine. These names are code names of drugs. Herring bone, phone, could be methadone.'

'And Joan d'Arc or Joan of Arc?' Beatrice asks.

'Heroin. A rhyme for heroin might be too obvious, but there's no bigger heroine in France than Joan. That's what they're doing; using their clothes' names to cover their drug jargon.'

'What about Hopping P and Toby J?'

'I don't know. Maybe they don't mean anything for us. Just there to build the picture.'

'And Nelson E? They say that several times.'

'That's Nelson Eddy's – readies – money. Cape of Good Hope means soap or perhaps dope. Probably just ordinary hash.'

The Commissaire's English isn't good enough to follow all this so Beatrice explains everything. They write down all the words so far and the Commissaire is getting very excited, gesticulating enthusiastically.

'Only someone from a rough part of London would know some of this stuff. I used to be stationed there. There's got to be a connection here with Bolton. Bolton is half French and half Londoner.'

They go through the transcripts in more detail, picking out the suspect words.

'Why should he do this? Isn't there the risk someone might cotton on?' Beatrice asks.

'Don't know. Maybe he's just being cocky and thinks he's so clever no-one will notice. No French person is ever likely to.'

'There's still no connection with Bolton, and the force doesn't have enough officers to follow all these people for days or weeks. They are checking their phones and emails all the time,' relates Beatrice. 'They could just be taking these messages round to the next man by hand or by fax machine. Nothing to trace that way.'

Ian thinks for a moment. 'What about shortwave?' he asks. 'When he was 13 or 14, Bolton was keen on radio ham stuff. Maybe he's gone back to it. It's all on different frequencies. I know it's old fashioned so maybe they think it won't be noticed.'

'How do you know this? I read all the files; that wasn't in them,' says Beatrice.

'No, but details about his school were and I dug out one of his teachers and spoke to him. He said how Bolton was a decent lad then and keen to learn all sorts of things. Even built his own radio out of a kit.'

Beatrice puts her face in her hands, then looks despairingly at Ian. 'If I had your brains and my eyelashes, and my tits, I could be ACC by now.'

'Your brain's good enough, you just need longer eyelashes.'

'Stop it!'

The Commissaire simply sits patiently waiting to be brought up to date here. Beatrice explains all and the Commissaire snaps into action immediately, calling the technical department and giving instructions.

'All right,' says the Commissaire, *'we need a break and lunch. You two go to the restaurant; I'll follow shortly. I'm going down to Technical first, just to check on everything. We'll see if any broadcasts are coming out of that building.'* He shows them out of the door and watches them walk through the main office, then he turns to Marie-Edith.

'Marie-Edith, that man is a genius. Marry him and that's an order. We need your children on the force.' Marie-Edith looks surprised, then pleased, then her typing speed increases considerably.

The Commissaire gives a large shrug with his shoulders and hands and walks to the stairs.

 ★ ★ ★

21

In Which a Breakthrough is Needed

After a further 24 hours, there's been no sign of any shortwave transmissions out of the building and the Commissaire decides to make a raid.

'As soon as we hear that all four of these men are in the flat, we move in. If we are to get any information out of them, we need to get it quickly before their arrest gets noticed.'

'We would like to come along as observers if you would allow it,' asks Beatrice tactfully.

'Perhaps. I'll check with Capitaine Charbonneau. He'll be in charge and you will have to follow all his instructions implicitly.'

'Of course.'

The four targets appear to be playing cards in the front room overlooking the street and the room can be seen from the police's observation room opposite. The front of the building is covered, and the police have to enter through the back. Beatrice and Ian are wearing protective vests and sitting with the Capitaine and his men in a plain vehicle down a side street. The briefing explains they have to enter quickly through the back door, which is at the top of steep flight to steps.

Ian speaks quietly to Beatrice; 'When we're close to these targets, we should not speak any English or they might guess we're after Bolton.' Beatrice nods.

They all leave the van and calmly walk down a path to approach the rear of the building, through a tall back gate and up to the steps.

An officer goes up the steps to try the door and finds it locked, so the Capitaine nods at the man with the battering ram.

'Sergeant, ask if I can try to open the door without all the noise.' She translates and the Capitaine looks surprised and sceptical.

'*Worth a try,*' she says.

The Capitaine shrugs and says, '*You have thirty seconds.*'

Ian runs up the steps and presses both hands against the door and pushes. When he hears some wood creak he motions Beatrice to come up the steps.

'Yes. I'll wait for the next train to pass. Tell them to come up the steps and be ready.'

With the officers moving up the steps, Ian gets in position to push on the door. A few seconds later, background noise increases and he pushes hard to the sound of splitting wood. The door flies open and as Ian tumbles through, all the police rush pass with guns drawn and into the other rooms. Three men are immediately restrained, and the forth is found on the next floor.

While the premises are being thoroughly searched for anybody else, the four are taken back to the station and held in separate interview rooms.

'Let's see if we can be spooky about this,' Ian says to Beatrice. 'Can you get the Commissaire to go into each room and ask them some brief questions and we'll see if we can find if one of them is a weak link?'

'Are you going to do another one of your stage acts?'

'You never know.'

By now, the Commissaire has heard about the business with the door and tolerates Ian being in the interview rooms, while Beatrice watches through the observation windows. The first prisoner is asked some basic questions about his name and jobs but in a couple of minutes Ian stands up to leave. It's the same with the next prisoner. With the third, Ian keeps his seat so the questions continue. Ian sits quietly, usually with his eyes closed. After ten minutes he scribbles something down on his notepad, nods to the Commissaire and stands to leave.

Outside the room, Ian hands the notebook to Beatrice. 'I reckon the next contact is here but I haven't got his name.'

Looking at the address the Commissaire says, *'This is a smart address in the 12th. Where did it come from?'*

'From the last interviewee, but not out loud.'

'Are you trying to tell me, the DC heard him think it?'

Beatrice puts on a sheepish expression and nods. *'He's done it before; it's worth taking seriously.'*

The Commissaire walks around in a circle a couple of times. *'But he doesn't even speak French!'*

'I think it's done with images,' says Beatrice defensively.

'I can't get a warrant and make a raid on the basis of

this. We can't start tapping phones and emails just like that, no more than you can.'

'How about just trying for the shortwave?' suggests Beatrice.

'Let's get back to my office.'

The Commissaire shows the address to a colleague in the general office with instructions to find out as much as he can about the occupants.

'Marie-Edith, can you get me Capitaine Charbonneau, please.'

The Capitaine is given instructions to observe the new address at the double-quick for any signs of short wave activity.

'Now we wait. My men are still searching that last building. You two might as well wander off for a while and I'll call as soon as there's anything.'

Beatrice and Ian thank him and leave the office. The Commissaire stands by Marie-Edith's desk with his arms folded and watches them leave. He's noticed several times the way Marie-Edith looks at Ian. *'Did you hear what happened?'*

'I heard about the door, sir.'

'Oh, it's much stranger than that now. If he's right and this works out, I'm going to have you two married by the weekend.' He waves his finger at her and smiles.

Marie-Edith holds her hand over her mouth to help suppress her laughter.

Beatrice and Ian go to the nearest park area and in the café get served with drinks. Beatrice can drink coffee at almost any time without it affecting her sleep but for

Ian it has to be only in the morning. He goes for hot chocolate, which he finds amazing in France.

Lounging in their chairs, Beatrice puffs out her breath. 'What a day. If that address works out, I think they'll give you a special certificate. He wasn't convinced was he?'

After the rest, Beatrice suggest they go and find Leo and stop him from working.

'I'll disappear shall I, if you two would rather be all a-l-o-n-e?'

'No of course not. We won't turn you into a gooseberry.'

'What, all green and hairy?'

'That's the one.'

After another excellent evening meal, the three of them are sitting in a busy street enjoying the atmosphere of the city, when Beatrice gets a call.

'Beatrice, it's Maurice Albert. Incredible. Things are looking good. There have been two shortwave transmissions from that address and we've tracked where they're going. We've now got the new location under observation as well. The man living there goes under the name Baroche with a wife and two children. Come round in the morning and get up to date.'

'Thank you; that's brilliant. Bye.'

Beatrice keeps a straight face as she puts her phone away. She carries on looking around the street, while Ian and Leo look at Beatrice then at each other, then back at Beatrice.

'Leo, how long will this go on for?'

'Pretend you don't care. Just ignore her; she hates that.'

Beatrice laughs and gives him a gentle push. 'We're going to have to put up with Ian's head swelling. He was right about the address and right about the shortwave. Now they've got a new contact.'

Ian says casually, 'Insufferable aren't I?'

In the Commissaire's office next morning, Beatrice is silently reading the full transcript of the radio conversations.

'Don't mind me Sergeant. Just pretend I'm not here,' says Ian.

'All right then. In the meantime, I'll translate. Bits of friendly chat about family and radio reception. Then Vergne says, "I'm still waiting for communication from the usual". And this morning, he says, "Still no word. I will speak to you after my holiday. Goodbye".

'*That last piece sounds like code for breaking off all contact for now,*' says the Commissaire.

'*Yes I agree.*' says Beatrice.

'*We're keeping a watch on both premises now so we need to wait. Excuse me for moment while I read these papers.*'

Five minutes later Marie-Edith enters the office. She's wearing a skirt a little shorter than usual and the shoes have more of a heal to them. Ian watches her walking towards the Commissaire's desk and thinks, My, she's got good legs, and she's not too skinny either.

'*These photographs have just come through from Surveillance 2, sir.*'

The Commissaire looks at the photographs and hands them to Beatrice while he goes into one of his files.

'It's Bolton,' she says, then passes them to Ian.

'Yes that's him, that's Bolton.'

'You English, you are so calm about it. Beatrice, where's the French in you; shouldn't you be more emotional?'

'We had complete faith in you Commissaire. We were always confident of the outcome.'

Marie-Edith sniggers as she leaves the room.

The Commissaire smiles and says, 'Well after I've sacked Marie-Edith for enjoying your comments, we'll pick up Bolton at the first opportunity, and that other chap, Francis Vergne. We can't risk them having an escape route. This case is now much broader and I must report everything higher up. First, I'm off to Communications. You two can relax and I'll call you as soon as we have Bolton here. I'm sure you'll want the satisfaction of seeing him.'

An hour later they are all back in the office.

'Finger prints match but we'll wait for DNA results just to make extra sure. 'It's good he's on a double murder charge as well. You never know with these big drug cases. There's so much money and violence, all sorts of strange things can go on behind the scenes; evidence going missing, some technical irregularity in the arrest suddenly appears.'

'Oh yes, we get that too.'

'But a double murder charge is more clear cut.'

'My chief did tick me off for arresting Bolton so soon. Says we should've spent much more time watching and listening, but Bolton's using lots of encryption and it *might be weeks before he makes a mistake we can pick up on.'*

'And how would it look if you let a double murderer slip away?'

'Quite.'

Bolton is in the interview room, still wearing handcuffs and sitting quietly at a table with a lawyer beside him. Two police officers are standing to one side.

Bolton has a confident smirk on his face as the Commissaire, Beatrice and Ian walk in the room and sit down. They look at him for half a minute, then the Commissaire speaks first. *'I'm Commissaire Albert Maurice and this is . . . '*

Ian interrupts, putting on an east London accent. 'Watchyer mate. How's the Screaming Alice and the Cape of Good Hope?'

Bolton stops smirking and turns to the Commissaire, *'Who's the clown and the tart?'*

'Detective Sergeant Walker and Detective Constable Stanton from the Bristol police.'

'Just a pair of wooden tops – one clown and one tart,' adds Beatrice.

'Extradition proceedings will start immediately but our investigations into your drug activities might take some time. That's all for now. Take him back to the cells.'

Beatrice finds a quiet corner and calls Chief Inspector Chandler back home in Bristol.

'DS Walker, sir. Success. Bolton is under arrest.'

'Excellent, fantastic. Send me the details and I'll get things moving at this end.'

'One snag; Bolton's been involved in big-time drug

dealing. The French are still investigating, so they might have claim on him also.'

'That doesn't matter. As long as he's always locked up. Did it all go smoothly?'

'Pretty exciting one way and another. DC Stanton is awesome He's like some sort of magician sir. He could make millions in Las Vegas. If he's not made Inspector after this I'm going to join a nunnery.'

'With your husband visiting at weekends?'

'Well maybe not, but you get the point.'

Ian and Beatrice walk away from the police station with their arms around each others shoulders, feeling triumphant.

'There's a good café bar not far. We'll get some drinks and I'll call Leo.'

They sit down side-by-side on a bench seat looking into the room.

'They've got one of my favourite plonks so we'll start with a bottle of that. We'll deal with food when Leo gets here, but as this is a sort of celebration lunch, drink must take centre stage.' Beatrice is soon on to her second glass, while Ian, not being much of a drinker, just sips at his.

'It's all right for you. You can celebrate by getting laid tonight,' says Ian.

'Now you're being vulgar.'

'Really, are you going to tell me that won't happen.'

'I'll record it on my phone if you like.'

'Now who's being vulgar?'

It's not long before Beatrice has had a little too much to drink.

'Ian, I might regret saying this but I'm sure you are gentleman enough to forget it by tomorrow, but you remember the time you saved my life in that shoot-out?

'Of course.'

'Well if I had been single and perhaps a few reckless years younger, I think I would have insisted on fucking you as a proper thank you.'

Ian puffs out his cheeks.

'I'm sure I would have been too scared to have sex with you at any time of life.'

'You wouldn't have been able to get away with that excuse; I can be very educational.' She takes another gulp of wine.

'Well just to embarrass you further, it would take brain surgery to make me forget such an offer. In fact, I am going to put this incident in my memoirs, word for word.'

'You do and I guarantee you'll be dead before you hit the ground.' She puts her arm round him and kisses him on the cheek. Just then Leo walks into the café. 'Looks like I've arrived in the nick of time.'

'Your wife has just threatened to exterminate me.'

'She must have had at least three glasses then.'

Beatrice gives Leo a hello kiss and pours him a glass of wine. 'This bottle's nearly empty. It's probably Ian when I'm not watching.' She unpins her hair, gives her head a good shake and beams a smile at both of them in turn.

'Let's get food organised shall we, then you can fill in all the details of your triumph,' suggests Leo.

★

Three hours later in the afternoon, Beatrice makes a call to the Commissaire.

'Ah hello. Firstly a man from the British Embassy is coming over tomorrow afternoon to check details on the Bolton matter. I think you should be here, about 2.30. Secondly the whole drug case has been taken over by the drugs department. They are both pleased and embarrassed that they had no wind of this operation. It's good for us. We get plenty of credit and we don't have to try and untangle all the connections.'

'Cigars all round then,' adds Beatrice.

'Precisely. Some of the people here would like to see you and Ian before you disappear so perhaps after the Embassy business is finished?'

'Certainly.'

'And finally, I would like to invite the three of you to dinner at my house tomorrow evening. My wife is a wonderful cook and she and my daughter would love to meet you all – you, Ian and your husband.'

'Yes, that sounds lovely, thank you.'

'One thing, could you wear the same clothes you wore when you first arrived. You looked spectacular and my daughter loves fashion.'

'Of course, we'll try not to let the side down. Now I've just heard that Bolton's brother has gone missing. You never know, he might be over here now as part of their network. They are sending over details and photos.'

'Good, see you tomorrow afternoon then.'

Over breakfast the next morning, Beatrice stretches and says, 'Well boys and girls, we have the morning off so I suggest we visit the Musée de Cluny, which is mega ace-wicked for medieval art. I haven't been there for ages.'

'I'll have to join you later. I've got a meeting over the wire. Will you be there all morning?'

'Either there or in a café somewhere. You all right for some mediaeval education, Ian?'

'Sounds good to me. One can never have too much mediaeval education, that's what I say,' agrees Ian.

'Right, and after lunch it's back to the station. I'm off to get changed. See you in reception in ten.'

Beatrice strides into reception in strike-'em-dead outfit number two. The buccaneer boots, tight green trousers, short black jacket and a mid-green pullover, close-fitting and very fluffy, and her long hair let down.

Ian looks her up a down for a proper inspection. 'Ready to take on the SWAT team are you?'

'Yes, if they dare,' replies Beatrice with a large smile.

Ian opens the front of her jacket to have a better look at the pullover.

'That jumper has "Please stroke me" written all over it.'

'No, it says "Stroke me and I'll bite your hand off".'

Ian runs his hands over her tummy and Beatrice looks surprised. Leo watches all this and says, 'Ian, you are the only person I know who can be cheeky to Beatrice, and she'd be afraid to smack around the head.'

'Don't tell him that. You'll destroy one of my best defences. Just behave yourselves you two.'

'Now now children, no squabbling. Off you go and I'll see you later.'

Among the laughter, Leo goes off to his computer work, while the other two head for the museum. Beatrice has been there several times in the past and has some favourite items to look at. Ian is intrigued by the exhibits especially as Beatrice gives him a personal lecture on many of the treasures.

22

IN WHICH THERE ARE STRAIGHT ARMS

Beatrice and Ian are in the Commissaire's office to meet the Embassy official. After dealing with a little administration, the official goes off to visit another department.

'Beatrice, I want to ask you a favour. See what you think of this. Our section assistant Marie-Edith is in a bit of a tizzy, over Ian, although she tries to cover it up.'

'I've noticed,' she smiles.

'I've never really seen her like this before. Well, I know the three of you will be spending tomorrow around Paris. How about if Marie-Edith joins you? Now she might look a little serious, but she's not like that at all. She speaks decent English so we could suggest she might like to spend some time with you to practise her English.'

'And we might be doing a bit of matchmaking?'

'Exactly. She's very good natured, hard working and efficient and quite amusing when you get to know her.'

'I think Ian might be more nervous of her than facing a gunman, but I'm sure it'll be all right. Don't you need her in the office?'

'I'll give her the day off – she rarely takes a break. I haven't put it to her yet. Perhaps I could say you

have invited her along then I'll give her a gentle order to go.'

The Commissaire calls Marie-Edith into his office.

'Marie-Edith, Beatrice wants to invite you to join the three of them tomorrow for a day out. They will be speaking English all the time; you speak the language quite well and it would be some good practice for you.'

'Do come along please,' agrees Beatrice.

Marie-Edith feels she must make a little protest just out of diplomatic prevarication.

'Oh, but, but, there's a lot to do here sir,' she says, and manages to avoid looking at Ian.

'That's all right, you can just work twice as hard the next day. What time tomorrow Beatrice?'

'We'll meet you at 10 o'clock in reception.'

'Good. That's settled then and it won't go down as one of your days off. We'll call it a training day.'

'Thank you sir.' She leaves the office and feels excited as she sits back at her desk.

'Now, Beatrice, as I told you, some of the men want to see you and thank you before you disappear. I'll just give Capitaine Charbonneau a call.'

Beatrice takes off her jacket and hangs it over a chair. Ian knows what she's up to – she wants to give that jumper full effect. It certainly displays her full breasts much better than a loose blouse. Ian raises his eyebrows as he looks at Beatrice then down at her pullover. Beatrice smiles and pokes a little bit of tongue out at him.

The Capitaine, with several of his men, enters the room, followed by a couple of people from the main office and Marie-Edith. Some of the men have only seen Beatrice in more functional everyday clothes, but here she is, looking like perfect sex on legs. There are surreptitious looks between some of them.

The Commissaire takes a bottle of champagne from a cupboard, he quickly pops out the cork and starts pouring into plastic cups. *'We shouldn't really be doing this, but just a little, and as no Frenchman would ever put champagne into a plastic cup this obviously can't be champagne. Marie-Edith, if you wouldn't mind.'* She starts handing them round. When she takes cups over to Ian and Beatrice, Ian takes a cup with his right hand and with his left he deliberately touches her hand.

'No real speech here, I just want to say what a pleasure this visit by DS Beatrice Walker and DC Ian Stanton has been. Dare I say it has been exciting at times and they have both proved to be wonderful colleagues. There have been successful arrests, a drug ring discovered, and we are relieved of a complicated case, thanks to the drug squad.

'Finally, any time the British police need assistance in catching your big criminals, just give us a call.' There is laughter and clapping from the small audience and Beatrice laughs cheerfully.

One of the police officers speaks to the Capitaine, who then speaks out. *'Ah yes, Pascal reminds me, we are all curious to know how you managed to push open that locked door.'*

Beatrice translates this for Ian, who looks around for a few moments, considering the request, then smiles and nods. He waves for the officer to come closer.

'Beatrice, I'm going to hold my arm out like this, and when I'm ready he has to put his hands on my wrist and pull my arm down.' She translates.

Ian holds his arm out straight horizontally and looks ahead. After 10 seconds he says, 'Ready now.'

Officer Guipont tries to pull his arm down but the arm doesn't move. He then uses both hands to pull but the arm still doesn't move. Soon the officer has his feet off the ground, with all his weight pulling down, but still the arm stays horizontal and Ian looks completely relaxed.

As Ian stops the process, he says, 'All right, now it's your turn.' There is mild applause from everyone in the room. This is a new trick even for Beatrice.

Pascal holds his arm out straight the same way, but Ian can pull it down with virtually no effort.

'Keep it up,' Ian says. He pulls again, Pascal starts to use strength but the arm still gets pulled down easily. 'Keep it up,' but still he can't.

Ian gestures for Beatrice to come closer. Ian starts talking very softly to Pascal.

'Are you married?' Beatrice translates quietly so no-one else can hear.

'Yes,' he says.

'Any children?'

'One daughter.'

'How old?'

'Nine.'

'What's her name?'

'Florence.'

'Is she wonderful and perfect?'

'Yes, absolutely perfect,' he says with pride in his voice and on his face.

'Okay, I want you to see your wonderful and perfect daughter on the other side of that wall. Hold your arm up; nothing else, just see your perfect daughter the other side of that wall.'

Ian waits half a minute, and gently pulls his arm down.

'Your perfect Florence the other side of that wall is the whole universe.'

Pascal stays relaxed and with Ian pulling again he meets some resistance this time. 'Close your eyes. See your perfect Florence the other side of that wall.'

Ian waits another half minute and then pulls again and now there is complete resistance. He uses both hands, and almost has his feet off the ground before Pascal's arm starts to move down a little.

Ian stops pulling, claps his hands once and slaps Pascal on the shoulder.

'That's it, you did it.' Pascal's overjoyed and everyone watching claps enthusiastically. Ian finishes by saying quietly to Pascal, 'There we are, the straight arm doesn't exist; the locked door doesn't exist; there is only your perfect Florence.'

Pascal gives strong handshakes to Ian and Beatrice, then goes back to his friends while making small fist pumps. Beatrice gives a little wink and nod to Ian, while Marie-Edith, in her excitement, she's feeling just a little bit wet.

The Capitaine says, *Wonderful, but what about the rest of us?*' Beatrice translates again.

Ian shrugs; 'Too complicated; next time perhaps.'

'Well everyone, let us say our Goodbyes and then we get back to work,' concludes the Commissaire.

That's all the invitation the men need, so they queue up to shake hands with Beatrice and give her kisses and hugs. And there are enthusiastic handshakes for Ian and some embraces as well.

Beatrice starts to put her jacket back on, raises her eyebrows and whispers to Ian, 'And how is it Marie-Edith blushed so much when she handed you that drink?'

'Did she? I didn't notice it.'

'She'll be joining us tomorrow.'

'What?'

'On our day out tomorrow, I've invited Marie-Edith to come along with us.'

'Oh, right; good.'

'Thank you Commissaire, we'll see you tonight then, 7.30,' says Beatrice as she shakes his hand. On the way out, she twiddles her fingers at Marie-Edith as a goodbye and gives her a bright smile.

At seven thirty, the three of them are welcomed into the Commissaire's house. Leo hands a huge bunch of flowers to Colette, the Commissaire's wife. Beatrice and Maurice shake hands warmly while Colette looks Beatrice up and down several times. Beatrice and Colette greet each other and shakes hands, and one is smiling more than the other. As Beatrice turns to their daughter, Bernadette, Colette looks at the husband. To Ian that look says "So this is what you have been involved with for the last week is it? We will have words later".

Beatrice is introduced to Bernadette whose eyes are popping. After shaking hands, Beatrice takes hold of Bernadette's left hand and keeps hold of it. Leo and Ian seem almost like afterthoughts as they shakes hands all around.

They soon sit down at the table with Bernadette helping her mother while Maurice takes charge of the wine. It doesn't bother Ian that he can't understand the conversation; he's happy to sit there without talking and simply enjoy the food. Early conversation is small talk about the three visitors' trip to Paris and about the police operation.

When there's a lull, Bernadette asks, *'Papa, may I have some boots like that for my birthday?'*

'Certainly not.'

'Perhaps when you're older, Bernadette. Boots like this can drive men wild.'

'Beatrice, please, you are corrupting the young,' says Leo. *'Do you have any favourite subjects at school, Bernadette?'*

'Yes, mathematics and music. I play the clarinet and I'm learning the harp, but it's very difficult.'

'Do you have your own instrument?'

'Yes, a basic one for learning.'

'Ah, Ian plays the harp, don't you Ian? Would you like to hear him play?' Beatrice asks.

'Oooo please.'

'How about that Ian?'

'What?'

'Bernadette is learning the harp and I was just saying you play the harp and how you'd love to play for us later.'

'No, no, I can only play an English harp, not a French harp.'

'If I say you will be playing the harp, you will be. Tell him Leo.'

'What sort of punishment would you prefer if you refuse?' advises Leo. 'She'll start at your toenails and work her way up.'

Ian simply looks to the ceiling and nods with a sigh. 'So, I would love to play some harp later.'

'Maurice says how impressed they were with that demonstration with Pascal,' says Beatrice.

'So was I,' says Ian. 'I was amazed. I didn't expect him to be able to do it so well and so quickly.' When Beatrice translates this, Maurice nods with approval.

The meal and all the relaxed conversation take some time, but eventually, Maurice goes to bring Bernadette's harp downstairs to the living room. Ian goes there also to try it out and to get his fingers warmed up.

When everyone gathers round to listen, Ian speaks first, 'I will do what I can but it won't be a concert performance. I'm only doing this because I am so frightened of the Sergeant.'

Beatrice translates the first sentence, then say, *'I won't translate the last bit.'*

'I will,' says Colette, and she does, to general laughter.

Ian plays two of his party pieces, which are fast with a good range of chords. Everyone is very impressed, and the Commissaire says, *'Heavens, it's like John McLaughlin on the harp.'*

By the time they leave, it's well past Bernadette's normal bedtime. Beatrice gives her a big hug and they hold hands a lot, while Colette has now quite taken to Beatrice. The three of them decide to walk for a while enjoying the atmosphere of the streets before entering a Metro station.

23

In Which it's a Day among the Trees

At the agreed time, Beatrice arrives at the police station to meet Marie-Edith, while Ian and Leo wait outside. Marie-Edith is wearing tight leggings which are bright red with small white diamond shapes over them. To go with them, she wears a quality dove-grey pullover, a bright red shoulder bag and a little more make-up than she uses for work.

'Wow, you look tremendous, very striking. Beatrice takes hold of her arm and winks as she says, 'I might have to throw a bucket of cold water over the boys.'

Leo notices Ian taking some sly looks at her legs and bottom and gives him some of the old nudge-wink business. Beatrice hears their schoolboy giggling.

'What are you two laughing at?'

'Nothing dear,' says Leo.

'Ignore them Marie-Edith. They are probably just being childish.'

First things first; all four of them are sitting outside a smart café in a local park having morning coffee and croissants.

'Now what to do,' says Beatrice, getting into organising mode. 'I'm sure Marie-Edith doesn't want to spend today walking around some museum or art gallery, do you?'

'Not really, I spend so much time indoors, and I do love trees.'

'Can you ride a bicycle?'

'Yes.'

'Good. Now how about if we get a taxi to the Forêt Domaniele de Meudon. I know where we can hire some bikes and we could cycle around the forest, stopping at every café we come across.'

'Lovely,' says Marie-Edith.

'And you are being treated for the day so don't even think about going near your purse.'

They cycle around the forest, getting a bit lost at times, but that doesn't matter at all. In due course they find a rustic café for lunch.

Marie-Edith asks, 'Are you all staying in Paris for longer then?'

'Leo and I are staying for a few more days and Leo will have to suffer a diet of mediaeval art and culture, and sore feet probably. He knows it's for his own good so he won't complain, will you dear?'

'If you say I won't then I certainly won't, honestly.'

'Ian is going back tomorrow. It was arranged that he would return as soon as this job was finished.'

'What this means, Marie-Edith, is that when I get back I will be writing the police report. I will have to explain how Sergeant Walker spent all her time in café bars drinking champagne and cognac, while all the work was done by the French police and myself. By the time she returns, it'll be Constable Walker, in uniform and on night duty.'

Beatrice has a tight-lipped expression as she looks at the other three in turn. Marie-Edith laughs and Leo smiles even with Beatrice giving him one of her stern looks.

'Do you see the sabotage I have to endure from junior officers?'

'Shocking,' agrees Marie-Edith. 'But very funny.'

'I think that's enough persiflage for now, before I get stabbed by someone's stilettos,' says Ian.

'Persiflage?' queries Beatrice.

'A French word I think.'

'From persifler, but where did you get a word like that?'

'From PG Wodehouse.'

'We'll make a linguist out of you yet.'

Amusement all round.

'May I photograph you all please, on my phone,' asks Marie Edith.

'Of course, let's sit together on this side.' Beatrice sits between Leo and Ian.

'Now all four of us must be together,' says Beatrice. 'I'll ask this man over here to help.'

A smile and a request from Beatrice is enough for most people. The four of them sit close together around a table. 'You sit here Marie-Edith and I'll hold this hand and Ian will hold the other.' The man takes the photo on Marie-Edith's phone and then another on Beatrice's.

All back at the table Ian whispers to Leo, 'Beatrice could get the devil to say please and thank you.'

'Why do you think I married her.' And the pair of them snigger.

Marie-Edith asks, 'You must have been to Paris dozens of times Beatrice?'

'At least.'

'And with Leo?'

'Quite often yes.'

'Have you ever been to Disneyland? Ian asks. 'You look shifty. Did you see that Marie-Edith?'

'Yes I certainly did and this is a triumph for your interrogating skills. A minister once called Disneyland a cultural Chernobyl.'

'We went with my nieces and nephews.'

'You haven't got any brothers or sisters, so how could you have any nieces and nephews?'

'I have cousins and they have little ones; and Leo has a brother.'

'She's getting desperate now.'

'Will you report this when you get back Ian, how Sergeant Beatrice, Madam Ice-cool, loves Disneyland?' Leo asks.

'Certainly. It'll be in the newsletter; might even make the front page.'

'I've only one thing to say to you DC Stanton.'

'What's that?'

'Stilettos.'

'Ooops. My lips are sealed. Quickly changing the subject, I see you are left handed Marie-Edith?'

'All the best people are left handed.'

'That's exactly what Ian says,' adds Beatrice.

'Are you left handed as well then?'

'Yes of course. Beatrice isn't, nor is Leo.'

'Sad, but we should not mock their misfortune.'

'No, one can only offer sympathy.'

'What is this, a music hall double-act?' from Leo. Marie-Edith and Ian simply smile.

They cycle around some more and stop by a lake to sit on the grass. The sun sparkles on the ripples as ducks swim along, while a heron circles on the other side of the lake and lands at the water's edge.

'This is good; it's almost full countryside. I don't get enough country. If you like trees Marie-Edith, what's that one called?' Ian asks.'

'Eric.'

'Eric!' And the others laugh.

'He's a very old friend of mine.'

'You haven't got it confused with Henry have you?' suggests Ian.

'Of course not. That's Henry over there.'

'Does it have any other name?'

'Yes – Quercus petraea.'

Ian raises his eyebrows at Beatrice, hoping for a translation.

'That means Sessile Oak,' says Beatrice.

'And Henry over there?'

'Henry is a Fraxinus excelsior,' say Marie-Edith.

'That means Common Ash,' confirms Beatrice.

'Leo, do you think I'd better shut up?'

'Could be less confusing, unless you want to learn Latin.'

'It's a strain being surrounded by clever clogs isn't it?' Ian says.

'When the numbness sets in, you stop noticing.'

Beatrice gives him a friendly tap on the arm.

'Marie-Edith, let's take a little wander over there.'

'Yes, and you can tell me what clever clogs means.' The two of them start to walk around the lake.

As they walk away, Ian says quietly to Leo, 'She's certainly got a neat firm body. Marie-Edith's not bad either.'

'I was thinking the same the other way round,' says Leo and there's more schoolboy giggling from the pair of them.

'I suppose you checked up on our records when we arrived?' Beatrice asks Marie-Edith as they walk on.

'I was only following orders, Monsieur Judge.' She laughs.

'Well I suggest you never mention some of the more dramatic incidents in Ian's record. He doesn't like to talk about them.'

'But he even saved your life once, didn't he?'

'Yes, but he never mentions it, although I think about it a lot. Certainly don't mention the shopping mall massacre.'

'And not even the Sovereign Medal?'

'How do you know about that? That's not supposed to be open on the records.'

Marie-Edith looks up and around with an innocent expression and she shrugs. 'Oh, I'm quite good with computers.'

'And dangerous too by the sound of it,' with a smile.

'And deadly.'

'What!? . . . . . Anyway it would be best to keep those

matters to yourself unless Ian speaks of them first.'

'But Beatrice, we don't understand this at the station. How can Ian have such a good record, bravery medals and loads of commendations and still be the lowest rank of constable? I mean, you are a Sergeant now and might be an Inspector soon and he hasn't moved.'

'Odd isn't it. I know he was questioned about being a Sergeant at the London station we were in. Said he wasn't interested; wanted to stay as a constable. He didn't seem to want more responsibility, which I know he could cope with. I'm sure that will change soon.'

Late afternoon, they return the bicycles and head back to the city by taxi. And it's yet another stop in a café bar.

'Now Leo and I are going to visit my aunt. Why don't you two go off somewhere and have supper together? Would that be all right?'

Marie-Edith looks pleased and Ian says, 'Fine.'

'I'm sure you can find somewhere interesting can't you Marie-Edith?'

'I should think so, but I don't know a lot about restaurants really.'

'There was a great Algerian place we went to last time we were in Paris. It's probably still there. In Rue de Tobliac.'

'Good, we'll try there first.'

Beatrice and Leo stand up to go. 'Right.' Beatrice gives Marie-Edith a couple of kisses, and Leo shakes her hand. 'And you, airport bus, 10 o'clock tomorrow.'

'Yes boss, bye'

'I do like the way he says that, even if he is taking

the P,' says Beatrice to Leo as they walk off. Once well out of earshot, Beatrice says, 'They are a couple already aren't they,'

'Looks like it. Well done.'

24

In Which it's Dinner for Two

Marie-Edith finds the Algerian restaurant, with its warm and moody atmosphere. The food is good, the people friendly and the two of them seem to find plenty to talk about.

'How far is your apartment from here Marie-Edith?'

'About three kilometres.'

'Shall we walk a bit of the way until we find a taxi?'

'Certainly.'

Leaving the restaurant, Marie-Edith holds Ian's arm and Ian puts his hand on hers. The evening light is fading and the pavements are not too busy as they walk casually along.

'We turn down here, and I just want to go in this shop quickly. You wait here and watch out for those two women across the road.' She winks at him and goes in the shop.

Soon returning, she smiles at Ian. 'You survived.'

'I can guessed what they are. Were you testing me?'

'I had no doubts for a moment, come along.'

'Here's a taxi. Shall we catch it?'

'Definitely.'

In the cab, Ian says, 'Are you going to show me your apartment?'

'If you like.'

'I certainly do. Now it's my turn to test you; to see if you are neat and tidy or if you haven't done the washing up since last week.'

'It'll be fine. The servants will have finished by now.'

And indeed it is neat, clean and comfortable.

'Would you like coffee or is it too late for that now?'

'It is for me. I'd like some hot water though.'

In the kitchen, Marie-Edith puts water in the kettle and takes two mugs from the shelf. When she turns round and smiles at Ian he approaches and puts his arms around her. She responds the same way. When she looks at him, he kisses her gently on the lips.

In the living room, they sit side by side on the sofa and Ian holds her hand. Taking a sip of water, he says, 'This is excellent hot water; you are obviously a good cook.'

She laughs. 'Actually I am quite a good cook but lazy. I don't bother much for myself.'

'You know when we went to the Commissaire's house last night, the food was excellent and beautifully laid out.'

'I've never been to his house but I have met Colette and Bernadette.'

'Beatrice was wearing the outfit you saw when we arrived. It was funny. Young Bernadette was completely speechless and couldn't take her eyes off her. Colette saw Beatrice and she gave the Commissaire such a look; I nearly laughed.'

'Surely she doesn't suspect something there?'

'No, but looking at Beatrice does raise questions doesn't it?'

After a minute's silence, Ian says, 'Now I am going to offer you an ultimatum. Do you know the word?'

'It's the same word in French I think. This sounds serious.'

'It is. Either you throw me out now and forever, or you let me stay for breakfast.'

Marie-Edith looks at him with a neutral expression then looks up at the ceiling. 'I'm thinking about it.'

'No you are not. You've made your decision. If you were going to throw me out, you would've done it by now, and possibly slapped me as well.'

'Oh, you, you, detective, you. I've given too much away already. All right, there's the bedroom – come on.'

Lying on the bed with some of their clothes scattered on the floor, Marie-Edith says, 'Why are you throwing our clothes all over the room?'

'It looks more exciting, as though our clothes have been torn off in a wild passion.'

'I didn't think the British did passion.'

'That's a rumour we spread out just to confuse the opposition and trick fair maidens. Have you got any massage oil?'

'No I haven't.'

'What a disgrace. Seducing me into your bedroom with no massage oil. Turn over will you and at least I can rub your back.' Ian spends some time rubbing Marie-Edith's back and her legs.

'You know your trouble, madam?'

'What?' she asks, sounding a little concerned.

'You've still got too many clothes on. Turn over will

you,' and as she turns over, he quickly pulls her knickers down and throws them on the floor. Then he rubs her breasts and tummy.

'You had better use one of these.' She stretches to the side table and picks up a packet of condoms from behind the clock.

'Do you always have a supply of these things ready?'

'No never.' She rolls on to her side away him. 'Oh you must think I'm some sort of . . . I don't even want to use the English word, an easy street woman.'

'Oh, I never have anything to do street woman, therefore you cannot be one. Problem solved.'

'I bought them when I went into the shop on the way home. It was really difficult; I didn't know what to do.' Marie-Edith looks more serious. 'I don't normally let men stay after one supper. I'm certainly not normally this easy.'

'You aren't easy at all and I think you're great,' and he kisses her neck.

'The trouble started when you smiled so brightly at me when you first arrived. I went all wobbly. I know I blushed and everyone noticed. And I've been getting worse since. I didn't think you even noticed me until you touched my hand when I handed you that champagne.'

'I noticed you all right, especially when you came into the Commissaire's office once; that was the first time I saw you standing up. And I thought, wow, what a good pair of legs, I bet she's a great lover with legs like that.'

'You cheap sexist. And as for great lovers, if you don't get at least nine out of ten, you will be out of the door. Now do something interesting.'

He kisses her breast and starts sucking one of her firm nipples. Marie-Edith flinches and her breathing gets faster as he rolls his tongue over each nipple in turn. After he gets ready with the condom he lifts her legs and opens them wide. He kisses and sucks her thighs, causing her to feel a surge of excitement. Giving her pussy a lick causes her to shiver, arch her back and gasp in surprise. He licks her again, holding a breast at the same time, with the same result. Marie-Edith has always seen herself as a calm person, but she's certainly not feeling calm now.

'Oh mon dieu, c'est fantastique, plus plus.'

He licks her then sucks her some more.

'C'est beau, suce moi, plus, plus dur, I'm starting, do it, please just do it.'

Ian puts his arms under her knees, lifts her legs and pushes into her. Her feelings are intense and she's feeling dizzy as he pushes hard for a second time. She feels a quivering inside her which ripples through her body. He pushes several times more and without realising it, she grabs his back, digging her nails into him, not out of violence but excitement and wanting it all to continue.

Ian finishes his climax and lies down on her. A few minutes later, and tucked up in bed, Ian has his arms around her.

'I love your body, Marie-Edith. Good shape, lovely soft skin, strong legs.'

'I go running and play squash sometimes.'

'Do you realise, we have just had sex and I don't even know your full name.'

'There we are, I must be an easy street woman.'

'No, a delicious hussy maybe, but no more.'

'What is a hussy?'

'A hussy is a light-hearted word for a woman of entertaining ways.'

'You mean like a whore?'

'No no, it's much more of a fun, friendly word, which you could even use in polite society.'

'All right, a hussy with no name.'

'You can tell me your last name if you like.'

'Perhaps not. Maybe I keep the mystery.'

'Or maybe I tickle you until you burst.' He lies on her and tickles her sides hard making her squeal.

'All right, It's Paul, Paul.'

'As in P-A-U-L.'

'Yes. Marie-Edith Simone Paul.'

'I think we've just discovered a new interrogation technique. Right, could you find some paper and a pen please.'

When suitably equipped, he starts writing. 'This is my full name, address, phone number at home and email. There, now you do the same please. And write down your birthday as well. Will you come and visit me soon, in August when everything in France closes anyway?'

'Yes of course, if you're serious.'

'Certainly. Do you think I'm just going to have you for the night and disappear?'

'Probably not, but it has been a fear of mine for the last couple of days. I was so excited when Beatrice asked me to join you on your day out, so I thought I'll have to take a gamble and buy those rubber things. If it only lasted one night, at least I would have a good memory.'

'Well fear not. I think I want you for at least two nights.'

'Sexist beast,' and she gives him a light punch on the chest. They lie quietly for a while.

'When I went to work yesterday morning, I thought it might be the last time I would see you and Beatrice, now here I am . . . . lying at your mercy,' and she gives a little laugh.

'And deliciously tasty you are that way too.'

'That's all right then. You know, it was very funny before you arrived. The Commissaire was a little bad-tempered.'

'Why's that?'

'He didn't want you here. He said we had your criminals then we're supposed to catch them as well. He doesn't speak too much English and he knew you would not know French and he would have to look after you. And your senior officer would arrive and criticise and try to take over. And everyone said how the English are always so badly dressed, and so on. Then when you two walked in, it was like a flash of lightning. You were so beautiful.'

'Beatrice was beautiful.'

'And so were you. Beatrice was like a movie star and the suit you were wearing was amazing.'

'Beatrice chose that; it's none of your cheap Armani rubbish. Beatrice knew how the French police would react, so she was determined to make an entrance and give a strong impression from the start. It was good our Inspector couldn't come because Beatrice was always going to be in charge because of her language.'

'You were beautiful too, and you smiled a lot; I never thought you would notice me.'

'I noticed you straight away. I saw your kind and intelligent face, then once I saw your legs, I thought, mmm I'd love to get them open.'

'As I said, sexist beast.'

'Don't give me that. I didn't hear many complaints ten minutes ago. It's what you wanted, be honest.'

'Yes, from the first day, but you are still a sexist beast.'

'I think your English is getting too good, knowing expressions like "sexist beast". Anyway, how did the office react after we went into the Commissaire's office?'

'It was very quiet, nobody spoke, we just looked at each other and slowly went back to work. It wasn't till later that people spoke about you and compared notes. Some of the men admitted they would be too scared of Beatrice, some pretended they would have a go. French men can be very machisme but I don't think that would work with Beatrice. Of the women I spoke to, they all wanted to have sex with both of you.'

'Well nothing happened and my hotel room wasn't locked. Why don't you tell them you've had sex with both of us?'

'That would be funny, wouldn't it? They would never know.'

'And the Commissaire changed his tune did he?'

'He wants you both on the force now.'

'It's certainly been quite a week. A murderer caught,

a drug ring exposed, seen a beautiful city for the first time and met a hot and sexy French maiden.'

'I don't think you have the order correct there. It's all a matter of importance.'

'You mean the hot and sexy French maiden comes first?'

'Naturally....Ian, you know when you licked me earlier?'

'What down below?'

'Yes.'

'Was it good?'

'It was wonderful. Absolute heaven. I've never had that before.'

'Really? You must have had some rotten lovers.'

'Mmmm. Poor me. Well could you do that every time please?'

'Not every time or you'll get spoilt or bored with it.'

'I am sure I will never get bored with it.'

'I'll save it as a special treat and when you least expect it.'

'All right, not every time, but often please.'

'With pleasure.'

She rolls on top of him. 'Well I'm not going to kiss you now – I know where your mouth has been.' She pushes herself up and says, 'Licking me and holding my breast at the same time, I was just about to burst when you did that. Where did you learn such a trick anyway? No no, don't answer that. There are some things a woman should not know.'

'I don't think I want to sleep tonight. I'll spend all night stroking your body; it's beautiful.' He runs his hand up and down her back several times, then rolls sideways. 'Good breasts too, and very firm nipples.'

'That's your fault; they aren't usually this hard.'

'Of course we'll have to see if you can pass the five tests.'

'What five tests?'

'The five crucial tests to be a perfect woman. We'll deal with them one at a time.'

'What's the first; to be good at sex?'

'No, that's not it.'

'To be good in the kitchen and have the dinner ready on time?'

'Now you're being crude. The first test is ... a perfect woman has to be good to cuddle.'

'What is cuddle?'

He puts his arms round her and cuddles her firmly. 'This is cuddle. Being good at sex is fine but you can't be doing that all the time, whereas cuddles can last for a lifetime.'

'Oh I see, and do I pass.'

'Easily, full marks.'

'What's the second test?'

'I'll tell you that in the morning.'

'What if I fail a test?'

'That'll be it I'm afraid. It has to be at least nine out of ten on every test or it's game over.'

'Well you got eight out of ten for our first sex.'

'Only eight, why only eight?'

'That's a very good score for our first time. And the licking took it up from six.'

'Six!?'

'Well, there has to be room left for improvement.'

'You are going to be a hard woman to satisfy.'

'Ian, about Beatrice, she is so impressive as a person and as a women, I can see that most men wouldn't be able to cope with her.'

'You're right, most men are pretty weak characters in spite of all their bull and bluff.'

'Is she really tough under the surface?'

'Yes she is. She's not as hard as nails but she is mentally strong. And physically, she's a real expert in ju jitsu. Do you know what that is?'

'Yes.'

'In a scrap, it's the other people who get the broken arms. She got caught out a few years ago with Sergeant Innes, but she's made damn sure that's never happened again. Why not go to sleep now and I'll just carry on stroking you all night.'

'Perfect.'

Over breakfast, Marie-Edith asks 'What happens now? Are we really going to see each other again or is it just the one night? Once you get home will you forget all about me?'

'I won't forget all about you on one condition – that we can have more sex right now.'

'You can have more sex with me on one condition.'

'Oh, you have conditions as well? Go on then.'

'That you lick me first, then you do it really hard and hurt me with it.'

'That's two conditions.'

'No, it's a package, take it or leave it.'

'But why should I want to hurt?'

'I want to be sore down below for several days, as a souvenir.'

'You are kinky.'

'What is kinky.'

'Strange, weird. I could always give you a baby as a souvenir.'

'Not today, thank you. Maybe next time.'

'What if you start begging for mercy?'

'Show me no mercy. Just do it harder.'

'Come on then, let's get those pretty knickers off.'

In the bedroom, there isn't much delay or build-up. Marie-Edith holds her legs up and Ian licks and sucks her again. She squeals and gasps at the pleasure of it. Once he starts shagging her she wraps her legs around him and locks them together.

'Harder, harder, push. Harder, harder push harder!'

Ian arches his back as he pushes.

He sees she's grimacing but still shouts 'HARDER HARDER'. Then he starts coming and soon finishes his climax.

When he relaxes down on her, she holds him tightly in her arms, and with a rough animal growl and pushing hard with one foot rolls them over so she's on top. Then she does a push up, grabbing his chest and digging her nails in, and starts working her hips up and down furiously. She puts a hand down between them to tickle her clit and starts to feel her organism coming. The thought flashes through her mind that it's been far too many years since the last time, and this is so much better than doing it on her own. Ian gives another lift of his hips in time with her shagging and squeezes her bottom hard as she climaxes, gasping and shouting out in her pleasure and excitement.

When finished, she flops down on to him and kicks her feet up and down with a few grunts and some heavy breathing.

'Was that hard enough for you then?'

'Just about but only just. How about you?'

'Heavenly, the best sex I've had all day.'

She pushes up a bit and slaps him on the shoulder.

'Monster.'

They laugh and cuddle.

'I was quite painful at times but beautifully painful. Thank you.'

'Do you think the neighbours heard?'

'I hope so; they think I'm dry and boring or at least a secret gay.'

'Well you are certainly not that.'

With a giggle she says, 'You wait until I really get going. I think we can give you nine out of ten now.' She whispers to him, 'I want to be fucked like that every day – no, twice a day.'

'Three times a day and that's my final offer.'

'Agreed.'

'And just how is it you know certain English swear words?'

'Well, when I was at school and learning English, some of us girls got together and made of point of learning all the crude English words. We collected them, the stronger the better and we even made up a few. So I know them all. We were only about 13, and basically scared of boys anyway, although we pretended not to be.'

'Just make sure you don't use those words in the wrong company.'

'No, I'll save them for when we're having sex. And I'll be trying most of them out of the first time on an Englishman. So what's the second test the perfect woman must pass?'

'Are you ready?'

'Yes, test me.'

'Your choice of chocolate biscuits.'

There's a pause then Marie-Edith rings out with laughter. 'You are crazy.'

'Quality chocolate biscuits are very important for a stable relationship.'

'Well I want ten out of ten straight away, because I told you last night my parents own a large delicatessen in Orléans and they stock some amazing chocolate biscuits.'

'That sounds good, but I am chief tester, judge, jury and inquisitor. You can bring the best with you when you come in August.'

'Agreed. I could lie here all day but must leave for work now and you have a plane to catch – and I hope it's not for ever.' She looks serious and worried.

'Now don't start that again. We've got it arranged, you are coming over to England in a few weeks. Don't worry, I won't change that plan and I hope you don't.' That brings a smile and a kiss.

Dressed and tidied, they have a big hug just before leaving the apartment. Walking down the stairs, Marie-Edith flinches at one point.

'You all right dear?"

'Just about. It's what I asked for,' she whispers. 'Perhaps we got a little carried away. I'm certainly sore now.'

'It's good to give satisfaction. You sure I'm not up to ten out of ten yet?'

'No not yet.'

Outside, they find a taxi for Ian; Marie-Edith gives instructions to the driver, and after watching it drive off, she takes the short walk to the Metro. Now she's in lover's dreamland. On her journey that morning, she's never known such pleasure in the Metro. Every object and every colour seem to display a new vibrancy and she can't help but smile at many of the strangers.

At work, the Commissaire asks how she enjoyed the day with the three visitors. Marie-Edith simply nods and seeing the glowing smile on her face and in her eyes, he doesn't need to enquire any further.

Ian is sitting with Leo in the hotel reception area.

'So how did you get on last night then?' asks Leo with a smirk.

'We are going to be laddish about this are we?'

'You bet. If I don't give Bea a blow by blow account, I'll be in dead trouble.'

'It's definitely been a week to remember, hasn't it?' Ian casts his eyes sideways to Leo but keeps him waiting with a 30 second pause.

'Marie-Edith sits at her desk quietly tapping away on the computer, with her hair tied back and looking so normal and quiet, but in actual fact, she's just a complete wild animal. I was lucky to survive. She's going to visit me in Bristol in a few weeks. And that's all you are going to get.'

'That's plenty. I can build that up into a reasonable drama.'

Beatrice steps out of the lift and approaches them. Ian and Leo stand and shake hands. Beatrice looks at Ian for a moment, wondering what's best, then gives him a big hug.

'See you then,' she says, 'and thanks,' and Ian gets the taxi to the airport.

Once the taxi is on its way, Beatrice says to Leo, 'Right, full report please. What happened?'

'I don't know. It was all so steamy, I'm not sure I can break such a confidence.'

'Don't be ridiculous. You know you can't get away with that.'

★ ★ ★

25

In Which it's Back to Bristol

For Ian, Time picks up its old rhythm . . . . .

Beatrice and Leo spend the next three days together; Bea leading them to some of her favourite restaurants and cultural places and new ones besides. Leo lets her indulge and absorbs some of the art, for his own good.

On the day of their leaving, Beatrice wants to say a final goodbye to the Commissaire and to Marie-Edith so calls Maurice at the police offices.

'Leo and I are leaving this afternoon and I just wanted to say thank you again and good bye.'

'Well your visit has certainly been interesting and eventful. We've found a big drug connection with these characters. More senior people will have to decide who gets Bolton first, us for the drugs or you for the murders. Either way he's likely to spend most of the rest of his life in gaol.'

'That's good to hear.'

'Now, I'm glad you've called. We have a cottage in the South of France and Colette and I would like you and Leo to come and stay with us some time. Bernadette would love it too of course. Perhaps August next year, if you could fit it in.'

'That sounds wonderful; we'd love to come, thank you.'

'Good, we'll be in touch nearer the time, if not before.'

'Finally, could I take Marie-Edith out for a quick coffee?'

'Yes, what have your done to her? She's a new woman, I've never seen her so happy.'

'Blame or credit DC Stanton for that. He said nothing to me so I need to interrogate Marie-Edith for all the real gossip.'

'Quite right. Give her the full works.'

'If you could ask her to meet me in the reception in ten minutes.'

'Certainly, she'll be there.'

Beatrice is in her full Superwoman outfit when she meets Marie-Edith in reception. Walking down the steps, Beatrice holds her arm affectionately. Entering the building at the same time is one of the female officers from the office. Marie-Edith gives her a generous smile, hoping to create some good gossip out of it.

In the café bar near the station.

'Now Marie-Edith.' Beatrice pauses and looks sternly at her while drumming her fingers on the table. 'Ian didn't say much about your evening together, but it went well did it?'

Marie-Edith just goes 'Mmmmm' and looks away with a slight smile.

'Look here, that's not good enough. I need details.' More drumming of fingers.

'Yes he stayed for breakfast and we got on really well. Didn't he tell you?'

'He said nothing to me and only a little to Leo. Ian did tell him you were an absolute wild animal.'

'What? Did he mean I have a bad temper?'

'No, I think he was referring to your bedroom performance.' Marie-Edit giggles and covers her face with her hands.

'He was a bit of a wild animal himself. I'm still sore.'

Beatrice laughs. 'Good, I'm glad to hear it.'

'He's very strong really – everywhere,' says Marie-Edith coyly. 'He says I should visit him in a few weeks but didn't set a date. Do you think he means it or is it a way to brush me off?'

'He would need to fix up some time off first and it'll depend on jobs back home. He will mean it. I cannot image Ian would lie to you. If he says he will meet you at the North Pole next year, July 9th at 2.30, he will be there. Now, Ian lives on his own and I know he's not used to spending long periods with someone. I suggest you plan to stay a few days rather than two weeks or so at first. You can always extend it if things go well.'

'All right, I'll do that. But I will still be nervous until he actually calls. Tell me, why did you ask me to join you that day?'

'I noticed the way you looked at him.'

'Do you think he noticed. Was I that obvious?'

'Not really. But Ian would have noticed. He sees things in people's face most will miss. Ian has such super-sensitive antennae, so he can see things in a person's body language even when they're certain they haven't given anything away. That's how he's solved some difficult cases. Did you hear how we found out the address for that Vergne character?'

'I thought you just got that from a normal inter-rogation.'

'Not quite. We had a few words with the first four men we arrested, and I rather insisted Ian should be in on the interviews. Ian wanted to stay with one of them. He saw him as a weak link, even though Ian speaks virtually no French. So there was the Commissaire, another officer and Ian, while I watched through the glass. During the interview, all in French of course, Ian wrote down an address. The man didn't say the address, only thought it, and probably looked at the street name in his mind's eye, but that was enough. The Commissaire was very doubtful at first but set up surveillance, then they got him.'

'You mean, Ian can read people's minds?'

'Sometimes; he's done it before. If the thoughts are strong enough, and he's amazing at smelling out lies in an interview.'

'That's scary.'

'So if ever you're thinking about a bit of hanky pinky on the side and a liaison, he will probably know about it before you do.'

'Gulp, oops' Marie-Edith gives Beatrice a wide-eye expression. 'Do you think Ian could ever learn French?'

'He told me once languages was his worst subject at school. He might learn French if he were locked in France and he couldn't speak anything else but Ian can do so much really well, if he can't learn French it might be better just to accept it. Now I left Leo on a park bench, probably eyeing up all the passing young women. We'll have lunch then head for the airport and we'll meet again in a few weeks. Bye for now.'

At the first opportunity, Marie-Edith pays a visit to her parents in Orléans. She doesn't normally talk about her police work but this time she can't wait to relate the whole episode of the visit by the British police. Her parents are intrigued to hear all the details of Beatrice, her clothes and appearance. They particularly enjoy looking at the photograph of them all together. Her mother notices the extra sparkle in Marie-Edith's eyes as she talks about Ian and both parents are hugely impressed by the medals for bravery.

When they are alone, her mother asks casually, '*And will you be seeing Ian the brave policeman again, dear?*' Marie-Edith tries to be as casual, '*Mmm, maybe.*'

In late July, DS Beatrice Walker is in the office of Chief Superintendent Wesley.

'You did well in the exam Sergeant, I mean Inspector. Congratulations. But that's no surprise really, especially after the success of the job in France.'

'Thank you sir. I would point out that much of the credit for the France job must go to DC Stanton. It would not have been a success without him.'

'Yes, I read the report. But remember you were the one who chose him in the first place. Not many people would have. That shows good management.'

'I've known him a long time; I know what he's capable of.'

'Now these mystical type of incidents. Shattering

that locked door just by pressing on it when the police were going to use a battering ram; and the business of mind-reading that criminal to get a crucial address. Did they actually happen like that?'

'Yes sir; just the way I said. He's done it before, although it's been brushed aside as only a fluky guess. And he can sniff out lies in an interview better than anyone I've come across. Many people are finding it strange he's still a DC.'

'I know, but he's made it clear he would not accept promotion. He's never taken the promotion exams but I'm sure he'd pass them easily enough.' The Chief Superintendent pauses. 'You know in cricket, I don't suppose you follow cricket? Anyway, there's often the question if a top bowler would make a good captain or would his bowling suffer because his attention was being divided in too many directions. And he'd want to be bowling himself all the time even when it's not in the best interests of the game. No, a top bowler is unlikely to make a good captain. It can happen but it's rare. Stanton's probably looking at it along those lines. As well as the fact that maybe he feels he won't be good enough being in charge and giving orders; not all police officers can do that. The same can happen in other jobs for that matter. In business, somebody is doing a good job so they get promoted, and the new job is slightly different and now they are above their level of ability.'

He pauses and looks out of the window. 'I'll have a word with a couple of people and see if there's a way round this. I know he gets those annuities from the George Cross but he's still on a constable's pay. 'I can certainly see that he gets a Commendation for his police work in Paris.'

'Thank you sir.'

'Although his position is mainly his choice, do you think he might be a little resentful of you being an Inspector now?'

'I'm not sure. Probably not. It's been fine so far with me as a Sergeant. In Paris it was like working with a good friend, but that's only one difference in rank. As an Inspector, it could be different.'

'I won't put Stanton in your team then. We'll see how it goes. Okay, there's no new office or desk for you at present, not until Inspector Cadwallader retires in a month or so, but your new duties will be coming through pretty quickly. Good luck Inspector.'

'Thank you sir. I'm looking forward to it. My husband says I've been practising by giving him orders for years.'

'I know just how he feels.'

Time bounces forward . . . . .

26

In Which Marie-Edith makes a Visit

It's the last week in August and Ian meets Marie-Edith at Bristol airport. They embrace in the manner of so many couples meeting after an absence. Once in the car, they kiss properly.

'You all right then?' he asks.

'Frightfully topping, thank you.'

'Where did you get an expression like that?'

'PG Wodehouse,' and they laugh indeed.

Ian starts the car and they head for the city.

'Now, if you are desperately hungry we could go for lunch straight away or we could go home first for some serious hugs. What do you think?'

'I think I am desperately hungry. . . for serious hugs.'

'That is the right answer.'

'And I have come fully prepared, so you won't need one of those horrid rubber things.'

'Beautiful, sexy and well organised; I'm in heaven already.' He squeezes her thigh.

She smacks his hand. 'Stop that and watch the road.'

After a whole list of unspeakable activities, they are lying peacefully in bed.

'Well in spite of your fears, here you are. I said you were worth more than one night. At least two nights and a bit extra in between.'

'So this is the bit in between, tonight will be the second night and then I get thrown out do I?'

'Or one of us turns into a frog or is it a prince, or do I chain you to the bed and keep you here forever – we shall see. Are you going to see Beatrice while you're here?'

'Yes. Are we all going to meet up?'

'No, I don't see Beatrice socially so it's best if you see her on your own.'

'But you're good friends aren't you and with Leo too.'

'Yes but our ranks are so different, and I can get too cheeky, which isn't a good idea at work. You know she's an Inspector now?'

'Yes, she said in an email.'

'Right, time for lunch. We'll go to the Waterfront and find somewhere there.'

Ian has put a large array of flower in a vase on the living room table. Marie-Edith is adjusting them slightly and says, 'Are you going to play some harp for me Ian?'

'I could have a little practice later, but it won't be a full performance.'

'And could we have fish and chips some time?' Marie-Edith asks.

'Fish and chips? Are you serious?'

'Yes, isn't it a British delicacy and tradition?'

'A tradition but I wouldn't exactly call it a delicacy. It usually gives me indigestion. I think it might offend your refined French palette. Do you want roast beef as well?'

'No, I don't eat that sort of meat do I.'

'How about Yorkshire pudding?'

'What's that?'

'Ah, a good Yorkshire pudding and gravy is a craft to be savoured and experienced, rather than talked about.'

'A bit like cricket?'

'What a clever answer.'

'And an English pub; we must go to a few of those.'

After lunch they spend the afternoon wandering around the city and then back home, and while Ian makes a pot of tea, Marie-Edith produces two boxes of biscuits.

She kneels on the settee next to Ian and starts unwrapping the first packet of biscuits. 'The trial begins,' she says. Taking out a dark chocolate biscuit, she holds it to Ian's mouth. 'Bite.' He bites and close his eyes, while chewing and savouring the moment. 'More,' he says. The process continues until the biscuit is finished.

Marie-Edith opens the second packet and the whole business is repeated. Ian smacks his lips and takes a sip of tea. Marie-Edith laughs at all this nonsense. 'Well, has the inquisition decided?'

'I must say, these biscuits are exquisite, excellent, near perfect.'

'Near perfect?'

'They taste nearly as good as your body, which gets 10 out of 10 and the biscuits get nine and a half out of ten.'

'Does that pass the test?'

'Of course,' and Marie-Edith claps enthusiastically.

'Come here and more biscuits please.'

'So what's the third test?'

'That test has been running all the time – decision pending.'

During supper in a pub, Marie-Edith asks, 'Are you a good cook Ian?'

'No, I can cook an adequate meal for myself but I wouldn't inflict it on anyone else. I can make a decent fruit cake and marmalade. In fact I make the best marmalade in the universe.'

'And who is the judge?'

'It doesn't need judges. It's one of the Laws of Nature, like gravity and microwave ovens. Look, Kings have lent me their daughters for a jar of my marmalade.'

'Do you have any left?'

'No, I have quite run out of King's daughters at the moment, but I do have jar of marmalade. We'll have it at breakfast.'

'I had best warn you, I make marmalade too.'

'No contest; you should surrender now to avoid embarrassment,' replies Ian with confidence.

'I said that wrong. It should be "I had better warn you". Ian I made a mistake and you said nothing.'

'No but I knew what you meant.'

'Do I often make mistakes?'

'Not often but sometimes.'

'Well you must correct me. Please, I do not want to speak with mistakes.'

'All right. I said that wrongly, not "I said that wrong".

Wrongly with a verb; wrong with a noun.'

'Yes of course, I know that, silly me. It's a funny thing about English. Some of it is so easy to learn, then it becomes difficult. It can be strange and complicated.'

'That's because English is an mixture and melting pot of so many languages and influences. Bits of Viking language, then German, then Normandy French, then French French, some spelling from the Huguenots, little bits of Latin and then a few other languages thrown in. We have "close" from the old French and "shut" from the old German and they both mean much the same thing, but it all amounts to about five million words. Only a few of us know them all of course,' and he laughs.

In the evening, Ian uncovers the harp and spends some time practicing before playing a couple of completed pieces for Marie-Edith's benefits. She certainly enjoys it and makes all the right complimentary comments.

Ian is keen on an early night and Marie-Edith makes no complaints. He lays a large bathroom towel over the bed and starts to undress Marie-Edith quickly.

'What's that towel for?'

'It might be for a special torture or a special treat. Lie face down please.'

'Won't the neighbours hear my screams?'

'Probably, but they're use to it. Come on lie down.'

Ian kneels beside her, picks up a bottle of massage oil, pours a large amount into one hand and starts massaging her back. It's a surprise for Marie-Edith and she lets out a loud sigh.

'Oh, this is wonderful. Is it lavender?'

'Yes, France is famous for its lavender.'

He spends the next 15 minutes massaging her back, bottom and legs, while Marie-Edith feels she is wallowing in a new world.

'You like this then?' he asks.

'Words cannot describe it.'

'Roll over now.' As soon as she's lying on her back, her breasts and tummy get the same treatment. Marie-Edith is in a complete dream-like state and she hardly notices when Ian opens her legs, gives her a few licks and they have very gentle sex.

Once tucked up in bed, Marie-Edith asks, 'Will you massage my back some more please?'

'I'll give it a little rub; more than that will have to wait until tomorrow night.'

'I've never had that before; well a couple of times in a gym but not from a lover and it feels ten times better from you. Will you do it every night please?'

'That purely depends on what entertainments you can provide.'

'Good. I have a passionately wicked imagination.'

The home-made marmalade takes centre place on the breakfast table.

'And it has a label "Sharp and Chunky". What is chunky,' she asks.

'Big, solid, large bits.'

'Then it's time for the tasting and testing.' Marie-Edith takes a sip of water and gargles.

'This tasting doesn't involve spitting does it?'

'No.'

She picks up a tea spoon and takes a spoonful of

marmalade. She pauses, looks up at the ceiling, rolls her mouth then takes another spoonful, wiggles her tongue in her mouth and then takes a third spoonful.'

'Well I'm very sorry but I have to say, and I hope this won't make trouble between us, but I truly must say, that this is better than mine.'

'A compliment from a French connoisseur is praise indeed.'

'Well, I must defend myself now. Tonight I will cook us supper.'

'Sounds good. Make a list and we'll hit the shops. I'll get some English sparkling wine and you can compare it with champagne.'

The following day, they are slouched on the sofa.

'Ian, I've only been here less than two days and we've had sex six times, most of them in a different position and I'm sore and tender. I'm not use to this sort of treatment.

'Well my dear, let's face it, the main reason you're here is to provide me with unlimited sex.'

'What? Why you . .' and she elbows him in the ribs. 'You might treat your British women like that, like some sex toy, but not this French woman. I decide when you have sex now. No more for you for two days.'

'I haven't heard any complaints so far, all I've heard is gasps and groans of pleasure. And if I don't get sex on demand, you don't get any cuddles,' and he gives her a theatrical snarl.

'That is criminal! You monster. Have you ever seen a French woman having a tantrum? It's worse than a hurricane, and you will be in the eye of the storm. I might even make you sleep in the spare room.'

'But it's my flat.'

'And it's my body, so I decide.'

'Ah. I think we need to have some international negotiations here.'

'Yes and I need more coffee. Go.' She snaps her fingers at him.

'Beatrice snaps her fingers like that.'

'That'll be the French in her – the sensible half. I said go.'

'You're getting as bossy as she is.'

'See it simply as a sign of affection. Now GO,' and she doesn't smile and snigger until he's in the kitchen, then she thinks to herself, Mmm that was fun.

Sitting quietly over their coffee, Ian ventures to make a little tentative conversation. 'I was thinking of going to my aikido class tonight if you aren't having a French woman's tantrum and maybe you would like to come along. Or we could do something else.'

'Oooo yes that would be good. I've never seen anything like that.'

Marie-Edith is impressed by the style of it – smart martial arts suits and long black robes. The elegant way they roll and fly through the air looks quite magical to her. At one point, Ian comes to sit beside her. 'What do you think?'

'It's amazing and beautiful and it looks so gentle.'

'At the moment, yes, until it matters and you're on the receiving end of it.'

'Are those real samurai swords there?'

'Yes. The higher grades are allowed to use them. I'm allowed but I won't go near them. We use wooden substitutes for training.'

'And how long have you been doing this now?'

'About 14 years but I don't practise as much as I should. Now I must get back in to the fray; another half hour yet.'

At bedtime, Marie-Edith feels she has to maintain her no-sex stance for a while. She kisses Ian on the cheek, gives him a cheerful "Good night" and turns to face the other way, not quite sure how he'll take it. She's delighted when, two minutes later, he puts some oil on his hand and starts rubbing her back.

'Do you want a cuddle?'

'What's the price? Do you expect me to pay with sex?'

'No. No charge. Just a cuddle.'

She rolls over and Ian puts his arm round her.

Over breakfast Ian suggests they could take a trip into Cornwall. 'There's good scenery, sea, cliffs and beaches. What do you think?'

'Oooo yes I love the sea but don't often get there.'

'And as an extra treat, we will have fish and chips sitting on the sea front.'

'Hurray.'

'And whatever happens you are not allowed to complain about the food.'

'You aren't selling this too well, you know?'

'Quite possibly. Now, August isn't the best time to go, with the school holidays still on, but it's towards the end of the month so we should find somewhere to stay.'

★

They end up in a comfortable Bed & Breakfast in Padstow, near the harbour, and it's a late lunch sitting by the harbour eating fish and chips out of the paper.

'This is good. I like this. Hot, fresh out of the pan and not greasy,' says Marie-Edith, licking her fingers.'

'Mmm, this is among the best I've tasted.'

The afternoon is spent wandering around the old town and among the rocks along the beach. They find a rustic pub in a side street, which will do nicely for supper.

'Now, as we are in the heart of the West Country, we have to start off with the local cider.'

'Cider?' says Marie-Edith, the tone of her voice showing a certain amount of horror.

'Now don't be a foody snob. See it as local wine, but from apples. I'll get two different types and if you really don't like it, you can have something else.'

They find a bench seat by a wall so they can sit side by side and look into the room. Ian returns with a glass of local clear cider and a glass of local cloudy cider, and two packets of dry roasted peanuts.

Marie-Edith takes several sips from both glasses, giving them the full lip-smacking treatment. 'Well, I must say, these are tasty; not what I expected at all. Do you think they are strong?'

'Usually yes. Half a pint should be enough. A whole pint and it'll be giggles all the way back to the digs. Try some of the dry roasted.'

Marie-Edith nibbles at the peanuts and starts to cough, resulting in Ian giving her some gentle slaps on the back.

'Ah, you can't take it, ay. Can't eat your peanuts with the men.'

'Apparently not. I'll stay with the girls and the pink jelly babies.'

Supper is local crab and vegetables and the rest of the evening is spent sitting by the sea watching the sky turn red.

Back at the Bed & Breakfast house, Ian comes out of the bathroom to find Marie-Edith lying face down on the bed, naked apart from her knickers. She rolls over and wriggles about a little, knowing she won't be able to keep the embargo up any longer. 'I always have trouble sleeping on a strange room, unless I get some special treatment to help me relax.'

'What about my headache?'

'You do not have a headache, believe me on this.'

'Well I couldn't possibly deny fair lady and it's a good job I brought that lavender massage oil.' He kneels on the bed. 'Let's get these knickers off first, shall we. Lift your bum.'

Just to surprise her, Ian instantly lifts her legs and licks her pussy several times, causing her to squeal and bite her knuckles. 'That's all for now, turn over and I'll massage your back.'

'Licking me like that doesn't exactly calm me down you know.'

'Good, you need to be well primed and desperate.'

After two days on beaches and walking around rocks and cliffs, they return to Bristol. Saturday morning and Marie-Edith is off to meet Beatrice and Leo for an early lunch.

'Where's Ian?' Beatrice asks.

'Not coming.'

Beatrice looks disappointed, glances quickly at Leo then back to Marie-Edith. 'Okay. It's wonderful to see you again.'

After lunch Leo tactfully says, 'Why don't I go off and play with my train set or something and you women can have a better chat. We'll see you again soon won't we? Here or Paris, at Christmas if not before?'

'I don't know. Nothing like that planned yet.'

Marie-Edith and Beatrice spend a happy two hours together.

That night, Marie-Edith decides to be a little bold and take a specific look at Ian's scars. She wants any sensitivity about the subject to be removed with a bit more frank-ness. Ian doesn't object as she looks at the scars closely and touches them.

'Ian, precious, do you find my seductive?'

'Of course, irresistibly so.'

'The best answer, but it puts you in a trap. Will you show me the medals please? I know you got something special.'

Ian hesitates, 'All right, wait here. You are not to talk about this, right?"

'Fine. I'm good at keeping secrets.'

Ian goes into the living room and returns a few minutes later with four boxes. He hands the first one to her, which she opens.

'My god, this is a George Cross. That's the highest isn't it?'

'Outside of the military, yes. This was for the terror attack way back when, with Sergeant Innes. I was a very new Constable then; I really only followed the Sergeant's instructions. 'This is the George Medal for the attack on Beatrice and Sergeant Innes again. And this for the shopping mall incident, which gave me all the scars.'

'Another George Cross, isn't it? And the other one?'

'You've never seen this right. This does not exist.'

Marie-Edith can see he's serious. 'Yes, I understand. Is this the Sovereign Medal?'

'How do you know about that?'

'You aren't the only one who can read minds you know.'

She opens the box which contains a large round medal with a red, white and blue ribbon. The medal is in gold and embossed with the royal coat of arms with the lion and unicorn. Underneath in small letters is engraved, "The Sovereign Medal". Around the edge is Ian's name and a date.

'I've never heard of this one before you came along.'

'No. It comes directly from the Queen and they aren't publicly announced. There are a few others, but no-one knows how many. If serious medal collectors even knew about these, they would pay millions for one.'

'And you met the Queen?'

'Yes, it was in early May. She didn't do any congratulations. She's a class act and knew cheers would be out of place with all that slaughter. My mother was there and just managed to avoid letting the tears flow until we got outside.'

'How did you get your mother not to talk about that terrorist attack, the Queen and the medals. It's the sort of thing any mother will want to boast about?'

'I convinced her that talking about it could get me killed. She can talk about the first one and the rescue with Sergeant Innes and Beatrice. That'll serve the same job and they're more public knowledge.'

Marie-Edith's visit has lasted a full week before she leaves, with arrangements made for Ian to go to Paris in October. And he's been ordered to meet Marie-Edith's parents, her adopted parents in fact, she never having known her real parents, in Orléans south of Paris.

At the airport, Marie-Edith is tearful about leaving but she's pleased to see that Ian's eyes are a little wet as well. As a final goodbye, he whispers in her ear, 'I can't wait to be licking you again,' so at least she's smiling cheerfully while entering the departure area and waving.

Time passes, just . . . . .

27

IN WHICH HIS LORDSHIP LORDS OVER IT

'Sergeant Thomas, come in,' says the Inspector. 'We've had a call from the Bristol Royal. The doctors have reported a case of what they're sure is domestic violence.'

'Shouldn't uniform be dealing with that?'

'Normally yes, but this is Lord and Lady somebody, de Bedivere, so we are supposed to be a little more discrete. Take DC Stanton with you.'

'We want this Lordship chap wiped out do we sir?'

'That'll do Sergeant. Here are the details. Just get on with it.'

'Yes sir, sorry sir.'

Sergeant Gwyneth Thomas and DC Stanton speak to their contact at the Royal, and get introduced to the doctor who examined Lady de Bedivere.

'What makes you think the injuries were caused by domestic violence rather than actually falling down the stairs?'

'We see all sorts of injuries every day, and you get to know the difference. The positions of the bruises, and bruises around the broken arm. It's most unlikely you're going to get a black eye from falling down the stairs. Falling down the stairs is a standard cover-up excuse for domestic violence. And she's been in before with a damaged face.'

'Right, well we need to speak to her.'

'Yes, she's in that side room, number 11.'

Standing outside the room, Sergeant Thomas says, 'Actually, Stanton it might be better if I saw her on my own. One person rather than two and woman to woman and so on.'

'Sure. I'll wait in the car.'

Lady de Bedivere claims she wasn't looking where she was going, so with no accusation, they can do little. 'We'll go and see the husband anyway. Our visit might make him more cautious.'

'Or even worse, who knows.'

The de Bediveres live in a large manor house on the edge of Bristol and there's also a farm and shooting estate in South Yorkshire. The two officers knock on the front door of the manor house. A middle-age man in old-fashioned butler's clothes opens the door.

'DS Thomas and DC Stanton from the police to see Lord de Bedivere,' says the Sergeant showing her badge.

'You will need to use the back entrance,' and he goes to close the door.

The Sergeant quickly steps forward and puts her hand on the door, while Stanton puts his foot in the way of the door. 'We do the front door, not the back. We would like to see him now please.'

'Come in and wait here.' He lets them into the hall

and goes down a corridor.

The hall is large and covered with wood panelling, with a wide staircase elaborately carved in wood. On one wall is a family tree chart, stretching up to the ceiling. Many of the names have Coats of Arm beside them. It's a good five minutes before Lord de Bedivere enters the hall while Ian is still studying the chart.

'That's my family tree going all the way back to William the Conqueror, and Percy de Bedivere. The property has been in my family since 1067.'

Ian only slightly turns his head as his eyes look at de Bedivere. 'William the Conqueror, also known as William the Bastard, a mass murdering psychopath who slaughtered hundreds of thousands of British. Anyone with land, property and money was killed and everything handed over to William's cronies. Perhaps we should fight for that land again and maybe win it back.'

'Damn impertinence. Who are you people? What do you want.' His manner is sharp.

Sergeant Thomas introduces themselves. 'We are here to ask you about the injuries sustained by your wife. The injuries she is being treated for right now in hospital.'

'Really, and what does she say about that?'

'We need to hear what you have say about it.'

'She slipped and fell on the stairs.' He indicates the stairs with a wave of the hand.

'How did she manage to slip on the stairs?'

'What rank did you say you were?'

'Detective Sergeant.'

'And you?'

'Detective Constable.'

'A constable and a female sergeant. Do you know who I am? It is unbecoming that I should be questioned by such junior officers.'

'Only serious criminals get interviewed by senior officers,' says Ian. 'We can arrange that. We can take you down to the station, put you in an interview room, get your lawyer there, then a Superintendent can do the interview with the recordings on.' He takes out his handcuffs. 'Or you can deal with our questions now. What's it to be then?'

'This is outrageous. I'll speak to the Chief Constable about your offensive behaviour; he's a personal friend.'

'Yes, Malcolm; he's a good friend of ours too. He's often in the station and is very supportive of his officers. Shall we carry on?' responds Ian in the same frosty manner.

Sergeant Thomas quickly steps in. 'How did she manage to slip on the stairs?'

'I don't know; wasn't looking where she was going I suppose, or tripped on a toy. The maid heard her fall and found her there.'

'The doctors say her injuries are not consistent with falling down stairs.'

'Well the doctors are wrong. Has my wife made a complaint?'

'No, the hospital called us. Lady de Bedivere says she fell on the stairs.'

'There you are then, she had an accident on the stairs and that's the end of the matter. Now get out.'

As he walks away he calls to the butler, 'Harris, show these people out.'

Back in the car and going down the drive, Ian says, 'He's a genuine AA – arrogant arsehole. Why doesn't she leave?'

'They've got three kids. If she leaves she probably won't see them again. He's rich, mean and violent enough to make sure she gets nothing. Are you always like that during interviews?'

'No, sometimes I'm in a bad mood then I can get stroppy.'

'Malcolm indeed. I was starting to see my pension go up in smoke and I'm only 32. No wonder people call you Deadly Dangerous.'

'I thought that tag had faded away. It was meant to be ironic and most people wouldn't dare say it to my face,' as he narrows his eyes at her in a comic manner and hisses.

'Yes, but I'm friendly with Beatrice Walker, and she says you are really just a big softy.'

'Heh, girly gossip ay? I can't have rumours like spreading around so I'll deal with Madam Walker later. Her eyes will roll and head will follow.'

'If his wife gets injured again like this, we will take him into the station and give him a proper interview, then the local papers might just happen to hear about it. That won't do his public standing any good even if there are no charges.'

'Won't he take it out on his wife?' Ian asks.

'He seems to do that anyway.'

'Can you imagine any of the women you know letting

themselves be kicked around like that? I certainly can't. He'd be lining himself up for a hunting accident.'

Time becomes pleasure . . . . .

28

In Which Ian Faces a new Challenge

By October, Beatrice has no doubt there's a certain distance between herself and Ian now. By email, Marie-Edith has told her about his up-coming trip to Paris and Beatrice wants to speak to him before he goes.

Passing him in the corridor, she says, 'DC Stanton, a word in my office please.'

They sit down either side of her desk. Ian is all right about calling her Inspector but refuses to call her ma'am, whether it's pronounced like ham or harm.

'So the jungle drums say you are off to Paris for a few days?'

'Yes, on Saturday, for nearly a week.'

'Now, about Marie-Edith, are you two going to get together on a more full-time basis?' Beatrice drums her fingers on the table, something she always does when expecting a proper answer to a nosy question.

'Is this an official police interview?' he asks.

'No, it's more serious than that – it's me being nosy.'

'Anyway, not sure. I could never get a job in France, and would she want to live here?'

'Her English is good enough to get a job here. She's never lived or worked anywhere other than in Paris and

Orléans so she probably wouldn't mind living here. A new adventure and all that, and Paris is not so far.'

'Thing is, you know what an insular, grumpy old sod I am. I've never spent a lot of time with one person before.'

'You are not old, you're not grumpy, usually; you're not a sod, usually; you can even be good company and amusing and if I hear you talking like that again, you are going to get a good thump, and I'll write it up as departmental discipline. You get on really well with Marie-Edith and you'll soon get use to her being around.'

'You could be right. I've got to meet the parents this time too – scary. Give me a violent criminal any time.'

'Good luck then and give Marie-Edith a big hug from me.'

'Sure, bye.'

Marie-Edith meets Ian at the airport and they return to Paris on the train. Ian talks to her quietly, 'When we get back, I am going to be absolutely animal with you. Don't give me any of this "respect my body" stuff. You can do that tomorrow if you like. Today you will have to grit your teeth and think of France. The only words you are allowed are "Yes and More".'

'How about harder, am I allowed to say harder.

'That's a good one; keep shouting "Plus dur". And then you can be in charge for the rest of the week.'

'All right, I'll accept all of that on one condition.'
'Go on.'
'That we can photograph and film it all.'
'You mean us hard at it in the bedroom?'

'Yes. I only see you every two months and I want more than just fading memories.'

'All right, my little kinky hussy, we'll film it.'

After a good hard session of physical devotion, they're lounging on the sofa looking at the movie results on Marie-Edith's little camera.

'Well it's atmospheric and full of action,' says Ian.

'I didn't realise I made all that noise.'

'Well don't change. I love all those sound effects and the way you kick your legs when you come. It's what you wanted then?'

'I'll play it every night when you aren't here.'

Soon after, while they're drinking tea, Marie-Edith asks, 'What about the third test; you know, of the five tests to be a perfect woman I have to pass?'

'Oh you passed that long ago, when I first met you.'

'What is it then?'

'Intelligence. The perfect woman has got to be intelligent. Glamorous looks are all very well, but if she's as thick as a brick, that soon gets boring. You are certainly not boring and I don't mind if you are more intelligent than me, although you'll probably have to learn how to make better marmalade. And custard, can you make proper egg custard?'

'I don't even know what that is.'

'This is not going well. I'll tell you later.'

She tickles him. 'So that's three down and two to go. What's number four?'

'All in good time. Don't harass the judge and jury.

★

After two days, they are off to Orléans.

'I had better warn you Marie-Edith, I can be very good with mothers, even in a foreign language.'

'You've met the mothers of lots of your lovers have you?'

'Oh yes, dozens.'

'Why haven't you married any of them then?'

'The mothers always felt their dear little daughters just weren't good enough for me.'

Marie-Edith laughs as she gives him a little dig with her elbow. 'Foolish boy, but you could be in trouble here?'

'Why's that?'

'Well my parents have bought me a new bed.'

'Meaning?'

'You see, I've always had a single bed at home and now they have bought me a double, so we can share a room. I had no idea my parents could be so open-minded.

'So they want us to share a bed, like a married couple. They're getting impatient to get you married aren't they?'

'Yes. They were always very protective of me in the past, now they're probably getting desperate. They think I'm getting too close to that left-over age.'

'I don't know how old you are but you're still young and healthy to me.'

'I'm nearly as old as you.'

'As bad as that is it? Checking up police records, ay? So you're thirty?'

'Twenty nine next March.'

'And they want to hear the sound of little baby feet.'

'That's it. This could be your most dangerous assignment ever.'

'Or I could get on the next plane home.'

'And miss out on all that unlimited sex I can give you?'

'Good point.'

Her parents turn out to be delightful and the trip is much more casual and easier than Ian had expected. The huge bunch of flowers Ian takes for her mother doubtless gets him off to a good start. Marie-Edith retaliates by complaining, '*He never buys me flowers like that,*' standing with her fists on her hips, scowling at him, much to the amusement of her father. She has to translate this for Ian who simply shrugs his shoulders, French style, and smiles.

On their first night, lying in the new double bed, Marie-Edith says, 'This feels very strange, in bed with a man, with my parents next door. I certainly did not expect this.'

'It feels a good bed. At least it doesn't squeak,' Ian says which makes them both laugh softly. 'I suppose any fun and games we have will have to be very delicate.'

'You can go without tonight, in fact all the time we're here. I couldn't bear it if we left a mark on the sheets. What you can do is tell me the fourth quality a perfect woman needs to have.'

'All right. Good boobs.'

'What are boobs?'

'These things here.'

'Is that a crude word for them?'

'No, it's an acceptable word. There are many crude words but boobs is not one of them.'

'And I suppose they have to be large and bursting out of the blouse.'

'No not too large. They need to be full and a decent shape. Yours are ideal, with good firm nipples when you get excited and very tasty they are too.'

Marie-Edith puffs out a loud breath and looks at the ceiling as she says, 'What am I dealing with here? Well it's a relief I pass the fourth test,' she sighs with a hint of boredom.

'Don't get so high and mighty madam, you're a fine one to talk. Some of your antics have been a real surprise, very creative. I certainly don't want to know your past history.'

'I haven't had much of a past history. It's simply late night fantasies of a lonely and innocent girl.'

'Maybe you should be writing romantic novels – with a extra spicy touch.'

They've been there a day when Marie-Edith asks, 'Ian, can you ride a horse?'

'No, I've never been on a horse.'

'I am shocked. I thought you could be everything.'

'Except speak French.'

'Except speak French and ride a horse.'

'And fly a helicopter.'

'And fly a…. All right. Anyway, my mother and I go horse riding. Do you want to come along?'

'Of course, as long as I don't have to try and ride.'

'No, sit and look at the scenery.'

The stables are a few kilometres away, and both Marie-Edith and her mother have their favourite horses, as long as someone else isn't using them at the time. The stables are owned and run by Charlotte and her husband Sébastien and horses are their life.

It's a quiet morning at the stables with only a couple of the horses out for rides, but only Mrs Paul's horse is in his box. While horses are being prepared with bridles and saddles for Marie-Edith and her mother, there's a commotion in one of the other boxes.

'*What's wrong there, Charlotte?*' asks Marie-Edith.

'*We bought that mare a week ago. The daughter doesn't ride her much and her father decided to sell her. She was supposed to be so docile. Sometimes she just stands with her head in a corner, sometimes she makes a lot of noise and kicks the walls. Perhaps she'll settle down in a while.*'

Ian walks over to the box with the troubled mare. The top half of the door is open and he stands close to the opening. He simply stands there and watches the horse. After a minute, the mare is making less braying noise and stops the kicking. Another minute and she puts her head to the open door, then puts her head through the door and moves closer to Ian. Gently he strokes her head and talks to her quietly.

Charlotte looks with surprise to Marie-Edith.

Ian turns to them and says, 'She's missing her friend.'

Charlotte speaks English so understands him, although she replies in French. '*She doesn't have a horse friend. She was the only horse there; there was only a . .*

. . there was only a donkey. The donkey!'

Charlotte looks from Marie-Edith to the mare. *'Oh dear. You go, I must talk to Sébastien.'* She hurries back into the house.

The two women go for their ride for half an hour, while Ian is quite happy to lie on the grass and watch the clouds pass across the blue sky. A couple of times he follows a sky lark rising and singing. It becomes a smaller and smaller dot then suddenly starts tumbling down towards the ground, to begin the cycle once more.

With the ride over and the horses back in their stables, Marie-Edith approaches him. 'Charlotte is trying to arrange to bring the donkey here to see if it makes a difference, then the owners are prepared to sell her.' She stands with her hands on her hips looking down at Ian. 'So if it's not criminals, it's horses.'

'Well, she's lonely and frightened. Poor little horse.'

'And you've spooked my mother. She doesn't know whether to admire you or be scared of you. Are you Saint or Satan?'

'Maybe I'm a saintly satan or perhaps a satanic saint, or even a satanic satan, or...'

'Stop it,' as she gives him a slight push with her foot. 'Come on, we're going to a café in town.'

That evening, they are sitting around after dinner when Mr Paul hands around a box of chocolates. Ian looks at Marie-Edith and says, 'I'm sure these are going to be good.' They are all wrapped in silver or gold foil. He takes one and savours it slowly, as he rolls the foil into a small ball. He takes Marie-Edith's piece of foil and adds it to his ball of foil. The chocolates are passed around again and Ian collects all the foil and finishes with two small balls of foil. The others watch him.

Ian has seen the cat sitting quietly to one side. The cat is a light cream colour with medium length fur and is called "Frou Frou". Ian notices they're all looking at him. He gets out of his chair, crouches down on the carpet about two metres away from the cat. Frou Frou watches him. Ian flicks one of the balls of foil towards the cat, who sticks out a paw and blocks the ball, just like a goalkeeper.

The cat crouches low down and starts wiggling her bottom as she gets ready for the next ball. Ian flicks the second ball and the cat springs up into the air, twists round and still manages to bat the ball back to him. The Paul family laugh and give mild cheers. Ian collects the two balls and flicks them again at the cat. One of the balls rolls passed Frou Frou and Ian says, 'Goal!' She starts to take the game seriously and keeps blocking and flicking the balls back to Ian. After a few minutes, the cat stops playing, obviously had enough of that, and as soon as Ian sits down, she jumps on his lap and lets Ian stroke her. Ian leans down to the cat and says, 'What's that? What not at all? For three weeks?'

He turns to Marie-Edith. 'Poor little puss hasn't been fed to three weeks!'

Marie-Edith laughs and translates for her parents, causing more laughter. Ian wraps his arms around Frou Frou, giving her a cuddle and scowls at the three of them. Frou Frou settles down and makes herself comfortable with Ian stroking her back.

'Well, you've certainly made a new friend there,' says Marie-Edith. 'That's horses and cats in one day; any more animals you can talk to?'

'I'm very good with goldfish and I've had a few encounters with dogs but that's too long a story for now.'

The following morning, while still lying in bed, Ian says, 'Why don't we have a very quiet and gentle romp before we get dressed, then we won't leave any evidence?'

'What a wicked idea. No licking or I'm certain to make too much noise.'

'No, it will just be a bit of quick basic sex. Your mother isn't likely to come in is she?'

'No. Come on. No build up. Let's just do it,' she says. It's certainly the quickest they've had and they get dressed immediately afterwards.

'A bit of extra tension added to the excitement, didn't it?'

Marie-Edith laughs. 'I think it took less than 20 seconds for us both to finish.'

'Well I'm sure we can beat that record some time,' and Ian laughs as well.

'I don't want to do it quicker.'

'More quickly.'

'That as well.'

A day later, Marie-Edith and Ian are just about to leave for the station to return to Paris when Charlotte of the stables rings Mrs Paul. They had brought the donkey to the stables and once together the donkey and the mare immediately started rubbing noses and holding their heads next to each other, like a pair of long-lost friends. The owners of the donkey made the most of the situation and charged more than double the normal price for the animal.

Time passes . . . . a busy time back in Bristol with more petty crime. Christmas approaching, crowded shops, crowded streets, good for shoplifters, old-fashioned pick-pockets, and mobile and bag snatchers.

29

IN WHICH EVERYONE GOES TO THE CONCERT

The band of Joe, Sarah, Ian, Jake and Petra have been meeting and practicing regularly under the musical control of Joe. Aiming for the next police Christmas concert, she has a new repertoire for them. She wants to start off with a revamped version of the old Chris Farlowe "Out of Time" hit – an upbeat number to get things going. Joe has added extra lyrics and modified the music to bring in all their instruments.

The next two numbers, Joe has written. The second piece she calls "Expanding Snowflakes" is more classical in style. The trumpet starts, followed by the drums getting louder, then the harp with several repeats, then the violin with the full 20 violin version. This gives Sarah plenty of time to do some of her gentle wiggles and body moves, which she has developed well. When the vocals come in, there's scope for her full range.

The third piece is more rock-based and at a faster pace. Joe titles it "Fast Moving Clouds", but the unusual combination of instruments make it unique. As is their style, the pieces merge into each other, meaning there won't be an opportunity for an audience reaction and applause until the end. Like on previous occasions, Joe wants them to make a recording and get a fully polished result.

Beatrice and Ian are having a rather rare talk on a street bench near the station.

'Is Marie-Edith coming over soon?' she asks.

'In a couple of weeks. Of course she went home for Christmas.'

'You see what a difference that suit made? Now you have Marie-Edith.'

'You mean she wouldn't even have noticed me but of this suit?'

'Yep. Not a chance.'

'Bitch. What a truly wonderful therapist you would make.'

Beatrice laughs. 'You're doubtless right, but admit it was money well spent.'

'Yes, she's worth every penny. And the Commissaire was impressed so it helped us catch that killer. Marie-Edith will be here for the concert, and at her parent's for Christmas.'

'All these passionate tête-à-têtes with Marie-Edith are becoming regular. Are they soon going to be more permanent?'

'I suppose permanent means I'll have to buy her a ring, marriage and all that stuff.'

'That's right and let her choose the ring.'

'You mean I have to let her go into a jewellery shop with a blank cheque?'

'No, go with her of course and give her some sort of limit to work to, and if you're lucky you might get some change.'

'Oh well, I dare say having sex with Marie-Edith on a regular basis will be worth a few hundred pounds.'

'That is the sort of joke men should keep among men. Say that to Marie-Edith and you could end up being seriously dead. In fact, I could use that to blackmail you if the need arises.' They both have a good laugh.

'Were you born bossy or did you have to practise?'

'Years of dedicated training.' After a brief silence, she asks, 'Has your mother met her yet?'

'No, not yet.'

'Well it's about time she did. She only lives six miles away now. Warn her first. If the pair of you just turn up suddenly and your mother can't give her a proper tea, she won't be pleased. And you could bring your mother to the concert.'

'Right.'

'So make sure you give your mum a call.

'Yes all right, stop nagging.'

'Say, yes boss.'

'Yes boss.'

'Good.'

'Do you treat Leo like this?'

'No, much worse. He has to call me Boudicca.' More laughter.

Beatrice doesn't say as much, but she's sure once his mother meets Marie-Edith, she'll be looking forward to grandchildren, and Ian won't have a chance. And this is the friendliest chat she has had with Ian for a long time.

'Meanwhile, what have you got on this morning?'

'Supposed to be going out with the Sergeant but he's got a dental emergency; that'll be this afternoon now.

So I'm a bit slack for a couple of hours.'

'Good, then you could come with me to ask a few questions. I'll clear it with your DI. Come on; I'll explain on the way. I hear you're getting good at domestic violence interviews.'

When Ian and Beatrice knock on the front door, it's soon opened by a woman in her early thirties. She looks stern and is dressed all in black – black leggings, long black jumper with a high neck and small black boots with silver metal fittings. With one hand on the door and the other on her hip, she gives an abrupt, 'Hello, yes.'

Ian is quick to speak first and says, Detective Inspector Walker and Detective Constable Stanton to see Zara Bryce.' He flashes his card briefly.

'It's Mizz Bryce and that's me. Come in.'

As she steps back and opens the door further, Ian gives the smallest of winks to Beatrice. She knows he's up to something.

In her office she says, 'Sit yer down,' in the same brusque manner.

Ian does the talking. 'You reported a case of domestic abuse.'

'That's right Inspector. My sister. She used to be very like me, now she's become weak, submissive, timid and extremely nervous. She had a bit of a whirlwind marriage. Her husband is all charm and too much smarm when you meet him and when you're all together, but once alone with her he's just a traditional bully. He ridicules and humiliates her, says how useless and pathetic she is.'

'How do you know? You've seen this yourself have you?'

'No, he's far too clever than that. She's told me in her more unguarded moments and I've seen the result with the changes in her. She's no self-esteem left and thinks she's worthless.'

'Mental and psychological abuse is a criminal offence and surprisingly common but can be difficult to prove. It's easy for outsiders to say, "Oh you are too sensitive – it's only banter".'

'And he's taking all her money. We were left quite well off when our father died. My share helped me set up my business, and Mary put her money into a better house and secure investments. He persuaded her to make all assets joint access, and he's been spending freely on big toys, gambling and other women.'

'Is there any physical abuse and violence?'

'He never leaves a mark that you could see, but he forces her to have sex. She's not interested any more and has too much depression, but he forces her any time and anywhere he fancies.'

'That might be easier to bring charges against. Any chance she'll make a complaint?'

'I keep nagging her over it, but she's too scared and timid now.'

'Has she got a job?' asks Ian.

'Yes, a good job, quite demanding, but one of the people there told me she isn't coping too well these days, and they might let her go or move her to something more routine.'

Beatrice speaks for the first time. 'Any chance she

could come and live with you to get her away from him?'

'Ah, the Constable is allowed to speak is she?' says Mizz Bryce with a sarcastic tone.

Ian replies, 'The Constable's been doing all the talking so far,' and nodding in Beatrice's direction continues, 'and the Inspector is allowed to speak as well.'

Mizz Bryce freezes with her mouth open. 'You mean you're the Inspector?'

'That's it; I'm Inspector Walker and this is Constable Stanton,' says Beatrice. 'Why should you assume the man was the Inspector?' she continues.

'Oh my god, I'm mortified, but that's the impression you gave.'

'I don't think so, but certain assumptions can be inbred,' says Ian.'

'Very funny, and you let me dig myself further into that hole?'

'Modern psychological interview techniques can be very devious,' says Ian with a smirk.

'If I pay you a million pounds will you promise not to tell anyone?'

'We are not allowed to accept bribes or gifts and I think you've suffered enough,' says Beatrice.

'Would that be a million pounds each?' Ian asks.

Beatrice gives him a mild slap on the arm with the back of her hand.

'Police as comedians now. Are you two married or lovers?'

'The last person to make such a suggestion is now doing three years.'

'Back to business. As Constable Stanton says, these

matters can be difficult to prove, but it must be stopped before something more serious happens. An effective way can be to make sound recordings of all the goings-on in the house. We couldn't do it, not without legal permission and for that we would need more proof of a crime, but I'm sure you could do it. Interested?'

'Definitely, how?'

'I'll give you two names. Both these companies can install secret listening devices. Don't bother with cameras; they're easier to find. Two or three bugs and the sound will be recorded at the firm's mission control. You'll need to convince them it's legitimate. Enough evidence of physical and mental abuse and we can prosecute. If she's forced to have sex, that is rape, even by a husband.' Beatrice hands her a small sheet of paper bearing the company names.

'Best not to tell your sister. It'll be too easy for her to slip up and give the game away,' says Ian.

'It's all rather underhand, but it's for her own good, as the saying goes.'

'It might save her life. And it's not uncommon for a woman to snap and she ends up doing the killing,' says Beatrice. 'Here's my number; keep me informed, often.'

On the way back to the car, Beatrice wants to laugh but in her position feels it's more appropriate to give Ian a frosty look.

'You and your fun and games, pulling that trick on her, on such a serious matter too.'

'Well, serves her right, a woman like her assuming the man to be the boss. It's a lesson she'll never forget. Lovers indeed. I think I let her off lightly.'

'I've often wondered what you'd be like as a lover.'

'Tramp!'

Now she laughs.

When Ian sees his mother next, he says how he'd like to bring Marie-Edith round for a visit.

'She's French and speaks excellent English so you won't have to shout or speak slowly, just speak normally. Let me write her name down for you.'

His mother asks various questions and appears to take it calmly. In fact she's very excited, not having met one of Ian's girlfriends for a long time. Her thoughts are already jumping forward to engagement, marriage, children and the rest.

When Ian turns up with Marie-Edith, his mother lays on a grand tea with all the trimmings. Marie-Edith is warm smiles and charm and with her delightful French accent, she's a great success. That's reinforced as they are leaving when Marie-Edith says goodbye the French way with a hug and two kisses.

Ian says, 'I'll send a taxi to bring you to the concert.'

'And I'll come in the taxi to take you there,' offers Marie-Edith.

In the car on the way home, Ian says, 'I've really had it now haven't I?'

'You certainly have mon pote' says Marie-Edith and she doubles up with laughter.

After they've gone, Mrs Stanton sits in her favourite chair with the cat on her lap and has a happy little weep.

★

With everyone taking their seats for the concert, Marie-Edith sits with Beatrice on her left and Mrs Stanton on her right. Beatrice says quietly to Marie-Edith, 'How do you get on with his mother?'

'Very well I think. Do you know what her first name is?' Beatrice shakes her head.

'Edith.'

'No! He is doomed.'

'Sad isn't it?'

Beatrice turns to Leo and whispers, 'Ian's mother, her first name is Edith.'

'Gosh, I wouldn't want you two as enemies.'

Marie-Edith has only heard a little practice playing by Ian and never the electric harp at its best, while his mother hasn't heard any of his playing for many years. Only Beatrice and Leo know what to expect and even they haven't seen the Baroque trumpet player and the new drummer.

As the curtains open to the band, the trumpet player has already started with the drums soon after. There's applause and some cheers, while Beatrice puts fingers in her mouth and gives a couple of loud whistles.

Marie-Edith's eyes are immediately drawn to Sarah rolling her body around. Sarah now feels the green leather suit is very much part of her, matched with the black boots, black leather gloves, the red wig and strong outlandish make-up. Green, black and white are still the bands theme colours. Marie-Edith is wide-eyed and open-mouthed.

'*Who's that woman in green leather?*' she asks Beatrice in French.

'Oh it's all right, she's only the band's groupie.'

'What? She's wicked hot.'

Beatrice gives a huge grin and nods.

'I'll kill her, and him.' She bears her grinding teeth.

Beatrice laughs and says, *'No – she and the violin player are partners.'*

Marie-Edith nudges her with her elbow for teasing.

'That's what they say. I'll kill her anyway just to be sure.'

The harp soon joins in with a strong electric blast followed by a full compliment of strings. Then Sarah's strong voice comes in over everything. At one point while the band is playing, Marie-Edith smiles at Mrs Stanton and holds her hand. Mrs Stanton is just about in tears while Ian and the others play.

After their set and once off stage, the five of them put their arms around each other's shoulders as a tight little group. They are feeling excited and their breathing is fairly heavy. Sarah is the first to speak. 'That was so exciting. Where are the bubbles? Then I'll need sex. All of you please, one at a time, any order.' They laugh as Jake says, 'I'll start with the bubbles,' while reaching for the sparkly wine.

With the end of the concert, all the performers walk around among the audience. As a loose group, the five musicians approach Beatrice and the others. Sarah, who's already managed a few glasses of champagne, puts her arm around Ian's shoulders and says, 'Is this your new squeeze Ian?'

'This is Marie-Edith and this is Sarah and she's an absolute demon.'

'Ian please, I'm much worse than that. She looks far too good for you.'

'You're probably right.'

Then Sarah goes all sexy and slides up to Marie-Edith. 'Would you like to stroke my leather, darling?'

Marie-Edith keeps a straight face, but runs her hand all the way down Sarah's back and squeezes her bottom hard. Sarah jumps, gives a little squeak of surprise and starts laughing. 'Oh, she's fun, I like her. Want to be my bitch? Ian can have Joe.'

Ian gently pulls Sarah away from Marie-Edith and says, 'That'll do; go and get some more champagne before Joe stabs all of us in the back.'

Sarah smacks a big kiss on Ian's cheek, leaving a lipstick smudge, gives a bright smile to Marie-Edith and Beatrice and walks away.

'Is she actually a police officer?' asks Marie-Edith with a sceptical tone in her voice.

'No. A support worker, and you know how crazy they are.'

'Certainly. With singing like that she can get away with most things but you can wipe that lipstick off your face if you like,' suggests Marie-Edith. 'Ian, what is a squeeze?'

'I've no idea; ask Beatrice. I'm going to change; won't be a minute.'

And now all of them are ready for something to eat.

Time drives super fast . . . . .

30

In Which Wheels roll Faster

Chief Superintendent Wesley is in his office and talking with Inspector Baxter.

'Next Thursday, it's going to be the anniversary of the shopping mall atrocity. A lot of our officers were involved in the aftermath of that, including yourself, weren't you?'

'Yes sir, one of the first on the scene, after the shooting had stopped.'

'There'll be a lot of talk about it and a lot of bad memories. There's going to be a service inside the centre, and we're sending a few officers to represent the station, only if they want to go of course. I'll have a word with DC Stanton. He might want to avoid the day altogether.'

'Surely he should be there more than anyone?'

'Unlikely – too much horror.'

'He should be able to cope sir; it's all part of the job.'

'Having a machine gun fight with three terrorists among a lot of dead bodies is not a routine event for most police officers. There are limits and I think you are being rather insensitive. Anyway, I'll leave the decision up to Stanton, but you'll probably be without him for the day. Thank you Inspector.'

Next, the Superintendent talks with DC Stanton.

'What are your feelings about Thursday, Stanton?'

'I'd like to avoid everything about it sir.'

'That's understandable; take the day off. Go out, visit friends, family whatever, do something interesting. Do you want to be your own or would you be better with people?

'Not sure. I'll need some distraction and avoid radio and TV, and all shopping centres.'

'All right, take it easy. If you need someone to talk to, don't forget the doctor. He's much more than a pills and injections man.'

An hour later, Ian passes Beatrice in the corridor.

'What you doing Thursday?' she asks. Ian shrugs.

'Well, there are certain things you need to avoid and you shouldn't be on your own with the risk of moping. How about if we go out for the day. Leo's just bought a new Jaguar F-Type in orange and it's Awesome. We could go in that?'

'Leo let's you drive his new Jaguar?'

'You see this thumb?' She holds out her thumb with it pointing down.

'I get it. Where shall we go?'

'Pembrokeshire coast. I've never been and it's a decent drive. Bring some chocolate biscuits will you.'

'Right you are.'

'I'll pick you up at nine.'

They both know the other will turn up on time, and as Ian steps on to the pavement at one minute to nine, Beatrice drives up.

'Morning.'

'Morning.'

While Ian is in smart casual, Beatrice wears a black jacket, tight black trousers and black shoes. Under the jacket is a scarlet pullover and she has scarlet lipstick with her hair long in good waves.

Ian looks her up and down. 'You look ...'

'What? I look what!?'

'You look the business and the part. I've never seen you wear scarlet lipstick before.'

They drive off straight away and Beatrice says, 'Think I look tarty enough?'

'Not a chance; that would be impossible.'

'Leo never pays me compliments the way you do.'

'Well he's your husband, I'm a bachelor, that makes a difference.'

'So why doesn't a married man pay compliments, to his wife I mean, not his mistress?'

'Perhaps he takes her for granted like a familiar old slipper.'

'So if you were married, you wouldn't pay your wife any compliments?'

'Well of course I would, but I'm sooooooo perfect.'

'Huh,' is Beatrice's only response to that.

'Are you wearing stilettos?'

'Not today; half heels.'

'Beautiful seats in this car; in fact beautiful everything,' says Ian.

As soon as they are clear of the bridge over the River Avon and there's an empty bit of road, Beatrice puts her foot down. In a few seconds they are doing over 140mph. 'Ah, that's better,' she says.

'Is this day out for my benefit or yours?'

'Ever the detective. Tell Leo I didn't go above 55 will you. If Leo were the passenger, he'd be biting his finger nails as soon as I turned the key, but you'll be all right. You might get worried about your life but you won't fret about the car and the car is the important thing, of course.'

'Indubitably. I hope you've got your warrant card with you. If we get stopped by the Bill, your smiles might not be enough.'

'But we are on an undercover operation to intercept an international drugs gang on the coast.'

'Of course, just the two of us.'

Beatrice has taken police advanced driving courses and can handle a car at speed very well. At times, she has to slow up drastically for traffic, but at the first opportunity it's heavy-on-the-pedal time.

'We'll get past the end of the M4, then stop for elevenses at some roadside coffee stop and bloat out on the chockies,' she says.

'Lunch in a country pub and tea in a quaint tea shop?'

'Perfect. Let's have some sounds. In there.'

'What do you want?'

'Loud and fast.'

'Bat out of Hell?'

'Fine.'

'You old rock queen.' Ian inserts the CD and presses Go, and Beatrice starts singing along with it.

Once they leave the M4 and travel on the A48, they stop at the first available roadside snack vehicle, where the site of a car like this and a beauty like Beatrice getting out of it are more than a little unusual among the lorries, vans and shabbily dressed drivers.

Ian returns from the refreshment van with two coffees to find Beatrice leaning against the car.

'There were certain comments and questions from the men there.'

'And what yarns did you spin them?'

'I said I bought you this car for your birthday.'

'As my husband or as my lover on a Thursday?'

'I left that one floating in the imagination, but when they asked if you're model or an actress, I told them you're a Chief Inspector in the police and that you have taken the police courses for high speed driving.   Now they are really scared of you.'

'You are so good to me. But I won't accept that post of DCI until you accept being an Inspector at least.'

'Have another biscuit and change the subject.'

'Where's our final destination going to be Mr Navigator?' Beatrice asks.

Ian opens the atlas on the roof of the car. 'If we aim to go all the way to the end peninsular, we'll never have time to get out of the car. I suggest we go to Tenby, mooch around there and find a pub for lunch. Then drive along towards Pembroke through a decent bit of countryside and find the sea and a beach.'

'Sounds good.'

'And of course if you let me drive then you can have a few glasses of wine somewhere.'

'I shall keep a stony silence at that remark,' says Beatrice with a smile.

With coffee finished, Ian takes her cup and goes back

to the passenger's seat. Beatrice is about to open her door when she looks towards to refreshment's vehicle with several drivers near it all looking at her. She raises her arms above her head and does a big snaky ripple with her body, giving rise to loud whistles and cheers from the audience. Once in the car, Ian simply shakes his head at her.

Beatrice looks at Ian and says, 'Perhaps I *am* just a tart really.' She screws up her face in a large cheeky grin, puts the car into Drive mode and pulls away at top speed.

The reaction at the coffee stop is repeated at the pub they visit, with the sight of Beatrice sliding out of such an eye-catching car providing a bonus to anyone looking out of the pub's window.

While Ian is getting drinks and the lunch menus, a young man propping up the bar says to him, 'Is that your wife there?'

'Yes.'

'She's beautiful.'

'Mmm, yes I suppose she is really. If I didn't have 16 million in the bank she'd probably leave me.'

Ian repeats the story to Beatrice. She gives him a frosty look, pauses, then says in a loud voice, 'You told me it was 30 million.'

'Calm down wench – you'll get us thrown out.'

'Then buy the pub and sack the staff.' She gives a lively smile to the young man at the bar, which brightens his day.

'Now that you've been boasting about being worth

16 million, it means you have no choice but to pay for the lunch.'

'Well of course I would have done that anyway, boss.'

The drive towards Pembroke leads them to the coast and sandy beaches. A quiet half hour is spent with bare feet on the sand and paddling in the extremely cold sea.

'Is this invigorating or foolishly giving us frostbite?' Beatrice asks.

'Both. Let's get back to the car and turn the heater on full blast.'

Taking someone else's fancy new car along all the narrow country lanes seemed too much of a risk, so it's a short drive to the country tea-room they saw earlier. The weather is sunny enough to sit outside, some of the passers-by being unsure which to look at more, the car or Beatrice.

When into his fourth Welsh scone and cream, Ian tries a second time; 'It's my turn to drive the Jag on the way back is it?'

'Afraid not. I think Leo had a mild heart attack letting me drive it; a second attack would finish him off.'

'Then you could drive it all the time, ho-ho.'

'What a good scheme,' and more laughter.

They arrive back at Ian's place in the early evening.

'Thank you, Beatrice, it's been wonderful and a much better day than I'd feared.' He squeezes her hand on the gear lever.

'You're welcome. I've enjoyed it too. I'll probably find Leo anxiously looking out of the window when I get home.'

'Will he be more concerned about the car than you?'

'Doubtless. Bye.'

Ian sits quietly looking at nothing in particular for a while, then decides to play some gentle harp music. He's only just started when the phone rings; it's Marie-Edith calling from France. She doesn't mention what day it is but of course she knows; it's just a friendly call.

A week later, Sarah is sitting in Ian's living room, feeling upset and sniffing a lot. 'She told me to get out, she was horrible to me. Says she's been seeing this other woman for a while, just as I knew all along really. Someone from work. I reckon it's been coming a long time. She's only waited this long because she wanted to do the Christmas show. The rotten slag.'

'You're lucky then.'

'Please don't say it means there is somebody better waiting for me.'

'Yes I will. Somebody who'll treat you properly. Man or woman who knows.'

'I suppose I've done more than enough skivvying for Joe.'

'There you are then; you can do better than that.'

'With a bit of luck her new tart will be a rotten cook. Joe can't cook. I've saved lots, so maybe I could buy something. You know, I can still remember how exciting it was having sex with you. You wouldn't like to dump your French frilly bit would you and look after me?'

'No I don't think so.'

'Oh don't be so boring; she's 200 miles away.'

'No she's not. Not in my mind, she isn't.'

'If I had known you were going to be frolicking and fornicating with a fancy French floozy I would have got myself pregnant the last time we had sex. Now you're with Marie-Edith I suppose we'll never have that baby.'

'No dear, you have a baby with someone else.'

'What has she got I haven't?'

'A delicious French accent.'

'Is that all?'

'All I'm going to say. It's not a suitable subject for comparison.'

'Have you had her on all fours yet?'

'We've done it in 23 different positions and now we're starting from the beginning again.'

'Dog!'

Sarah slouches back in the easy chair, pouting and sulking for a while.

'You can find someone much more suitable than me and you're going to be so much better off without Joe. She hasn't been good for you for a long time.'

'I never did have a copy of that photo you took of me; too scared of Joe finding it. And you never made me that stone plaque saying I am hot, juicy, sexy and great to fuck.'

'Well you can't have them now – you might blackmail me with them.'

'Too right.'

'For your singing, you could join a choir. There must be several in Bristol and singing among lots of others won't be scary and who knows whom you might meet. And wear some brighter clothes. You know no-one at work realises it was you on that stage. They're supposed to be investigators and detectives and nobody's worked it out. How about if you tried this. Now you've let your hair grow, dye it the colour of the wig and go in wearing that green leather jacket.'

'I could wear the whole outfit, the strides, boots, wig, make-up, the lot.'

'That might get you called into the manager's office, but it could be plan B. Start off with the green leather jacket, the boots, black tights, a short skirt and everyday make-up. You will get offers. Then you can work your way through them and pick the best.'

'You think that'll work.'

'You bet. You're very good natured, when you aren't being grumpy, like now. Good company, good in the kitchen and I'm sure you can keep anybody happy in the bedroom. Men and women saw how sexy you looked on stage.'

Two days later day, Sarah decides to be a little bold. She wears the green jacket, zipped all the way up the front, black tights, a short black skirt and the black boots. She's also wearing false nails painted a bright green to match the jacket. People start to notice. During the morning she finds an excuse to go into the general office where Ian is. She walks up to his desk and drops a folded sheet of paper in front of him. On it is written "This is just an excuse". She winks at him and walks away with everyone watching her. When she gets to the door, Ian calls out, 'Sarah'. She turns round. 'Give us a wiggle.'

She takes her glasses off, extends her arms and with a big smile she wiggles her hips as she did in the performance. Then she turns quickly and disappears. The others in the office look at each other, and one of them addresses Ian, pointing to the empty doorway.

'Err, was that...like at the concert...er...with you...er singing.'

'Yes that's her – Sarah Miller. Careful Peter, she's completely lethal. But someone could die happy being with her.'

'You survived then did you?'

'No, she spat me out for being inadequate.' The others laugh.

Time Struggles . . . . .

31

In Which a Tension Mounts

It's late February and certainly cold enough to make most people irritable. An evening raid is planned on a warehouse which, after careful surveillance, is known to be an important part of a counterfeit operation, dealing in high-end fashion clothes with designer labels and expensive but fake perfumes. It is timed to begin at 6.15, the same time as a raid is made on a house connected with the crime.

For the warehouse, the Chief Inspector is in charge and waiting with six uniformed officers. It should be more but there's a clash with a large football game. To add to the numbers, there are DI Walker with DC Collins and DS Melrose with DC Stanton.

Melrose and Stanton pull up near the building at 6.10, expecting the call to start the raid. By 6.20, nothing is happening. Ian has been feeling fairly short tempered for a few weeks.

'What's going on Sergeant?' Ian asks in an abrupt manner.

'Don't know. We can't move until we get the call.'

'They'll see us here. They've got cameras around the building.'

Two minutes later, the call comes. Melrose and Stanton jump out to cover a small side door. The main group of officers bursts into the front. The side door opens suddenly and a man runs out but is quickly restrained. Inside the building, progress is quick, with three people held and goods seized. Prisoners are put into a prisoner van and confiscated goods in other vans. The four detectives and some uniform officers go round checking and collecting computers and mobile phones. Then they pick up items which have been dropped in the rush. Stanton picks up a few coats and is taking them down a corridor where Walker and Melrose are. Suddenly a man runs out of a room and down the next corridor.

'Where did he come from?' shouts Sergeant Melrose.

Ian looks round to see a man running away. Inspector Walker turns and is blocking his way.

'Take these. Move!' he shouts, and pushes the coats into Walker's arms and pushes her hard out of the way, causing her to fall against the wall.

'He's going for our car,' shouts Melrose.

The man runs out of a side door and towards the police car, jumping into the driver's seat, fumbling for an ignition key. Ian is a fast runner and soon reaches the car, just as the man is getting out of the seat with a knife in his hand. Ian grabs the man's wrist, pulls him forward and punches him hard in the face then throws him to the ground. Without being too gentle, he twists his arms behind his back and puts cuffs on him. By now, Sergeant Melrose has arrived.

'Steady on now Stanton.'

Ian is angry. 'Don't give me that,' and with both fists he punches the Sergeant on the shoulders, causing him to step back to maintain his balance. 'He wasn't coming at you with that knife,' and Ian kicks the knife with its long thin blade towards Melrose. 'You can put him in the wagon if you want.'

Just then, Inspector Walker approaches them.

'Look, Stanton, I know we've known each other a long time and all that, but maybe you could show rank a little respect some time.'

'I'm not with you – how do you mean?'

'Throwing those clothes at me, shouting and shoving me against the wall, then punching the Sergeant like that.'

'Ah, well pardon me I'm sure. There was a minor emergency on. What should I have said, "Excuse me Inspector, ma'am, I know you outrank me and are far more worthy in every aspect, but would you mind frightfully, awfully, terribly holding these coats for a moment, while I chase after that villain and risk my life restraining him." How's that sound?'

Beatrice bites the inside of her cheek trying not to raise a grin. 'Yes, that sounds about right. Just remember that little speech for next time will you.' She manages to keep a straight face until she's turned her back on him.

Ian calls after her, 'And maybe when you become Superintendent then you can assign me to the sewers,' and there's quite a lot of bitterness in his tone which Beatrice isn't use to. She slows her walk and realises maybe she was coming on a bit grand.

When everything has calmed down, Melrose and Stanton get back in their vehicle. The Sergeant says, 'I'm going to make sure you are on a disciplinary for that. Punching me, speaking in that manner, and your rudeness to Inspector Walker was a disgrace. You should consider yourself suspended already.'

'You haven't got the rank to do that. But it would be good; at least I can have an early night. You'll enjoy doing all the paperwork.'

'You've said far too much. Now shut up.' The Sergeant looks for the key in the ignition, then in his pockets. 'The key's gone; that character must have taken it.'

'Then why didn't he drive off? Ian pauses. 'He hasn't got the key; it's here.' Ian throws it on to the dashboard. 'You left it in the ignition when you jumped out and I took it. Basic theft prevention, don't you know.'

The Sergeant says nothing but is embarrassed, as he starts the engine and drives off.

Back at the station, 'Inspector Walker and I will be dealing with you first thing in the morning.'

Ian doesn't normally work with Walker and Melrose, so the following morning he goes to his own section and carries on as normal.

Sergeant Melrose enters Inspector Walker's office bristling and ready for action.

'What are we going to do about DC Stanton now, ma'am?'

'We, Sergeant?'

'His behaviour last night was a disgrace, and in effect he assaulted both of us, and used excessive force restraining that man.

'The man wielding the knife, you mean?'

'If anyone had behaved like that at my Dundee station he would be out on his ear on the spot.'

'Enough!'

'I am not the slightest bit interested in that sort of speculation nor do I like you telling me how to deal with the matter.'

'No – sorry ma'am.'

'How long have you been at this station Sergeant?'

'About six months.'

'Right. I want you to go on to the police website, do a search for DC Ian Stanton, read everything there, although many things will have been redacted, then come back and see me. Do it now.'

'Yes, ma'am.

The Sergeant returns ten minutes later.

'Was that what you expected?'

'No ma'am, not at all. It's quite amazing really.'

'As I said, many details are redacted, but I can assure you that his actions have saved dozens of lives, including that shopping centre massacre and that's under the Official Secrets Act. Also, one incident some years ago when two uniforms got a bit careless and found themselves in a trap. There was a Sergeant and a WPC. They were badly beaten and would definitely have been killed. Fortunately, Stanton was tipped off that something was wrong and charged in, against four men with guns. He saved the lives of those two officers. I was that WPC. Stanton's behaviour last night was inexcusable and out of character, but there is no way I am going to put him on a disciplinary for having such a tantrum. It needs to be dealt with some other way. I'll look into it now.'

'Yes ma'am.' The Sergeant turns to go. 'Just one point ma'am.' He hesitates. 'When the call came to go in, we jumped out of the car and, like an idiot, I left the key in the ignition. Stanton noticed and quickly put it in his pocket or that character might have driven off.'

'Well, that's him all over. Thank you Sergeant.'

When Sergeant Melrose has left the office, Beatrice makes a call to the police doctor. It's the next day before she can see the him. After filling him in on all the details of Ian's past record, she relates the events of a couple of days ago.

'The tabloids claimed they had inside information from the ministry and that it was off-duty male and female SAS soldiers who were in the shopping mall having a burger,' recalls the doctor.

'Typical garbage from them but good for Stanton; keeps him out of the picture.'

'It sounds like basic post-traumatic stress. That can happen straight away or might not show for months or even years. It might stop there; the chances are it will get worse unless something is done. Wasn't he offered counselling at the time?'

'I don't know. But you know what men are like, they'll brush things off and say they're fine.'.

'Yes, some people can distance themselves from it. Some bottle it up and suddenly the cork can pop. Well he'll need some counselling now. Do you have any influence there?'

'Possibly. There's a bit of distant between us these

days, me being a DI and him a DC. But apart from that, underneath it all we are pretty close.'

'Who's his Inspector?'

'Baxter.'

'Oh.'

'Quite.' Beatrice puts on a deep voice. "Let him man-up and get on with it like everybody else". I'll have a word with him anyway. After all, they were his detectives last night. The raid had to be brought forward. Baxter was policing at the football match so I stepped in.'

'He probably won't listen to you, or to me for that matter. I'll write a report to the Chief Superintendent and go and see him as well. Stanton shouldn't be put on any jobs with excessive trauma.

That evening, Beatrice calls on Ian at home. Ian opens the door to find her there in a smart woollen winter coat, colourful woolly hat, and attractively flushed cheeks from the cold.

As he opens the door, 'Ah hello, come in.'

Once inside the flat, he asks, 'What's up Inspector'.

'Hello Ian. It's not Inspector, it's Beatrice.'

'Okay.'

'Say it. Say hello Beatrice it's good to see you. Say it, unless you want a good smack.'

Ian smiles, 'You're such a romantic. Whatever you say boss. Hello Beatrice, it's good to see you.'

Beatrice laughs, puts an arm round him and kisses him on the cheek. 'Don't I get a cup of tea.'

Ian returns with a tray, teapot, mugs and a plate of profiteroles.

'Ah profiteroles. You know what these are don't you?'

'How do you mean?'

'These are hard core seduction. If a woman takes one, fine. Two, just about. Three and all virtue is lost.'

'I've never heard that before, but help yourself vixen.'

'Leo told me that. Mind you, he only told me after I'd eaten six of them.'

'A butterfly caught in a net.'

'I was happy to be caught in that net at least.'

Ian is sitting on the front edge of the settee and looking down to the ground.

'Beatrice . . . . I'm sorry about the other day. I lost it a bit. I don't know what's happening to me at the moment. I hardly sleep at night, for weeks now and I get such pains in my head. Then I get patches of nausea, and . . . and, well it's awful.'

Beatrice comes over, sits next to him and puts an arm around his shoulder, giving him a firm hug.

'Let's pour this tea shall we?'

As they start drinking their mugs of tea and nibbling at the cakes, Beatrice relates her conversation with the doctor.

'Ultimately Ian, treatment becomes compulsory otherwise there's the risk you can end up a less effective officer, or pensioned off through sickness.'

'What's this treatment involve then.'

'Mainly talking therapy, like CBT and maybe mild medication. It all seems to work pretty well. Healthy living helps. You know, good diet, plenty of exercise, so you are all right on that score. And you've got your music and Marie-Edith to keep you human.'

'All right, stick your needles in; do whatever you like. I'll see it as preventive medicine.'

'If you see the station doctor tomorrow, he can give you the low-down. It's known as trauma-focused cognitive behavioural therapy. It's all talking and can be fairly subtle stuff. I knew someone at Eversley Road who had to do it. This was after you left. She only had about eight or ten sessions and she was fine, back to normal duties.'

They sit quietly for a while, topping up the tea cups and finishing off the cakes. Then Ian says, 'You might have had the decency to come here in daylight so the neighbours can see me visited by a glamorous woman.'

'They'd probably think I was an escort come for an hour's business.'

'I wouldn't be able to afford your prices.'

'I give discounts on a Tuesday.'

'Today's Wednesday.'

'Bad luck.' Laugh and laughter.

Beatrice has a word with Inspector Baxter, and his response was just as she expected. He is macho and expects all his officers to pull their weight, whatever their rank and circumstances.

Time hits a buffer . . . . .

32

IN WHICH TRAUMA STRIKES

A few days later, Ian gets a call from Joe and she invites herself round for a chat.

'There's one of the lecturers at the music college I still see. She has contacts. Among them is someone who works on the Proms, finding orchestras and new players. As well as all the regular classical stuff, they are always looking for something new which still fits their format. Anyway, I gave her recordings of three of our tunes: "Staring at Water", "Fast Moving Clouds" and "Expanding Snowflakes". And they want us to do an audition.'

Ian hesitates and says very slowly, 'You want us to audition with the hope of performing at the Proms? Are you mad?'

'Possibly, but it would be amazing wouldn't it?'

'But surely the Proms is all about the best musicians in the world?'

'Yes, that's us,' and she laughs. 'As a group we perform much better than our individual parts. We can do this. I mean, Sarah is good but she could hardly compete with the pros on an opera stage, but with the rest of us once she gets the bug and a full head of steam, she's brilliant. And the rest of us are good enough when at our best.'

'How long would a performance like that last?'

'I'm not sure. It would probably be in an afternoon. We certainly wouldn't be a headline act, more a filler between to more well-known performers.'

'Worth thinking about then. Have you seen Sarah recently?'

'I saw her once at a club; I think it was the Queen Tavern. With some tall blond woman.'

'I was speaking to her the other day; I don't think there was anything in that. The new one is a bit of a hunk.'

'Is she indeed.'

'He, actually.'

'He? She's with a man?'

'Yes, someone from the station.'

'The traitor. She's meant to be true to the cause.'

'Why should you care? You didn't want her any more.'

'That's no reason for her to commit treason.'

'She's having a good time.'

'Have you fucked her?'

'No. I have my lovely French woman.'

'That wouldn't bother most people with a partner hundreds of miles away and you know what the French are like for affairs.'

'No, she knows I can read minds so she wouldn't dare.'

'Just check how sore her clit is next time you see her.'

'Joe, you are outrageous and if you want Sarah and me to join you in this, especially Sarah, you'll have to be less prickly. No bitchy comments to her about her man and no catty remarks about Marie-Edith.'

'I'll try. Trouble is being catty is in my DNA.'

'Then blame it on your parents and rise above it.'

Joe is silent for a while. 'I'll be good.' Joe looks both intense and tense. 'Ian, please. This Proms attempt is really important to me. Please, can we try?'

'So we're going to have to practice those three pieces are we?'

'At least twice a week together and we have until the end of April. What do you think Sarah will think about the audition?

'She'll have enough time to get use to the idea, and she's singing in a large choir now which helps. I'll give her a call and pump her with sparkly booze before I mention the Proms and an audition.'

'Fill her with bubbly booze and she'll certainly want fucking, if I remember,' and she laughs.

'She's got someone else to do that for her. Now stop it, witch. Actually that could be an angle. Sarah has never invited her parents to any of the shows, and I think she'd like too, but they aren't keen on you.'

'So now there isn't this abnormal freak queering the pitch, it might be all right?'

'That's probably the way they'll see it.'

'Especially if she is with a hunk of a man with a proper dick and her parents can start thinking about a normal marriage.'

'You do have a unique turn of phrase to sum up a situation Joe.'

'Okay, you could try that sales pitch then.'

'I'm sure Sarah's appearance on stage will severely shock her parents, although she might leave out her more outlandish make-up. With a performance in the Proms no doubt everything will be forgiven, even you.'

* * *

Two uniformed officers in a patrol car are called to a domestic disturbance – never popular with the police. The street is on a rather run-down council estate with semi-detached houses, old cars in the street and too much rubbish in many of the gardens. They pull up to the house to see the front door open. Approaching the gate, the woman next door is looking out of her front door and calls to them.

'I called you. Such goings-on there; shouting and screams and he run out and ran down the street that way.'

The officers are on their guard as they enter the house. From the hall they go into the main room and see the horror – blood on the walls and over the floor and a dead woman among the blood. Immediately they go back into the hall and call Control. Once that's dealt with, they take out their tasers and search the house, finding nobody else, alive or dead.

At this point, Ian has had only one of his therapy sessions. DS Knox and DC Stanton are dealing with some shoplifting nearby and get the call to go to the crime scene. They go just inside the door of the living room and see the carnage.

Sergeant Knox says, 'The Inspector and scene of crime are on the way, lets get out of here.' He turns back to the hall and sees Ian hasn't moved. 'Stanton,

Stanton come on.'

Ian still doesn't move. Knox goes back to him and sees his blank face just looking at the body. 'Ian, come on, we leave this for scene of crime.'

Ian still doesn't move. A moment later, he collapses and Knox manages to catch him. Dragging him in to the hall, he calls, 'Kelly, Kelly! Grab his legs.'

'What's happened?'

'Don't know, he just collapsed. Lay him down here. Call an ambulance.'

PC Kelly calls for the ambulance as Knox puts Ian in the recovery position. Ian's face is still blank but tears have started to run down his face and he begins trembling.

Kelly says, 'She wants to know his symptoms.'

Knox stands closer to Kelly and shouts at the phone. 'This is Sergeant Knox! It's an injured police officer. Send an ambulance NOW.'

Scene of crime officers turn up soon after and the ambulance arrives surprisingly quickly. It has left before Inspector Baxter drives up.

When a police officer is in hospital, the news soon gets around. All Beatrice hears is "Stanton's in the Royal. Don't know what happened." She's walking down a corridor to find out more and sees DC Manze. 'What's this about Stanton?'

'He's in the Royal.'

'Yes I know that much. Why? What happened?'

'He and Sergeant Knox went to a domestic in Greenbank. Dead wife, stabbed and throat cut, blood everywhere. Stanton saw it, froze and collapsed.'

'He wasn't supposed to go to trauma scenes.'

'I don't know anything about that ma'am.'

Beatrice goes straight to the hospital.

Ian is in a side room and a young woman doctor is looking at a chart as Beatrice walks in and introduces herself.

'He's on a sedative at the moment and the drip is for extra minerals and vitamins.'

Beatrice says, 'The police doctor will be here soon, perhaps we should wait till he arrives for details.'

'Fine. I'll be along the corridor somewhere.'

When the doctor has left the room, Beatrice touches Ian's face and sits down, waiting quietly. Ten minutes later the police doctor walks in and they simply nod to each other.

'What do you make of all this doctor? Will he be all right?'

'Yes I'm sure he will be. Let's go and get a cuppa, shall we?'

Once in the corridor, he says, 'We need to bear in mind that it's likely he can hear what we say in there.'

'But he's unconscious or sedated surely?'

'Yes but the brain is a clever and strange thing and it can still take things in, even in that state.'

'Is it like a nervous breakdown?'

'That's not a medical term and it's too general, because the condition can be complicated. But it'll do for now.'

They find the doctor Beatrice was speaking to earlier. 'You'll need to give me some background.'

They outline Ian's history and the recent events which triggered this condition.

'All right, he froze because of traumatic shock. I'll try and get in touch with the specialist doctor. Why don't you two go to the coffee bar downstairs and I'll come and find you shortly.'

When sitting with their brews, the doctor says, 'Human Resources called his mother and are sending a car for her. She should be here shortly. I know Ian isn't married but has he got girlfriend or partner?'

'Yes, she's French, Marie-Edith. We met her when we did an assignment in Paris last June. We had to track down a double murderer.'

'Successfully?'

'Yes. Marie-Edith is delightful and intelligent. She's a support assistant at their station.'

'And is it serious between these two?'

'Oh yes, Marie-Edith and I made sure of that.' They both laugh.

'If she can pay a visit soon, that would be a good tonic,' says the doctor.

'Look, if Mrs Stanton is going to be here shortly, I think I'll go to Ian's room and wait for her and leave you medical boffins to it.'

'Sure; I'll come and see you when we've finished.'

Back at the station later, Inspector Walker walks into Inspector Baxter's office without knocking. He's there with a couple of his officers. Beatrice has a severe expression and says, 'I've just seen Stanton. Well done Baxter. If there weren't any witnesses, I'd punch you in the face.' She looks for a moment, then walks out.

★

Ian stays a few days in hospital and is put on sick leave until further notice. Leaving hospital with a course of treatment planned, Ian goes to stay with his mother for a while.

A couple of days later, Beatrice turns up for a visit. Mrs Stanton is glad to see her again, being a big fan of Beatrice's elegance and charm and she knows Ian has such a good ally at the station. While Edith Stanton is in the kitchen, Beatrice stays in the living room and says to Ian, 'Well this is luxury isn't it. Just like the old days. Tea and biscuits on tap, snap your fingers and a hot fish pie turns up.'

'I never snap my fingers at my mother. She's always ahead of me anyway.'

'Just like my mum.'

'How's life back at base camp then?'

'The same old chaos, mayhem and destruction. I bet you can't wait to get back.'

'Right now I'm enjoying the peace and quiet.'

Edith Stanton comes out of the kitchen with a tray of tea and biscuits and she's obviously enjoying herself as the hostess.

'You had better watch out mum, Beatrice is a gannet with chocolate biscuits.'

'Rubbish, I always draw the line at 19.'

'How do you keep such a perfect figure then?'

'Exercise and stress.'

'Do you think you could do me a small favour Bea? Well I suppose I mean another one really.'

'Sure, as long as it involves shooting Inspector Baxter.'

'No I'll do that. It would be good to have my harp

here. Do you think you could fetch it from my flat? It's a bit heavy and awkward, you might need some help.'

'No problem, I'll go there tonight with Leo. Got tolerant neighbours have you Edith?'

'It won't be loud and I love hearing it.'

'Yes, it'll be on soft domestic mode.'

After a couple of weeks of home cooking, Ian returns to his flat, with his mother being concerned he might return to the job too early.

Ian has had no contact with Marie-Edith recently; he's been feeling too withdrawn and languid to make the contact, but Beatrice has secretly been keeping her informed. She meets Marie-Edith at the airport and they go to the café area for a good chat.

'As you know, my father used to be in the army,' says Beatrice. 'He's retired now of course. He was a colonel; quite a high rank. He's always been interested in courage, bravery and fear. He would come across some people who had absolutely now fear, whatever the situation. No fear, no nervousness, no concern, nothing. They weren't callous or psychopathic. They could be very kind and sympathetic but were completely fearless in any dangerous situation. Should they get medals for bravery? Perhaps not, because they didn't need to show any courage.

'He found normal people had various levels of fear and courage. In spite of everything they would just get on with the job. Ian's like that. I know he gets scared but just does what he has to.

'That terrorist attack in the shopping centre, you won't have heard many of the details, will you?'

Marie-Edith shakes her head. 'I've never asked Ian and he hasn't talked about it.'

'Anyway, Ian was in a store on the first floor, the second floor as it's called in France. A terrorist ran in and started shooting. Ian jumped on him from behind, punch him and knocked him to the ground, grabbed his gun and shot him. He picked up some more ammunition and another gun and went to a side wall. There was a woman there frozen with fear. I spoke to her later. Ian told her he was police, said he was not a firearms officer but he would have to have go. She could see he was scared. He looked at her and said "My name is Ian. Have a good life". Then he ran out of the shop and had gun battles with the other two terrorists. He got them both and was seriously wounded. The woman said it seemed as though he thought he would die, but he had to do what he could. That's why he got the George Cross and the Sovereign Medal.

'My dad says people can eventually run out of their store of courage and can do nothing about it. Ian's just been unlucky to be involved in so many extreme incidents. I think Ian collapsing in that manner means his nervous system just couldn't take any more. It's different for those people in special forces or the Foreign Legion; most of those characters are varying degrees of psychopaths anyway. Ian's more sort of gently dangerous rather than deadly dangerous. As you'll know, much of police work is routine and solid plodding along with occasional peaks of drama. Ian's peaks seem to have been more dramatic than most.'

'Will he recover; will he be all right?'

'Yes, they reckon so. He'll get good support from the police and some private therapy.'

'Do you think he should leave the police? I don't want to be married to a ghost or a corps.'

'Married eh? We'll come back to that one. I think he's on overtime for survival. I think he will have to stop being on the front line. The very senior officers don't have to go to the crime scenes. Others gather the evidence and deal with any blood and gore. He should stick to all the clever stuff, interviewing, detection and mind reading.'

'Will he do that? Will he listen?'

'I reckon he will, if we both nag and bully him enough. He's always avoided promotion because he likes being at ground level and has always been nervous about being in charge and giving orders. He has some sort of insecurity in that direction, but he's been in the police for 10 years now, so with all that experience, he'll get use to it.'

Marie-Edith says, 'There's a saying "If life is eternal, then death is only another horizon". Possibly, but he should not put it to too much of a test any more.'

Beatrice continues, 'Quite right; make sure you repeat that to Ian. I've already had words with the Chief Superintendent and the Assistant Chief Constable. If they insist on promoting him to Inspector, he'll have to lump it, or leave, which I don't think he'll ever do. Come on, I'll drive you over there.'

Ian answers a ring at the door, to find Marie-Edith standing there in smart new colourful clothes holding a small bag.

'Marie-Edith! How wonderful; I wasn't expecting this.' Ian gives her a big hug. 'Great to see you. I love these clothes, you look tremendous. Beatrice has been speaking to you then.'

'Well detected.'

Sitting down to a pot of tea, she asks, 'Well how are you really?'

'A bit weak and fragile, but all right I suppose.'

'Have you been out today?'

'Just to the local shop for a couple of things.'

'It's beautiful outside. Why don't we go to the park and have some sandwiches for lunch?' So they head for the park. They are sitting quietly on a bench and Marie-Edith has her hands around his arm.

'I got your Valentine's card – thank you,' Ian says.

'You didn't send me one.'

'So you mean you didn't get any?'

'I got two actually. One from Richard at work and...'

'Who's this Richard bloke?'

'Oh just one of my many admirers.'

'I will have to sharpen my shotgun.'

'And the other one had an English stamp. It wasn't signed but I assume it could have come from you.'

'Quite possibly. We never sign our Valentine cards.'

'What never? Why not? How do you know where they've come from?'

'That's part of the fun. All part of the mystery. You have to guess and work it out.'

Marie-Edith is surprised. 'What an amazing idea. That is so clever and so romantic and so unBritish.'

'Also, if you get a card from someone you don't like

and it's signed, then that can be very awkward and embarrassing.'

'Double clever then. All right, you're forgiven.'

They sit quietly in the sun for a while.

'Marie-Edith, I know I said I like these clothes you're wearing but I much prefer you without them, so I'd better warn you that when we get back after lunch you are going to be ravaged without mercy.'

'Oh. And I had better warn you, that if you don't have me screaming with pain and pleasure, I will never speak to you again.'

'Righty-ho.'

'And it's about time you told me the fifth test for the perfect woman.'

'Yes indeedy, but in fact you've already passed the fifth test many times. And then comes the sixth test. Did I tell you about the sixth test?' A comment which gets him a mild elbow in the ribs.

'There will be no sixth test. Be sure about that.'

'Yes boss, I mean, no boss.'

So off they jolly well go.

The End
of Book One

Book Two
Quietly
Dangerous

ISBN 978-0-9957792-5-9

Printed in Great Britain
by Amazon

52490134R00169